THE TREE
HOUSE

SHAY LYNAM

Maggie -
Enjoy!

For my husband, Mike.

CONTENTS

ACKNOWLEDGMENTS

Thank you, God, for everything you have blessed me with.

A big thanks also to: my family and friends, for your support and putting up with me when I was stressing out about this whole process.

To my sister, Samantha Thompson, who helped with editing and my beta-reader, Chrissy Shelton for helping me to make this book the best it could be.

Finally, a huge thank you to my wonderful husband, Mike, who helped me write this story and supported me wholeheartedly every step of the way. I wouldn't be the person I am today without him.

CHAPTER ONE

One second, I'm sitting in my room working on a paper for my Psychology class and the next second, I've crammed myself into the crawl space behind my bed hearing the scared screams of my parents downstairs.

It's not as if I'm a wuss. It's not as if I didn't want to go down and see exactly what was going on. But rather, it's the fact that amidst all the screams, I clearly heard my dad yell, "Hailey, get out of here!"

Crouched here behind my bed, which I had slept in since I was four, 17 years ago, I felt as if I was once again, a little girl hiding from my daddy as he jokingly scoured my room looking for me to tuck in. Though now, things were much different. Now, instead of my dad opening small drawers in my child-sized vanity whispering 'is she in here?', there was a tall, strange man, ripping apart my closet, overturning my desk, smashing my computer in the process and cursing, yelling, "The girl's not in here!"

I watched as his big, black shoes clomped out of my

room and disappeared into the hallway. I waited and listened. Voices downstairs filled my ears.

"Are you sure you checked everywhere? Every room?" one asked.

"Yeah, I checked both bedrooms. No one was in either one. Not in the bathroom either."

"There has to be someone there. The man yelled up at someone. You don't yell upstairs at someone, if there's no one there."

"Maybe they were trying to trick us."

Then the men fell silent. I held my breath, straining my ears for any sounds of footsteps. Any indication as to whether or not, they were still downstairs.

My heart was pounding in my ears. Who were these guys? What happened to my parents? Were they alright? Were they dead? I had to get out of there. Whoever those people were would surely come back and check again.

As quietly as possible, I pulled myself out from under my bed keeping an eye on the hardwood floor outside of my bedroom, waiting for shadows to appear. Nothing. It was still dead silent downstairs. My dad's words echoed in my head. "Hailey, get out of here!" he had yelled.

I needed to do just that.

Without moving, I peered around my room. There was an empty duffel bag up on a shelf in my closet. A small pile of clean clothes sat on the side table next to my desk. My cellphone lay on the side table near my bed, and my purse sat beside my door.

"Why don't you check there one more time?" I heard one of them say from downstairs.

I had to get moving. Quickly, I went for the closet and grabbed the duffel bag. When I turned to reach for my cell phone, it was lit up and vibrating. My brother's face smiled at me from the screen and I watched in horror as it vibrated its way right off my table and landed hard on the floor with a loud thump. Crap.

Suddenly, there were two sets of pounding footsteps coming up the stairs. I glanced at the duffel bag in my hand. There was no time. I dropped it and started to reach for my phone, when the footsteps hit the top of the stairs. I froze.

"Which bedroom did that come from?"

"Sounded like this one."

I closed my eyes praying they were referring to my brother's old room and not mine. The footsteps started down the hall toward my open door. Please turn, please turn pleasepleaseplease.

They stopped walking. I opened my eyes again. Finding my doorway still empty, I breathed a quiet sigh of relief. The rustling noise of the two strangers came through the wall next to me. They were in my brother's room now. All I had to do was get out my door, sneak past my brother's and run down the stairs and out the door. Sounded simple enough. Why couldn't I have had the room with the window?

With every step I took toward the hallway, I stopped and listened to the ruckus going on in the room next to me. I heard them tearing apart my brother's closet. Hangers clanged together, junk was tossed out onto the floor. They were looking for me.

Finally, I reached the hallway and slid up against the wall. I had to make it past the open door without being seen. All I could think to do was run. And it needed to happen soon.

Without another thought, I lunged from the wall, right past the open doorway.

"There she is!" I heard from behind me.

My feet hit the stairs and I raced down them stumbling and skipping three at a time. By the time I hit the ground floor, they were almost at my heels. No time to unlock the front door. I darted left into the kitchen and eyed the sliding glass door just ahead of me. It was open slightly. Enough that I could slip through and out into the shadowy backyard.

"Stop!"

I jerked around to see two tall men in suits, both holding handguns. Both pointed directly at my head. I stood there, my heart pounding, my breath ragged and hands shaking. My mind was racing. Do I surrender? Do I try and make a break for the sliding door? These guys looked like they've shot a gun before.

"What do you want?" My voice quivered.

"We just need you to come with us," the one on the left replied failing to sound convincing.

"Where are my parents?"

"We'll bring you to them," he said.

I didn't believe him. Not for one second. I knew right then, if I wanted to get a chance at saving my parents, at figuring out what it was that these guys wanted, I had to get out of there. I had to try.

Not wasting another second, I turned on my heel and lurched for the sliding glass door. Two shots rang out and I dove. The glass exploded around me as I lunged through the door, feeling it cut me in a billion places.

I landed hard on the concrete patio and scurried to my feet as more shots were fired. The icy wind whipped through my hair and the freshly torn holes in my jeans as I sprinted through the backyard toward the chain link fence. Bullets whizzed past my head. No time to look back. I grabbed the top of the fence, stabbing my palm with a stray wire, and vaulted over. As soon as my feet hit the sidewalk, I was flying. Across the street, through three yards, down an alley and finally into a half full garbage can, before I let myself catch my breath. The sickly sweet smell of week old garbage had never felt so inviting to me.

They wouldn't find me in here. They couldn't. Who would look in a garbage can? As if in answer, the faint sound of running footsteps crunching on gravel entered my ears and grew louder as they came closer. Without changing pace, the footsteps went past me and faded again into silence.

I needed to do something. I needed to tell someone what was going on. The police? Would they think I was crazy to tell them I was being chased by two guys in suits? I counted to one hundred in my head before opening the lid and peering out into the alley. Lights suspended from a few scattered garage roofs illuminated the street enough for me to know that it was empty and I was alone. I stood up, pushing the lid all the way back and inhaling the sweet, less-rotten smell of the air above the garbage can.

I hopped out, brushed the loose pieces of trash off my jacket and looked around.

Now what? I couldn't go home. They might have people there waiting for me. There could be someone waiting for me at all of my relatives' houses. At my friends' houses. At the college. Where could I go? I hadn't had time to grab any money. I'm sure someone grabbed my phone and my wallet. My ID. I wasn't safe.

They had all of my contacts. No one I knew was safe.

Sickness grew in the pit of my stomach, welling up like a volcano about to erupt. I felt lightheaded. Like I needed to eat something. Like I needed to sit down. Like I needed to know just what the heck was going on.

Inadvertently, I began to walk. Only when I heard something crash to my left, did it really occur to me that a back alley, in the middle of a sketchy suburb outside of

Seattle might not have been the safest place for an unaccompanied, young woman to be walking. My pace quickened and I almost tripped over a stray cat as it ran across my path.

I made it out of the alley and came out on Genessee Street, one of the main streets that ran toward the center of the city. The night was young enough that there was still some traffic. Being the middle of winter, the sidewalks were devoid of people. Well, except for me. I needed to get off the streets and find somewhere to hide. I had no idea how far those guys had thought I'd gone. They were probably hunting around my neighborhood and before too long, they were going to make it out to this stretch of road.

With that thought in mind, I started making my way toward the center of town. If I could make it to the bus station, and catch a bus, I could get to Seattle where it would be much easier to blend in among the hustle and bustle of the busy city.

Walking alone on the dark streets of Columbia City made every shadow look like one of those gunmen in the suits. Every noise sounded like their hushed voices, as they waited for me around the corner.

I had been walking for a good ten minutes and I still had another five before I would reach the center of town where the bus station was located. I wasn't even sure how I was going to pay for it yet. My bus pass was in my wallet at home along with any cash I would have been carrying. The only items I could find when I dug hastily through my pockets was a small piece of paper and a couple pennies.

The icy wind was biting at my face and arms. I hadn't had to time to grab a heavy coat or anything before I had run out the door. Luckily, it had been a little cool in my room when I was working on my paper, so I had put on a black hoodie. At least I wasn't completely exposed to the elements. Though the freshly torn holes in my clothing from smashing through the glass door and skidding on the pavement wasn't really helping the situation.

As I passed a connecting street, movement out of the corner of my eye caught my attention. I turned my head just as two shadowy figures looked in my direction.

"There she is!"

With a pant I took off running down the street. Houses rushed past me in a blur and the wind threw my heavy dark hair behind me as I ran. I could hear the two men behind me.

"Stop!"

Please, don't shoot. I thought as the wind whipped past my ears.

As if on cue, a bullet flew by my head, barely missing my cheek. I let out a squeal and veered left, cutting into Genessee Park. I hoped, with every fiber of my being, that I could get lost in there.

The trees cut out any moonlight that had been able to break through the clouds, making it pitch dark as I tried to navigate through the woods. If there was ever a time to be completely scared out of my mind, this was it. Not only did I have two trigger happy gunmen after me, but I was in the area most well-known for its muggings and kidnappings. Though I must say, I would have been glad to meet a punk or two rather than be caught by the two lunatics chasing me.

I broke out of the trees and found myself in one of the four playgrounds within Genessee Park. The place was deserted, no surprise there. Behind me, sticks snapped as footsteps grew closer. There was no time to make it across to the other side and back into the woods.

In a panic, I ran toward the the ladder leading up to the slide. Once at the top, I shimmied my way into the tunnel and plastered myself up against the side, trying not to lose my footing on the slippery plastic.

Just as I pulled my leg back in and out of view, the two guys appeared at the edge of the trees. I held my breath and pressed myself back against the plastic wall of the tube slide. From where I was, I couldn't see them at all. I just hoped they couldn't see me either.

"Where could she have gone?" the one with the lower voice muttered.

"Paulson, we have to find her soon. We were given strict orders to wipe out the neighborhood of any and all of these pests," the other replied. "If we leave even one..."

"Pests?"

"Did you hear something?" Paulson asked.

I held my breath. Leaves rustled deep in the woods. The silence told me it was going to snow tonight. It seemed like an eternity before either spoke.

"Alright, let's move on," he said.

I heard the two begin to make their way past the slide that I was hiding in. My heart quickened and I was sure they could hear the sound of it echoing up and down the inside of the tube.

Suddenly, a hand appeared at the bottom of the slide. I backed my way out slowly as another hand appeared next to it. My breath quivered as I tried to hold back a whimper. They got me.

"Adams!" Paulson yelled from a little ways away. "Come on, we have to catch up to her."

Just then the hands disappeared and I heard the reassuring crunch of feet on gravel as he walked away to join his partner.

Only after it had been silent for a good five minutes, I felt I could come out from my hiding place. I had been right about the weather. No sooner had my feet hit the gravel than the first flakes of winter started to fall like ash from the sky.

I remembered my mom bringing me and Ryan here as kids whenever it snowed. We would clumsily make our way to the top of the slide then launch out the bottom like we were being shot from a cannon.

Now, sitting here shivering in the bitter wind, I began to wonder if my parents were even alive. I wondered if Ryan, off at school in Nashville, was aware of what had happened at home. Maybe they got him too. Maybe I was the only one left.

With another gust of icy, snowy wind, I slid down the slide, glumly reliving my childhood memories. I had to find somewhere warmer. This jacket wasn't going to keep the cold out, and my body heat in for much longer.

With rapidly stiffening joints, I began treading my way through the already snow-covered ground. I planned to cut through the park and come out on 42nd. The bus station was just four blocks away from there and I could get to Seattle and away from Paulson and Adams.

The thought of sitting on a bus, surrounded by strangers who weren't out to kill me cleared my head enough that I could navigate through Genessee Park.

I came out on 42nd just like I had planned. The snow had started falling in sheets and by now the whole street was covered in white. Everything sparkled.

There were only a few blocks separating me from the transit station. I glanced at the watch on my wrist. The only bus for Seattle was going to be there in eight minutes. I needed to move faster if I wanted to get out of here.

I broke into a jog, being careful not to slip on the icy sidewalk. I'd never been in this part of town by myself. It was a bit nerve racking as I hurried down the silent road.

From half a block away, I watched the bus pull up to the station. One person stood by the bench waiting for it to come to a complete stop. The air was filled with the sound of the hydraulic breaks as the bus slowed to a halt and the doors opened with a loud whoosh.

I jogged the rest of the way there and made my way around the front of the bus. When I reached the steps, I looked up and made eye contact with the driver.

"It's a little late for a young one like yourself to be out alone, don't you think?" he asked me. His face was kind.

"Well," I started. "I'm in a bit of a jam. I don't have my pass or anywhere to go."

"I'm sorry, miss, I can't let you on without your pass," the man gave a sympathetic shrug.

"Please." I could feel my lip quivering. "I have nowhere to go."

The bus driver looked at me with sympathetic eyes. I bit my lip trying to hold back tears. I was so close.

He let out a big belly sized sigh. "Where do you need to go?"

"Seattle."

"Well, I can't take you that far without a pass." He scratched his ear. "I could get in big trouble."

I nodded. "No, I understand," I said, toeing the bottom step with my foot.

"But,"

I looked up at him again hopeful.

"I can bring you as far as North Beacon, and then we'll see about finding somewhere warm for you. How's that sound?"

A smile stretched across my face and I nodded. "That would be great," I said. "Thank you so much."

"Sure, sure." He motioned with his head for me to get on board.

I took a seat directly behind him and sighed with relief as the door closed and the bus pulled away from the station. As we turned to get onto the freeway, I looked back and saw two dark figures emerge from the alley just next to the bus stop.

CHAPTER TWO

"So, what's in Seattle?" the driver asked me after we had been on the freeway for a little while.

"I don't know yet," I replied watching his reflection in the window. "I just needed to get away."

Actually two men were trying to kill me and had probably already killed my family, but I wasn't about to tell him that.

"Sometimes you just need to start over, ya know?"

"Yeah. I know."

"Like when my wife decided to go off with our young, trim and fit gardener to Vegas, I knew I needed to get out of that town and start fresh, ya know? I needed to make a new life for myself. So I packed everything up and headed for Seattle..." his voice faded into the background.

The lights flickered overhead and I looked around. There weren't many other people on the bus. Only four others.

There was a kid, probably in high school, in dark

clothes listening to his iPod and staring out the window. The older person I had seen get on the bus before me sat near the middle on the left looking down at his lap, most likely reading a newspaper. Then there was a couple who looked to be a bit older than me, the woman with her head resting on the man's shoulder.

At that moment, I wished so much that I had managed to grab my cellphone. I wanted so badly to be able to talk to Ryan in Nashville and let him know what was going on. I just wanted to let him know that I was alright, and was hoping that he was alright too. I just needed to hear his voice.

"...and then they asked me if I wanted the job and, well, I said yes. And here I am."

I hadn't even realized the bus driver was still talking to me. I looked ahead again and caught his eyes in the review mirror.

"What's your name, dear?" he asked me.

"Hailey."

"Hailey, you look like you've been through a lot tonight."

I felt tears well up in my eyes. "Kind of."

"I see." He cleared his throat and set his eyes again on the road.

It seemed he didn't want to dig and I appreciated it. I wasn't sure I could tell him that I was being chased by two men with the intent to kill. We drove for another couple minutes before the bus began to slow to a crawl. It came to a stop with a loud whoosh and the driver turned around in his seat.

"This is as far as I can take you without getting in too much trouble."

I smiled. "Thanks...?"

"Charlie."

"Thanks, Charlie," I said. "It was nice meeting you."

"You too, kid," he replied and pulled the lever, opening the doors.

I stood up, brushing myself off and started down the stairs.

"Hailey." I turned around and stared at his outstretched hand. There was a crumpled ten and a five sticking out of his fingers. "Why don't you go get yourself something to eat?" He lifted his hand toward me.

"Charlie, I couldn't..." I shook my head.

"Come on now." He held the money out closer to me. "There's a 24 hour diner just down the block. Just stay off the street until it gets light out."

I reached out and took the money, feeling the soft, worn paper between my fingers. "Thanks," I whispered. "I really appreciate it."

"Sure thing," Charlie answered clearing his throat and sitting forward again.

When I hit the bottom step, I turned to look one last time at the bus driver. He smiled at me. "Take care, Hailey."

"You too, Charlie." I gave a little wave before I turned away and started down the sidewalk with the fifteen dollars clutched tightly in my hand.

I found the all-night diner Charlie had been talking about a few buildings down from where I had been let off. It was surprisingly crowded for how late it was. As eyes locked on me, I realized that I must have looked like a mess. Having just crashed through a glass door and running for several blocks, I'm sure I looked nothing short of insane. So, with my head down and my eyes glued to the floor, I hurried to the bathroom. When I got inside, I checked under all of the stalls to make sure I was alone. I was.

I took a look in the mirror and let out a gasp,

dropping the money in my hand. There was a streak of dried blood down the side of my face from where I had hit the sliding door. My jacket was ripped, dirty and sparkling with bits of glass. I shook my head and pieces rained down over my face and shoulders. What had Charlie thought when he saw me? No wonder he pitied me and had given me money for food. I must have looked like an escaped mental patient to him.

Without warning, I burst into tears and sunk to the floor. Now that I was as safe as I could get, the night's events came crashing down on me. I wished I knew where my parents were. I wished I knew what was going on and what I would do when I got to Seattle. Would those guys be waiting for me there? And why had they called me a pest? Why were they trying to get rid of me and people like me? What was I? What were they?

Just then, the door opened and an old woman came in. She stopped when she saw me and just stared for a minute. "I'm okay," I whispered.

With that, the woman hurried to the farthest stall and shut and latched the door. Quickly, I snatched up my money and got up off the floor. After scrubbing my face and tying my torn jacket around my waist, I felt I was satisfactory enough to keep people from staring.

Once out of the bathroom, I looked around at the other people in the restaurant. No eyes met mine. I sighed with relief and made my way to the bar. I sat two seats away from the nearest guy and asked for a cup of coffee.

When it arrived, I took my time drinking it, letting the warmth bring feeling back into my hands and face. The smell and taste reminded me of home. Of the few mornings I shared with my parents during my winter break, drinking coffee and chatting before they both went off to their jobs and I went upstairs to work on homework.

"You look like you've had a rough night." I looked to my left to find a guy sitting two seats from me staring into his glass. Had he said that to me? When his eyes met mine, I knew he had. I looked away.

I really didn't feel like talking to anybody.

"So?" I glanced at him again. The boy looked to be my age. Maybe a little bit older. He had dark hair that hung in his eyes and skin that hinted of a sunny, tropical place.

"So, what?" I asked, my voice cracking a bit.

"Have you?"

"Have I what?"

"Had a rough night," he replied.

I sighed, pushing a strand of my wet hair out of my face. "You should have seen me before I cleaned myself up." I let out a pathetic chuckle.

"I did." I met his eyes again. They looked tired and sad. Like I wasn't the only one having a bad night. I didn't notice the waiter come up to me.

"Did you want to order anything to eat, dear?" he asked me as he dried out a wine glass with a white towel.

I had jumped a little when he'd started talking. "Oh, um..." I hadn't even looked at a menu. I didn't even see one near me. The guy next to me slid a laminated menu across the bar. I grabbed it and rattled off the first thing I saw for under five bucks. "I'll just have a turkey sandwich."

"Sure," the waiter replied and walked away.

I looked back down at my half full cup of coffee. The guy next to me hadn't said anything in a little while. He still hadn't opened his mouth by the time the sandwich got to me. I glanced over and saw him staring at something in his hands. "What's that?"

He quickly drew his hand inside his coat, hiding it from view. As he did this, I saw it flash in the light. Like something made of metal. "So, what's your story?" he asked me.

I looked back up at his face again. For the first time I noticed the lovely shade of green his eyes were. They were set in a hard stare. Almost as if he was trying to will me to forget what I had seen in his hand. "I don't have one." I took a bite of the sandwich. It tasted like diner food.

Once again the guy was silent. When I looked over at him again, his expression had changed to an almost amused half-smile. His green eyes said yeah right. "You come in here in the wee hours of the morning, bloody and all roughed up, order the cheapest thing on the menu and expect me to believe this is just your Friday night routine?"

I dropped the sandwich back on the plate and swiveled my chair to look at this guy. "When a girl says that they don't have a story, that usually means they don't want to talk about it," I replied narrowing my eyes.

"I see." He smiled. "Sorry for the misunderstanding." His voice dripped with sarcasm.

I sighed and sat back in my chair. "What's your name?"

"What's yours?" he retorted with another smirk.

I rolled my eyes and swiveled back to face the bar. As I turned, I noticed a payphone hidden in the corner near the bathrooms. I turned back to him. "Do you have any change?"

"Why?"

"I need to check my messages."

"Where's your phone?" he questioned with the same smile on his face.

I kept my mouth shut. The last thing this kid needed was for someone to go along with his games.

"Tell you what." The guy leaned his elbow on the

bar. "I will give you change for the phone, for something in return,"

I raised an eyebrow. Great, I picked a seat next to the perv.

"Tell me your name."

His request caught me off guard causing me to stammer a bit. "Ha-Hailey." I cleared my throat. "My name is Hailey."

"Hailey," he smiled. "I like that."

"Thanks, now can I please have some change so I can use the phone?" I asked trying not to sound too desperate. Without another word, the guy dug into his pocket and pulled out two quarters. I held his gaze as I took them carefully almost expecting him to snatch them back. He didn't.

"What's your name?" I asked.

"I'm afraid that will cost you fifty cents," he replied and faced the bar again taking a drink of his beer.

I rolled my eyes again. Whatever. I made my way to the payphone and put the two quarters in. Ryan and I talked on the phone at least three times a week. It had been hard when he moved to Nashville. Because we were the same age, we'd always been really close. I glanced at the clock as my fingers dialed my number. What could he have been wanting to call me for at 3:30 in the morning his time?

I skipped over the familiar recording and went straight to my newest message. His voice sounded hoarse and short of breath like he was running.

"Hailey? Please pick up...Hailey someone's after me." My heart stopped for a second. "I think someone may be after you too," Ryan said.

I heard gunfire in the background and my hand slapped over my mouth to keep a scream from escaping. My brother's ragged breathing entered my ear.

Listen, Hailey," he whispered. "I don't know what's going on, but I met someone who might. He told me to get to the Tree House. It's in Seattle, so I need you to get there." I heard muffled yelling coming from behind him. "Crap," he whispered. "I hope you have your phone, Hailey. Call me so I know you're safe. I love you."

Nothing.

With frustration, I slammed the phone down onto the holder.

"Hey!" the bartender called irritated.

I looked up and saw that people were looking at me. "Sorry," I said quietly. "Sorry."

Everyone turned back to their own business. My knees went weak and I felt like I was going to be ill. They got Ryan. My brother. The only other person I had.

Feeling defeated, I started making my way back to the bar to sit next to No-name, who was staring at me with a look of concern. Before I reached my seat, I heard the door open and the bells on the handle jingle. My eyes tore away from No-name and settled on the two men that had just entered the bar. Their eyes locked on mine.

I froze where I was. Were they going to pull out their guns and just start shooting up the place? They seemed to realize the situation they were in. I looked back at No-name and his face was completely turned away from the situation. Thanks for the help, hero.

With Adams' and Paulson's eyes fixed on me, Paulson gave me a look that said "let's not make a scene" and motioned with his head for me to follow them. There was no way I was going anywhere with these guys. Before anything else could happen, mystery boy sprung from his chair and rushed the two suited men. They didn't have time to react before he barreled into both of them taking them down to the floor.

This, I'm guessing, was my chance to escape. I didn't

waste any time. As people began getting out of their seats to see just what could be happening in this podunk diner this early in the morning, I shot for the kitchen, hoping to God that there was another way out of the place.

I burst through the door almost taking down a waitress with a tray of drinks. "Watch it!" she yelled, plastering herself against the wall just in time.

"Sorry," I called over my shoulder.

Being late at night, there was only one cook, and he didn't really have much time to yell at me before I reached the other side of the kitchen and threw myself at the back door. It flew open and I stumbled out into an alley.

There were a couple teenagers smoking, leaning against the wall giving me a curious look. Other than that, the alley was deserted.

I didn't know how much time mystery boy had given me, but I wasn't taking chances. I bolted for the street, snatching one of the kid's hats off their head.

"Just gonna borrow this," I said quickly and dashed out of the alley. I tugged the worn baseball cap down onto my head, covering my face as much as possible. There were a couple other people out and about, but not enough for me to get lost in a crowd.

Snow was still falling lightly. The ground was already covered and beginning to freeze. I looked back behind me. The street was almost empty with the exception of the small group of kids from the alley, walking the opposite way. I wondered how long I had before Paulson and Adams appeared. Had they hurt that boy? He hadn't looked scrawny or anything, but there was no way one person could hold off two guys like that for very long.

I ducked down another alley, unwrapping my jacket from around my waist and pulling it on. I flipped the hood up over my head to conceal my face a bit more. The next street I came out on was just as empty as the first.

I needed a plan. I needed to figure out what my next move was going to be. Seattle, I felt, was still my best option. At least as the next step. From there, hopefully I could find a way to get on a train or something and head east or maybe north to Canada.

As I walked, the conversation with my brother started playing in my head. What had he meant by the Tree House? Was it like an actual house up in the trees? In Seattle? There are no trees in Seattle other than those lining the streets and scattered in people's yards and in public parks. Not exactly safe and inconspicuous sounding to me.

Whoever had been following him had surely gotten him. I felt my face cringe up as tears formed in my eyes. I ducked into another alley and leaned back against the wall.

I had no idea what time it was. Probably closer to two. It had gotten colder since I'd been in the diner and this jacket wasn't going to be enough to keep me from turning into a popsicle. The tears running down my face were warm on my cheeks, but turned icy cold as soon as the wind picked up. I needed to get out of the weather. I couldn't go back to the diner for obvious reasons, and I didn't know my way around this suburb.

As I stepped back out of the alley, I was grabbed and pushed back up against the wall. I couldn't see who the figure was, but with everything I was going through, I wasn't about to let them take advantage of me. I jerked hard back and forth trying to get loose.

"Get off of me!" I screamed throwing my arms out in front of me. My hands hit a solid chest and didn't even budge the person an inch.

"Hey." They pushed me against the wall again.

"Stop, it's me." I stopped struggling and looked up into the dark face of the stranger. No-name stared back at me with his relentless, green eyes. His arm was braced across my chest keeping both my shoulders pinned against the wall.

"Get off of me!" I tried to shove him away.

"Keep your voice down!" he hissed looking around the corner.

I shut my mouth and listened. Everything was silent. The snow muted any sound that would have been coming from the freeway. "Are they coming?" I whispered.

"Shh."

I rolled my eyes and slumped back against the wall, shoving his arm away from me. No-name was preoccupied and either didn't notice or didn't care. "Will you tell me what's going on?"

"I don't know if I was followed," he explained. "I think I lost them back at the diner, but I'm not sure."

"What happened back there?"

This time the boy didn't respond. With a sigh, I turned away from the street and started walking deeper into the alley. I shoved my hands down into my pockets trying to gain some feeling back in my fingertips. I was halfway down the alley when No-name raced past me grabbing my arm in the process and pulling me behind him.

I looked back over my shoulder in time to see Paulson aiming his pistol at us. "Come on!" No-name yelled veering around the corner and out onto another street.

We made it out of the alley just in time for a bullet to bite a big chunk out of the corner of a building where I had been only moments before. No-name wrenched me after him, down another street and pulled me down behind a lifted truck.

"Are you ever going to tell me your name?" I asked after we had slid down onto our bellies and crawled under the vehicle.

"This really isn't the time for that," he replied in a harsh whisper as he peered out from underneath the bumper. Two pairs of shoes came around the corner and stopped not too far from our hiding place. I held my breath and peeked over at No-name. He had his finger up to his lips and was still peering out from under the truck.

"We lost her again," I heard Paulson say.

Adams walked over and leaned against the front bumper. I shut my eyes hoping he couldn't see our shadows under his feet.

"Yeah, another one of them was with her," Paulson said. He must have been talking to someone on a phone. "No," he muttered, "I didn't recognize him. He must have been one of the 25."

I kept my eyes locked on No-name, waiting for his expression to change. He remained stone-faced.

"Yes, we got her brother," Paulson said. "Right, we'll keep an eye on places she might go. Of course."

I heard a beep as he hung up the phone. "They want us to report back," he said to Adams. "Let's go."

"What about the girl?"

"We'll worry about her later," he said and started down the street with Adams following after him like a puppy.

We waited for several moments after the two had disappeared before we came out from our hiding place. No-name got to his feet immediately and held out his hand to help me up. I sat back against one of the front tires and wrapped my arms around my knees, hugging them against my chest. "You need to get going," he said to me.

I didn't say anything back, just stared at the ground

in front of me. They had my brother. Any hope I had that he had fought and gotten away was gone. What had they done to him? Was he still alive?

"Hailey."

Finally, I looked up at No-name and pursed my lips.

"If I'm not allowed to know your name, you aren't allowed to say mine," I fumed and shoved his hand away. "Just give me a minute."

He didn't say another word. While I sat there letting my heart slow back down and pondering my next move, No-name leaned back against the side of the truck and started digging into the ice with his shoe.

Once my butt was good and frozen, I got up and brushed myself off. The boy had a decent sized hole dug into the snow by this time.

"Are you ever going to tell me your name?" I asked crossing my arms over my chest.

No-name smirked not looking away from his handiwork. "Is it really that important to you?" he inquired meeting my eyes.

"Well, what am I supposed to call you?"

"Whatever you want to call me." He shoved his hands in his pockets and pushed away from the car.

I watched him start down the street.

"Fine!" I let out an irritated huff when I couldn't come up with a good name. "Brat," I finally muttered under my breath. I heard him chuckle. "Where are you going?"

No-name stopped walking and half-turned around. "I don't need you following me," he said.

"Why not?"

"It'd be safer for you to travel alone."

"Are you being serious right now?" I yelled letting out a pathetic laugh. The boy turned all the way around and stared. "Have you been off in lala land for the past hour? The only reason I got away from those lunatics was because of you." The feeling of panic washed over me making my heart pound in my ears. I stood there silent, staring No-name down, waiting for him to say something.

"I just can't take on that responsibility right now," he finally said shrugging his shoulders sadly then turned again and started walking.

I stood there trying to steady my breathing, watching my only hope fade into the distance. "Hey!" I jogged after him. "You can't just leave me here."

"Look, Hailey," he said turning around. The sadness in his eyes was gone. "It's okay if you don't like me. I don't mind being the bad guy here." I kept my mouth shut. "But you aren't safe with me. Just find some place to lay low for a while."

I threw my hands in the air. "And then what?"

No-name shook his head and turned away. I could feel the fear welling up in my throat. He couldn't leave me here alone. Not with Paulson and Adams after me. I had to get to Seattle. I had to find that place Ryan had told me about.

"What's the Tree House?" This stopped him dead in his tracks. "My brother told me that I needed to get to the Tree House," I said. No-name turned back around and looked at me. I closed the last few feet separating us. "Is that where you're going?" I asked him. "If it is, I need to come with you. I have to help my family."

"You won't find your family there," No-name said shaking his head. "Your brother told you about that place because there is nowhere else for you to go. You need to accept that you won't be seeing any of them again."

I shifted nervously on my feet and shook my head, trying to understand. "Are they dead?" I whispered feeling my throat close up.

"I couldn't say," No-name replied softly then looked

me in the eye and bit the inside of his cheek. "Alright," he finally muttered.

"You'll take me there?" I asked not even trying to hide the desperation in my voice.

"Yeah, I'll take you there. But we need to get out of here now." No-name glanced around. "Those two may be gone, but they could still be watching us."

"Who are those people?"

"I can't explain that now," he said and picked up the pace.

I didn't say another word as I tried to keep up with him.

Paulson and Adams had managed to chase us to the center of town so it took us a while to get back to the bus stop. By the time we rounded the last corner, my feet were dragging and I could barely keep my eyes open. I couldn't feel my hands or most of my face, but the rest of my body ached from the cold and lack of sleep. As we waited for the bus, No-name took off his coat and wrapped it around me, then told me to sit down. I slumped onto the bench and laid my head against the plastic cover. Every part of me was shaking. No-name stood on the curb with his head down and his shoulders hunched. As the wind picked up, it rustled his sleeves and he dug his hands further down into his pockets.

"You aren't very good at being the bad guy," I said trying to keep my teeth from chattering with little success.

An amused smile cracked on his face, but he didn't say anything.

I don't know how long we waited there for the bus. I might have dozed off buried in his heavy coat. Even as I watched the bus pull up, the sound of the hydraulic brakes made me jump. No-name motioned with his head for me to get up then waited for me to board the bus before he stepped on and gave the driver some money. I slumped down onto a seat near the front of the bus. We were the only passengers. No-name sat on the seat across from me.

I sat with my back against the window and studied this strange boy. Why wouldn't he tell me his name? Why did he want to remain such a mystery?

His eyes met mine and he leaned back against his window clasping his hands together behind his head. "What happened to you tonight?"

"Why do you get to ask all the questions?"

"I saved your life, I believe that is merit enough."

I raised an eyebrow. "You're the hero now? I thought you said you were the bad guy."

"You can call me whatever you want to call me."

"That's getting real old, you know." I sneered. No-name smiled again then turned his head and looked out his window. I watched his smile fade and his eyes become sad, as if he were reminiscing. My nose twitched as my face began to regain some feeling. "Will you answer one of my questions if I answer yours?"

"Depends on the question," he said not looking away from the passing street lights. I bit my lip thoughtfully. He obviously wasn't going to tell me his name, and judging by his attempts at hiding that shining object earlier, he wasn't going to want to tell me the story behind that either.

"Why are these guys chasing me?" I finally asked him.

No-name turned his head and squinted his eyes at me. Almost like he had expected a more personal question. He opened his mouth to say something, then closed it again. A quiet chuckle escaped his throat. "You have no idea what you are."

CHAPTER THREE

No-name refused to tell me anything else until we got to where we were going. I knew it was going to be a quiet ride to Seattle, so I let my mind wander. My thoughts of Ryan and my parents materialized into nightmares of the horrendous things that could be happening to them. I imagined my brother laying on a table, paralyzed as doctors cut open his body and tore apart his insides. My dad being tortured with water and knives as my mom watched on in horror from behind a glass wall, screaming to not tell the suited men anything about the whereabouts of their daughter.

I was jarred awake by the sound of the breaks as we came to a stop. No-name was up and already headed toward the front of the bus. I scrambled up and clumsily followed him down the aisle and off onto the street. My mind was still foggy and my body still ached from my abrupt awakening.

"How much further?" I asked, my voice cracking.

"Just a little while longer," No-name replied taking

my arm and pulling me down the sidewalk.

I shut my eyes and shook my head, trying to clear some of the fogginess from my mind. "Where even is it?" I asked letting him pull me down the street.

"Other side of town."

"Is a cab out of the question?" I muttered.

No-name didn't answer me and I knew to take that as a "yes". The sky was still very black. Luckily, in a big city, the streets are never dark. Neon signs, streetlights and lighted windows kept our surroundings lit well enough for me to see where we were going. I started feeling dizzy looking up at the tall skyscrapers and I stopped walking. No-name let go of my arm.

I sat down on the curb exhausted. "Dude, I'm so tired."

"Dude, eh?"

"Unless you think of something better for me to call you, shut up," I grumbled and put my head down on my knees.

The bill of the hat I was still wearing caught on my shin knocking hard into my forehead. With an irritated growl I yanked the hat off and threw it into the street. I could feel angry tears welling in my eyes and I blinked hard to clear them. No-name wasn't going to see me cry.

He didn't say anything as I sat there staring at the hat in the snow. Just then, a car passed by crushing it under it's wheels and disappeared around the corner.

No-name came to stand beside me. "Should we get going then?" he asked.

Without another word, I stood up and started down the street in the direction we had been heading. We were still in down town. Getting to the other side of town was going to take all night on foot. The thought made my eyelids droop dangerously low and I started feeling dizzy again. I must have stumbled then because I found No-name's hands on my arms trying to steady me.

"Can we please just find somewhere that I can rest?" I asked looking him in the eyes.

I think I had finally gotten through to him. Whether it was the tiredness in my bloodshot eyes or the way I sounded, No-name nodded and led me down a few buildings until we reached some obscurely named hole-in-the-wall and went in.

The place was slightly busier than the diner in North Beacon. Nonetheless, it was quiet so we found a booth near the back and I slid in. The cracked vinyl felt like a goose-down comforter and scratched table, like a soft pillow. No-name sat down across from me.

"I'll take a coffee and Sleepy here will have water," I heard him say, though his words were muddling together as darkness took over.

I had only just started to doze off when No-name grabbed a hold of my arm jolting me awake. "What? What?" I grumbled yanking it away.

"I shouldn't have given in," he said under his breath and staring past me.

"What?"

"I should have made you keep going." By this point I was confused and growing angry. No-name's eyes flicked to mine. "We've got company."

My stomach dropped and I turned my head slowly, following his eyes. A man in dark clothes sat at the bar watching us. I turned back to look at No-name. The waitress came with our drinks and set them down in front of us. I didn't speak until she had walked away. "What do we do?" My voice was already growing shaky.

"Nothing." He took a drink of his coffee. "He won't do anything in here. Not with all these people around."

"But when we go outside-"

He cut me off. "I'm thinking."

I shut my mouth and pulled the sleeves of his coat down over my quivering hands. It was just one thing after another tonight. Were we ever really going to be safe? I looked back up at No-name. He was staring hard at the man. I couldn't see the guy so I could only assume he was staring right back.

"Do you trust me?" he asked under his breath.

"More than that guy."

"Good. That's what I needed to hear." No-name slid out of the booth. "When it's clear, I want you to run."

Before I could say anything to stop him, he walked to the bar and sat in the stool next to the guy. He had to be crazy. I couldn't tell what No-name was saying. Not even when I tried straining my ears to listen. He was obviously talking low. Low enough that not even the bartender, standing three feet away, could hear. I was still trying to figure out what No-name had meant when he said "when it's clear..." when he and the man got up and made their way through the back exit.

What the heck?!

Suddenly, my head was dizzy. Had he really just given in that easily? Perhaps he was doing this to save my life. Maybe I had underestimated him. Now it was my turn. I slid out of the booth keeping my eyes glued to that back exit as I backed toward the front door. The waitress was standing by another table glaring at me so I pulled a bill out of No-name's coat pocket and put it in her hand.

"Keep the change," I muttered then whirled around and burst out through the door and into the icy night.

I made my way, as fast as I could without breaking into a run, down the street creating as much distance between me and the diner as possible. A couple strangers exchanged looks as I passed them. Surely the look of terror on my face gave them the idea that I was some sort of schizophrenic.

Where was No-name?

I rounded a corner into an alley, no longer knowing or caring if I was going the right way, and skidded to a halt. Standing a few feet in front of me was another big man dressed all in black.

"Don't try to run, Hailey," he said calmly. I stood there unable to move. My heart was pounding so hard his words were muted. My eyes darted around as I tried to think of a way to escape. "I have a gun and will shoot you if you make any sudden movements. Understand?"

I gave a small nod. He nodded back, his eyes piercing mine.

"Here's what's going to happen," the man said. "We're going to walk calmly out of this alley and to a car that is waiting a block down. You are not going to talk to anybody, and we are going to get in the car. Still with me?"

I gave another nod, not tearing my eyes away from his. I was going to die. This was the end of the line. Only a few hours into the worst night of my life, and this was where it was going to end.

"Excuse me?"

My captor and I turned our heads at the same time and I almost whimpered with relief. No-name stood in the entrance to the alley looking from me to the big guy.

"Hailey, right?" he asked pointing at me. "We met in the diner."

"Yeah, yeah," I cracked, my voice shaking.

"You ran out of there so fast, I didn't get the chance to ask for your number." He took a step toward us into the alley. That's when he acknowledged the man standing behind me. "Is everything alright?"

"Yeah, everything is fine," my assailant said calmly. "I was just explaining to her that something has happened and she needs to come with me."

My eyes didn't leave No-name's face as he locked eyes with the guy. Where was he going with this?

"An emergency?" No-name raised an eyebrow.

"Yes, an emergency. She needs to come with me now."

No-name flicked a glance at me then looked back at him. "I don't think she wants to go with you."

"Boy, it's none of your business. This is a personal matter that needs to be dealt with and you are just making things difficult." The man sounded slightly annoyed.

"Alright, alright," No-name replied holding his hands up. "I'll just go then."

My heart sank into my stomach.

"Can I just have my coat back, Hailey?" he asked me, closing the space between us, then turned to my captor. "It's pretty ridiculous out here, yeah?

"Yeah." The man was getting impatient.

I let No-name lift the coat from my shoulders. Tears were stinging my eyes. This was it. He was just going to let them take me. I felt a hand pull one sleeve down my arm while the other reached into a pocket inside the coat. Suddenly, his hand yanked free and a loud crack split the night air.

I stood there frozen with my mouth gaping open, matching my assailant's expression. His eyes locked on mine as blood began dripping down his face from the bullet hole in his forehead. No-name stood beside me, a shiny, smoking pistol clutched tightly in his hand, still pointed at the man, finger still holding down the trigger. The man fell to his knees then forward and lay still on the pavement.

"Jack," No-name whispered.

"What?" I was so breathless and so shaky that the word was almost inaudible.

"My name," he replied locking his green eyes on

mine, "is Jack."

There wasn't any time to hide the body. That shot could have been heard for miles in all directions and it wouldn't be long before the cops showed up. We made our way quickly, down the alley and out onto another street. Sirens were already blaring off in the distance.

After a few more turns, Jack finally slowed to a fast walk. He still had the gun gripped tightly in his hand.

"Could you put that away?" I asked quietly. "It's making me nervous."

Without saying anything, he tucked the gun into the waist of his jeans and pulled his shirt down over it.

The two of us walked in silence for a long time. I still had his coat on. To think that I had had a gun with me this whole time sent shivers down my spine. I could only assume that the guy Jack had taken out of the diner had suffered the same fate as my assailant. Even though I had only known this boy for a few hours, it had never occurred to me that he could be dangerous.

After we had been walking for a while, I began to get anxious. "Are we heading in the right direction?"

Jack kept looking straight ahead. "We have to make one stop before we go to the Tree House."

"Where?"

"I need to get a list."

"A list of what?"

"You sure ask a lot of questions," Jack said sounding annoyed.

"Well, you aren't giving me many answers," I huffed and shoved my hands into the pockets of his coat. "Have any other weapons in here?" I asked sarcastically and began patting myself down.

Jack stopped walking and looked at me.

"Any grenades? Machine guns? Nukes?" I asked.

My hand found another pocket inside the coat and I pulled out something small. It was a ring. A bulky ring like the ones you get when you graduate high school. There was a large blue stone set in the center and small engravings etched all around it and up the sides. Before I could see what they were, it was snatched out of my hand. Jack's face was in mine in seconds.

"You don't touch that," he snarled. "Got it? You don't ever touch that."

"Okay." I nodded a bit in shock. "Okay, I'm sorry. I won't. I promise," I stammered.

Jack held my eyes for a second then turned away and continued walking. I pursed my lips shut and followed after him in silence.

After walking for a while longer, an icy wind started blowing. Even as I walked a few paces behind Jack, I could see him shivering.

"Do you want your coat back?" I asked quietly.

"No," he said not looking back at me. "Then you would be cold." Just then he stopped walking almost causing me to run into him. "We're here," he said.

I looked up at the building we were standing in front of. It was mostly windows so I could see in. The place looked dark and deserted. Closed down for the night. "How do we get in?" I asked.

Without answering, Jack grabbed the handle and I heard some latch click into place. He pushed the door open and went inside. I followed behind cautiously. I could just picture another ambush in here. Big guys clad in black popping out from behind doors and bursting out of closets, surrounding us in seconds. Surely Jack's gun wouldn't have enough bullets to take all of them down.

"This way," he said and headed down a hallway.

I stuck close as we passed a couple closed doors until Jack finally turned around and looked at me.

Judging by the curious look in his eyes, he was no longer mad.

"What's your last name?" he asked me under his breath.

The closeness was making me feel uncomfortable and I had to back up against a closed door. "Roemer," I replied suddenly feeling nervous.

"I'll be right back," he said then turned and went through the door he had been standing in front of leaving me alone in the hallway.

What was he doing? What did he need my last name for? I was tempted to peek into that room and see what he was doing, but then I remembered how he had reacted when I'd found that ring and decided against it. It's like he was trying so hard to keep everything a secret from me. His name, the ring, the list, and apparently the answer to why I was being chased around Seattle. I could feel myself getting angry. Angry at Jack for keeping me in the dark while dragging me all over the city.

Before I could make myself any more aggravated, Jack stepped out into the hall and closed the door behind him. "Where's the list?" I asked through gritted teeth.

"Don't need it." He shrugged. "You check out."

"I check out?"

"Yep, now let's get going. We don't want to be out and about when the sun comes up," Jack said almost cheerfully and started back down the hall toward the entrance.

I looked after him in astonishment. Was this guy bi-polar? I almost expected him to start skipping to the door.

"Why is that, you a vampire?" I asked following sullenly after him.

He smiled holding the door open for me. "Can't tell you."

I let out an annoyed groan and stomped out into the

snow. I made sure to stay at least two steps in front of Jack for the rest of the block.

The sky was still dark, though it had lightened a few shades and some of the stars were beginning to fade away. I glanced at a clock hanging on a wall inside a store and saw that it was nearing five thirty. Anytime now the streets would start filling with cars as people headed to work to start their long monotonous shifts.

"Pick up the pace," Jack said. I could hear his amused smile.

"You're a jerk," I grumbled.

He let out a chuckle. "You have no sense of humor."

I turned around to look at him. "I do too have a sense of humor. For example, I'd laugh hysterically if you got ran over."

By this time I was fuming. The initial sadness and fear for my life had subsided by this time and now I was just feeling dangerous. If either of the two suited men had shown up now, I would have run at them, fists swinging. At the moment I was just trying to keep myself from hitting Jack square in the jaw. It's what he deserved.

I had just met him a couple hours earlier and he had already taken me on his crazy emotional roller coaster. What was his problem anyway? One minute he's shooting guys in the face for me, and the next I'm the last person in the world he wants to be stuck with. What right did he have? What had happened that could have turned him so sour? God help me if this was his normal attitude.

"Are we getting close?" I asked looking around.

Everything looked the same.

"You sound like an impatient child on a car ride," Jack chuckled from a few steps behind me.

That was the last straw. I whipped around grabbing him by the front of his shirt and pushed him hard up against the wall. "That's it!" A look of sheer astonishment broke out across Jack's face as I leaned in close so our noses were almost touching. "You will tell me what is going on," I spat staring hard into his eyes. "And you will tell me what the Tree House is. Now!"

He didn't say anything for a while. I think when I smacked him against the wall I had knocked the wind out of him because he stood there breathing heavily.

"No need," he finally said hoarsely.

"Why?" I asked through gritted teeth.

"Because we're here."

CHAPTER FOUR

I let go of the front of Jack's shirt and stared up at the building we were standing in front of. It was just a plain old four story brick building. It looked a little worse for wear with a couple broken windows and some of the bricks missing. I couldn't at all figure out why it would be called "The Tree House."

"This is it?" I finally asked, still looking up at the tall building.

"Yep," Jack replied with his hands in his pockets.

"This is the Tree House?"

"Yeah."

I looked back down at Jack and just stared for a second. "Well, I'm stumped." I threw my hands up in the air exasperated.

A smile cracked on his face and he grabbed the handle. He flipped another little secret switch and pushed on the door. "It'll all make sense once you're inside."

I stepped inside and found myself in a dingy dark colored room. A flight of stairs led up to the second floor and past that was a hallway leading somewhere into darkness. A door stood on either side of us. One marked "Janitor's Closet" and the other blank.

"Oh yeah, it all makes sense now," I said sarcastically.

Jack let out a chuckle and made his way down the hallway. "This way," he said. "I'll show you."

I followed after him, stepping around a small pile of boards. He stopped in an open doorway then turned and waited for me to get next to him. "Does that answer your question?" he asked pointing with his head to the back wall.

I followed his direction and gazed into the room at the wall. I couldn't believe what was there right in front of my eyes. There growing through the wall and twisting up into a hole in the ceiling, was a big, oak tree. Large, thick limbs stretched out like arms into the spacious room and climbed up the wall like vines. There weren't any leaves on any of the branches or the ground. I didn't know if that was because it was the dead of Winter or if the tree itself was dead.

"This," I breathed with astonishment, "is incredible."

I stepped inside the room and looked up behind me. The ceiling was even draped with branches and vines. It made the room feel alive. As if I had entered through a passageway into Narnia.

"When you said 'Tree House' I figured a house in a tree," I said. "Not a tree in a house!"

"We get that a lot," Jack replied folding his arms across his chest and leaning against the door frame.

"How is this even possible?" I was still staring up at the big tree.

"It happens sometimes. A seedling grows under the foundation long enough, it eventually gets strong enough and big enough to start pushing through the concrete."

"I can't believe it," I whispered still in shock.

"Usually places like this get demolished before the tree can grow to be this big," Jack said. "This place was condemned at one point, but Sy made a deal with the city."

I turned toward Jack with a look of confusion on my face. "Who's Sy?" I asked him.

Jack smiled and pushed off the door frame spinning on his heels. "This way," he said and headed back down the hall.

I followed eagerly behind feeling excited about one of my questions finally being answered. Jack was already heading up the stairs when I got there. The top step let off onto a platform which turned leading up another flight of stairs. Once at the top, we were standing at the end of a narrow hallway. Several doors stood on either side and at the end was another wooden staircase leading up to another level. "What's behind all these doors?" I asked feeling the need to be quiet.

I hadn't heard or seen any signs of life since I had stepped through the front door. "Bedrooms," Jack replied under his breath.

"Is one of them yours?"

He nodded at the door on the left, closest to the staircase. Knowing that there was possibly a comfortable bed only a few yards away made my eyes droop. Jack looked at me. "You've had a long night," he said putting his hands on my arms and pushing me gently down the hall. "Maybe get some sleep, then you can meet Sy."

"And then I'll get some answers?" I asked feeling sleepier with every step.

"Yes, then you'll get some answers," he replied.

Jack opened the door and let me go in first. The room resembled that of a dorm room, minus the few branches slithering in from a couple holes in the walls, which were painted a crisp white color. The whole room was lit by an electric camping lantern sitting on a desk which, along with a tall bookcase, sat against one wall and two twin beds against the other.

"Why two beds?" I asked.

"One for you, of course," Jack replied pulling his coat off of me and I sat on the closest bed.

His answer didn't make any sense, but I was too tired to argue. He hung up the coat on a nail then pulled my shoes off my feet. Dim, gray light filtered in from behind the curtain hung over the window. I lay down on the bed and pulled the covers up to my chin. I hadn't noticed before how cold it was in the building. Though I suppose if a place is condemned, it wouldn't have heat or electricity. The last thing I saw was Jack sit down at his desk and pull the shiny object out of his pocket. Then everything faded to black as sleep took over.

I woke up to bright sunlight streaming into the room. It took me a minute to remember where I was and what had happened. Only after it all came back to me did I recognize that I was alone. I slipped out from under the covers and padded across the floor to the desk where my shoes and Jack's coat sat neatly on top. There was ruckus above my head on the third floor. Someone said something, though it sounded murky to me, which caused laughing. There must have been several people living here with Jack.

When I reached the desk, there was a piece of paper with a quick note scribbled on it in black ink.

Come find me.

I hoped he wasn't planning on leaving me to explore the place on my own. Although maybe I could finally get some answers. Renewed with energy, I quickly put on my shoes and slipped Jack's coat on over my shoulders. It was still pretty cold, even with the sun shining in and I had no idea what time it was. I went out into the hall and up the stairs, following the sound of the chatter and laughing.

When I reached the top of the stairs, I found myself in a big room. It took up the entire floor. The first thing I noticed was the small bonfire in the middle of the room. The smoke floated up and into a hole in the ceiling. This must have been the house's heat supply. Up here more branches spread out from the tree reaching around to cover every wall. Books and other trinkets sat on the branches making them more like shelves. A hammock hung between two sturdy branches and there were a couple couches in the middle of the room, surrounding the fire. The people occupying these couches stopped talking to each other and gazed at me. A blond, tattooed boy and a hippie looking girl sitting in the hammock were staring at me too. Jack wasn't in the crowd. It seemed we were all waiting for the other to say something.

"H-hi," I croaked. My voice was still hoarse with sleep so I cleared my throat. "I'm Hailey." I sounded a little better that time.

No one else said anything for several moments.

Before things could get any more awkward, the sound of footsteps broke the silence. They all turned to look at the staircase across the room leading up the top floor. A pair of shoes appeared, followed by jeans, a shirt and finally the kind face of an older man. I was taken back by how much older he was than everyone else here. While these other people looked my age, the man standing in front of us looked twice that.

"How's everyone doing today?" he asked. "You all sleep fine?"

There were some murmured responses.

I couldn't stop staring at the man. There was

something odd about him. About his demeanor. About his eyes.

"How's David?" one of the boys on the couch asked and pushed his glasses up his nose.

"Okay for now," the man replied nodding solemnly.

"What about you, Sy?"

So this was Sy.

"So far so good," he answered then his eyes flicked over to me. "Ah, I see Jack was successful in getting our newest member here safely."

Everyone's heads turned to look at me again and I froze. "Hi again," I muttered and gave a small wave. This would be so much easier if Jack were here.

"Alright, let's get down to business," Sy said addressing everyone else again.

They turned back around and I relaxed my muscles. I wasn't sure if I was supposed to take a seat so I just found a spot against the wall and started fiddling with a branch while I tried to listen. Sy pulled a small notebook out of his back pocket and opened it, taking out a pen.

"Melody and Arie," he started, acknowledging the couple in the hammock, "we are running low on our general medical supplies. We're going to need more Vicodin, bandages and rubbing alcohol, as well as a new tarp for the roof and gasoline for the generators. Got that?"

The two nodded in response.

"Keeta," he said to the dark-haired girl on the couch. "according to Jack, there were two agents killed last night. Find out all you can about how Eli will be handling this. Will there be serious measures taken, a change to their strategies? Other than that, continue with what you have been researching. Find out all that you can about the chip."

The chip? What kind of chip? The girl nodded,

causing a small metal hoop in her lip to catch the firelight.

"And finally, Root and Logan, continue with your work as well. Any questions?" he asked looking around the room.

No one said anything. Some shook their heads in reply.

"Good," Sy said with a satisfied nod. "If you have any concerns, you'll know where to find me." Then he started toward the stairs again.

"Sy," someone said causing him to stop. It was Melody. "What about Jack?" she asked with a hint of sadness in her voice.

Sy's eyes flicked to me then back to the hippie girl in the hammock. "We will talk about that later tonight," he said. "For now, let's get our jobs done. Hailey, please come with me."

With that he started up the stairs again. I pushed off the wall and followed quickly past the curious eyes and up the stairs to the top level.

Sy led me down a hallway, around a corner and through an open door. We ended up in a big bedroom similar to Jack's. He went over to his desk and opened a drawer. I watched him take out a folder.

"Everyone else read this when they got here. It explains a bit," he said handing me the folder. "I'll give you some privacy."

With that, Sy left the room, closing the door behind him. I stood there for a moment letting everything sink in. This folder in my hands contained information as to why I was being chased. Why my brother and parents had been taken from me. Why Jack had said I wasn't normal.

I walked over and sat on the chair behind Sy's desk, laying the folder down in front of me. With a deep breath, I opened the folder to find a letter. It was addressed to Sy.

After doing some quick math in my head, according to the date stamped on the top right corner, he would have been close to my age when he got this.

Dear Mr. Sylvester Adams,   *May 15, 1990*

     This letter has been written to inform you of your current medical condition. Please read it thoroughly and contact us with any questions you may have. I encourage you to read this letter with a loved one present. This may not be easy to comprehend.

     At your birth an unsterilized instrument was used to cut your umbilical cord. This resulted in a disease known as Neonatal Tetanus to grow in you as an infant. You were then transported immediately to our facility here in Seattle, Washington. We currently have the technology that has allowed us to create an electronic chip that blocks the disease from entering your nervous system. This chip is called an EPI Medic chip (Electronic Postnatal Illness Medical chip). This chip was implanted in you upon your arrival to Seattle. For the past 18 years we have been monitoring you throughout your doctoral visits. Of the ten trial runs, the chip has had a 100% success rate. Your condition is stable and has had no abnormalities.

     The chip is inserted behind the cerebral cortex and connects directly to the central nervous system through the spinal column. In a way, the chip has become fused with your brain allowing its full potential to protect you from the virus. We have no intention of removing the chip as it has had no side effects on any of our patients.

  Your biological mother's identity has been kept private as well as the country or state you were born in. After the chip was safely planted in your brain, you were taken to E. Scott Pharmaceuticals and placed with a prescreened family who was part of the program "Adopt to Save". This program gives infants the medical care they need to survive by adopting them into an American home where the care can be provided.

  If you are interested more in this procedure please contact us. We will be starting another trial of 100 patients soon and appreciate your cooperation. Please stay in close contact with your doctor. They have been informed of your knowledge of your condition and will be able to answer any questions you have.

  Sincerely,
  Eli Scott
  CEO of E. Scott Pharmaceuticals

I read it a second time to make sure my eyes weren't playing tricks on me. This chip that Sy had mentioned during the meeting this morning was inside me? In my body? All my life I had believed I was just a normal girl. A normal girl with normal parents and a normal twin brother. But now...now the shattering truth hit me like a semi-truck. Now, I was a science experiment. I didn't even know my real family. I could see it now. Being born, possibly halfway across the world where sterilization was a luxury they couldn't acquire. Where something like a rusty scalpel could have had me rushed to Seattle by a desperate mother only wishing that her child could have a chance. To think what she had given up. If these doctors had saved my life, if this chip had cured me from this horrible disease, why were they coming after me now? What could have happened that would make them start ending the very lives they had originally been trying to save? Just then there was a knock on the door, breaking my thought process.

"Yeah?" I whimpered realizing there were tears on my face.

The door opened quietly and for the first time all morning, I saw Jack's face appear. "Hey."

"Hi," I whispered.

He came in and closed the door behind him. "I see you read the letter," he said leaning back against the door.

I just nodded in reply looking down at the paper in my hands. Jack walked over and leaned on the desk next to me.

"What is this about?" I asked wiping a tear from my cheek with the back of my hand.

"Well," Jack started, "something happened a few years ago."

"Something with the chip?"

He nodded. "It started to fail."

"What?" I asked astonished. "It was working fine all this time then..."

"There were ten patients in the first trial," he explained. "Sy and David were two of them. And now they're the only two still alive."

"What happened?"

"The chip was working fine. The doctors thought that this was the start to something miraculous. They were already well into their second trial and were in the process of developing a similar chip that could fend off every type of terminal illness. Even cancer. In fact, as the patients in the second trial, we were supposed to be told of our condition at the age of 18 when we were legal adults."

"But why weren't we?" I asked feeling angry that this had been kept a secret from me for all this time.

"When we hit 18, odd symptoms started appearing in some of the first ten patients. It freaked the doctors out and they decided not to tell us until they could figure out what was wrong." He shook his head. "Within a couple of weeks of the first showing symptoms, he died," Jack said staring straight into my eyes. "The others followed soon after."

My eyes widened as the horror unfolded in my mind. "There was nothing to protect them from the full-blown disease," I whispered.

I had learned a bit about tetanus in high school. It gave the infected person seizures that were so powerful, they could literally fold a person in half, breaking their back rendering them paralyzed or dead from a punctured lung. I covered my mouth to keep from crying out at the thought of this happening to me.

"Why are they trying to kill us?" I finally asked shakily.

"Think about it, Hailey," Jack said. "If the word got out about what they had done. About how many people they were killing with this chip, they would have lawsuits flying at them left and right. The company would go belly-up and Eli Scott's name would be ruined."

"So instead of taking the fall for their own idiot mistake," I muttered, "they're covering their butts and hoping no one notices when a hundred people go missing."

"This is the world we live in," Jack replied with a bitter chuckle.

Attaining all this information was making me dizzy.

Black spots appeared in my vision and I could feel myself getting ill. "I'm gonna be sick," I croaked and rushed out of the room.

Luckily, the bathroom was just down the hall. I barely made it to the toilet before everything I had eaten in the last couple days came up and splattered into the water. By the time I was done heaving, my face was dripping with sweat and tears. I sat back against the wall breathing heavily. My head was swimming with all this new information.

There was a soft knock on the door.

"Not right now, Jack," I called holding my head in my hands.

The door opened a crack and a blonde, curly head popped in.

"Jack wanted me to make sure you were alright." Melody came all the way in. She held a towel out to me.

"Thanks," I said taking it from her.

It was cold and damp, which felt soothing on my feverish skin. Melody closed the door and sat down against it, her bracelets clanking together.

"I thought you were going to get supplies."

"Arie and I were just leaving when Jack came and found me," she said. "I remember finding everything out when I first got here. It's a lot to take in."

"No kidding."

Melody chuckled then we sat there in silence.

"You can go ahead and go," I said. "Thanks for this." I held the towel up.

She cracked a smile. "No problem. We take care of each other here." Then she turned to leave.

"Melody, what was that earlier you said about Jack?" I asked her. "Did something happen?"

She turned back around in the doorway and looked at me.

"Has he mentioned anything to you about Ben?"

I shook my head in reply.

"Maybe ask him about it." Then she gave me a small nod and left, closing the door behind her.

It seemed odd to me that there was running water in a condemned building, but I wasn't complaining. I took this opportunity to take a shower. It took a while to get the remaining shards of glass out of my hair and to clean the cuts on my arms, but afterward, even putting on the same dirty clothes, I felt refreshed. Now it was time to go find Jack.

I went downstairs back into the big meeting room. The place was pretty much deserted except for two boys hunched over a table in the back corner, kitchen area. I remembered Root being the one with the glasses so the blond boy must have been Logan.

Root glanced up for a second to see who had disturbed their meeting.

"Hailey," he dragged out my name lightheartedly as he looked over whatever was on the table.

"What's all this?" I asked feeling a little shy.

There was a map of Washington spread out across the table top with different colored lines following different roads and boundaries. A laptop sat in the farthest corner open in front of Logan so I couldn't really tell what was on the screen.

"Planning our escape," he said, his eyes not leaving the computer.

"Escape?" But I just got here.

"Sy wants us out of Seattle soon," Root explained pushing his glasses back in place. "The farther we are from the company, the harder it will be for them to find us."

"How soon?" I asked.

He looked up from the map at me then shared a glance with Logan.

"We aren't sure," he replied hesitantly. "Sy hasn't mentioned an exact date to us yet."

"He just keeps saying soon," Logan added and took a bite of an apple.

My eyes followed the apple as he put it back down on the table. Root chuckled at my lack of discretion. "Hungry?" he asked me.

"A bit," I replied, "It was a long night."

"Help yourself," he said then got back to tracing routes with a highlighter.

There was a bowl of fruit on the counter with oranges and apples like the one Logan was eating so I grabbed one and took a bite. "Have either of you seen Jack?" I asked chewing the apple.

"I think he's on the roof with David," Logan replied, his eyes still glued to the screen.

"Thanks."

I headed back up the stairs and onto the top level. I hadn't seen any stairs between here and Sy's room so I continued on down the hall. When I turned another corner, I saw another room, this one larger than Sy's. There was a big hole in the floor and a trail of smoke was drifting up from the level below and out another hole, this one leading outside. Gray light filtered down illuminating the smoke, making it look like a lit tunnel. I could hear voices coming from the hole above me. I recognized Jack's immediately.

I finally found the stairs leading up to the roof and took them two at a time. A door stood at the top of the stairs and I opened it, revealing a flat, concrete rooftop. Jack was helping another older man shake out a tattered old tarp and fold it neatly until it was small enough for one person to handle. As I got closer to them, Jack looked up.

"David, this is Hailey," he said acknowledging me with his head.

David extended his hand and I shook it. "Nice to meet you, Hailey," he said with a small smile.

"You too," I answered.

As we shook hands, his tensed up all of a sudden crushing my fingers together. I yelped pulling my hand back and flexing my fingers.

"Sorry," David winced shaking his hand. "I'm sorry," he said again. "These spasms are getting worse."

"Spasms?" I asked.

"David's chip is failing," Jack said solemnly and took the tarp from under his friend's arm.

I didn't know what to say to that so I just stood back eating my apple and let them work. Other than that spasm, David seemed to be okay. He was obviously glum about the fact and scared as well, I'm sure. I would be. Jack said something quietly to David, then handed him the folded up tarp. David nodded and threw me another apologetic smile and headed down the stairs. Jack came and sat down next to me.

"He's going to die soon, yeah?" I asked looking out at the cars on the distant freeway.

"Yeah," Jack muttered.

We sat in silence for several moments before either of us spoke again.

"Who's Ben?" I asked cautiously.

If Melody hadn't wanted to tell me, it must have been a touchy subject. Jack's jaw clenched letting me know that it was. I wasn't sure if he was going to answer. Finally, he let out a sigh.

"He was my brother."

"You have a brother?" I asked remembering the guys I had met so far since I'd gotten here.

"I said 'was'," Jack snapped, his eyes piercing mine.

I was taken back by his sudden change in attitude. He got up and walked over to the edge of the roof. I almost expected him to jump, but instead he turned around to look at me.

"He was killed while we were out looking for you," Jack raised his voice over the wind. It whipped his hair into his eyes and made the sleeves of his shirt shutter.

"What?" I whispered. I got up and went to stand next to him. "How long were you looking for me?"

"A few days. I don't really want to talk about it," Jack said quietly now that I was closer, not meeting my eyes.

"I'm really sorry, Jack," I said touching his arm.

He shrugged me off. "I know."

I looked out at the street down below. There were no buildings as tall as this one and it sat on a deserted street lined with other closed down buildings. It seemed this was the best place to hide out.

"How did Sy find this place?" I asked changing the subject.

"I'm not sure," Jack said. "It was condemned because the tree had started growing up through the floor. Sy is...well off. He was able to keep the city from tearing the place down."

"How do we have running water?"

"David is a really great handyman. He rigged it so we're 'borrowing' water from a hydrant across the alley," he explained. "We just have to limit ourselves so no one notices."

"Good to know." I dropped my apple core off the ledge and we watched it fall and hit the pavement below. It broke apart, bits of apple flying in every direction.

"I want to show you something," Jack said after a little while.

He turned away from the ledge and headed for the stairs. I followed him down through the top level to the next set of stairs. Through the third level, past Logan and Root still wrapped up in their research and down the next flight. Down into the empty second level and finally down the stairs to the bottom level where everything still looked deserted and in disarray. He took me down the hallway and back into the big room with the tree. The image was still just as breathtaking, I had to stop and take it all in again. This time, the sun was up making the view even more exquisite. Someone had placed a large planter by the trunk with dozens of brightly colored flowers, making it look like a garden sitting at the base of the tree.

"This way," Jack said quietly, trying not to disturb the moment.

I followed him past the tree and out an old, worn looking blue door with a brass handle. It didn't really fit in with the rest of the house, but seemed appropriate for this room.

The door led outside into a very small grassy yard. It couldn't have been more than ten feet wide and across. The alley was cut off by a tall wall of plywood and scaffolding, making the area seem more like a room with no roof. I could see from here that most of the tree was growing inside, but a portion of the trunk was on this side of the wall with branches extending out above my head. The ground was still white with snow, but a real garden was planted on this side of the wall with poinsettias, primrose and lilies. A snow covered bench sat next to it.

"It's beautiful out here," I said taking it all in.

"It is pretty nice here," Jack replied with his hands in his pockets. "Sy and David really wanted the place to feel as little like a prison as possible."

"But can't you come and go as you please"

"We have to keep this place a secret, so we don't get

to go out much," he explained. "There's only one day a week usually where Melody and Arie go out for supplies. And Keeta only a couple times a week."

"What about you?" I asked going over to the bench and sitting on the back.

"With me, it's a different story." He sat down below me on the seat. "I'm gone for weeks at a time usually. My brother and I. Then we're here for another week, and then gone again."

"How do you know who to look for?"

"There's a list of patients," Jack said.

"So you had to check to make sure I was on the list the other night."

He nodded.

"You could have told me instead of keeping me in the dark about everything," I said irritatedly and nudged him hard with my foot.

He laughed. "I was just taking the necessary precautions."

"While being a jerk," I muttered shoving my hands in my pockets to warm them up.

The sun was shining today and there wasn't a cloud in the sky, but the wind was icy and nipped at my face.

"Is this the same list the company has?" I asked.

Jack nodded again.

I remembered last night when Paulson had told whoever was on the phone that Jack wasn't in their database. "Why aren't you on it?"

"It's a long story," he said.

I shrugged, "I've got nowhere to be."

CHAPTER FIVE

"There was this woman, Allison, who worked for E. Scott Pharmaceuticals," Jack started. "She started around the time that David and Sy learned about the trial. It didn't take long for her and David to fall in love. But they had to keep it a secret."

"Why?" I asked.

"It's similar to people not being able to date their therapists," he explained. "Plus, if a doctor and patient are romantically involved and the test fails, it could complicate things."

I nodded. "That makes sense, I suppose."

"Yeah, so anyway, they were able to keep their romance on the down low. Things seemed to be going well for a long time. The chip worked like it was supposed to. Allison talked about leaving the company so they could get married and start a family. Then she was put in charge of keeping the records updated for the patients from the second trial run."

"She was in charge of the list?"

"Yeah, it was her job to keep up on things like change of address and sending out the letters when we turned 18. Then the first patient from the first trial started getting strange symptoms."

"Spasms?" I asked.

"Spasms, stiffness in his joints, lockjaw, restlessness. Everything pointed to tetanus which meant the chip was failing. Allison was told not to send out the letters until they were able to get the chip working again. Well, they never did, so the letter was never sent," Jack said. "There was no way to fix the problem. If they tried to replace the chip, there was risk of the disease spreading before they could get the new one in after the first was taken out. Finally, patients just started dying."

"From the tetanus?"

"Some," he replied looking me straight in the eye. "David told me that Allison called him one night in a panic, saying that some of the patients' families were threatening to sue them for all they had. Eli was afraid of losing the entire practice. Then the patients started to disappear," Jack said. "They would go in for emergency visits and never come back out. The doctors just said that they died from the failed chip, but Allison had seen first hand what was really going on, so she warned David, who in turn warned Sy. The two of them left their homes without telling anyone, so when it was their turn to come in for an 'emergency visit' they never showed. Allison knew that if Eli was taking such extreme measures with the first set of patients, it would only be a matter of time before he came after us. She was the only one in contact with David and she knew that he was our only chance. So she emailed him the original list of names and addresses of the patients in hopes that he could at least warn us of what was coming."

By this time I had slid down onto the seat next to

Jack and was staring down at the snow under my feet. This was a lot to take in. If Allison had been as cold hearted as the other doctors and scientists, I would be dead right now. Jack and all the others would be dead.

"So," I started, "how did you and Ben get off the list?"

Jack shivered and I offered him his coat, but he shook his head causing his hair to fall into his face.

"It was Allison's attempt at saving as many of us as she could on her own," he said. "She began deleting names off the list in hopes that she could replace them with fake names and fake addresses."

"But?"

"But she got caught before she could change all of them," Jack said. "Allison was able to send David the new list so he would know which of us were safe. There are 25 of us around the Seattle area that are no longer on the list. The other 75 are in danger, a lot of them already dead."

"What happened to Allison?" I asked already knowing the answer.

"She was killed."

I thought so. "So, if you were safe," I said, "why did David and Sy come find you?"

"We were the first two of the missing names on the list," Jack explained. "They were going to try and get those that were safe to help in searching for the others that weren't. They stopped after finding us. Ben told them that getting the missing kids to help find the ones on the list would bring attention to themselves and Allison's sacrifice would have been for nothing. So the two of us took on the job of finding the others ourselves while David and Sy tried to find a place to keep people safe. Hence..." He lifted his hands up as if presenting me with the Tree House.

I looked up at the building above us. It seemed like the perfect place to hide. Right under Eli's nose where he wouldn't think to look.

"So you guys have found seven of us so far," I said bending down and picking a small pink flower from under the tree.

"Alive," Jack muttered and took the flower from my hand. "Most of the time we've gotten there too late." I watched as he began picking the petals off and letting them fall to the ground.

"Wow," I whispered my stomach sinking at the thought of these other scared kids. The last thing they see, being the barrel of a gun between their eyes.

"I think that's enough information for today," Jack said quietly.

I hadn't even noticed the tears on my cheeks.

"Sorry," I whispered wiping them away.

"Are you hungry?" he asked me.

I turned my head to look at him with astonishment. "Not after hearing all that!"

We ended up going back inside to help David and Sy with more work around the building. I volunteered to clean the bathrooms, especially since I had made a mess of the one on Sy and David's floor, and Jack went off with David somewhere to help him fix something too technical sounding for me to understand. I didn't really know what Sy was up to. I had heard him mention something about finances before he disappeared into his room.

When I was done with the bathrooms, I went up and started on the kitchen. Keeta returned then and went to the fourth floor to update Sy with any new information she had learned about the chip or the company. Jack told me that he would inform us at the meeting the next morning if they had learned anything new.

I had moved on to scrubbing at the stained tile counter when Melody and Arie came up the stairs, their backpacks bulging with supplies. I brushed my hair back from my forehead and exchanged a smile with Melody.

"Get everything we needed?" I asked awkwardly.

Melody nodded. "Almost everything," she said. "We'll get the rest tomorrow."

"I'm starving," Arie added putting his backpack on the couch and reaching back to stretch his arms. His shirt lifted showing a strip of bare skin and black ink. I looked away quickly before either of them caught me staring. "What's for dinner, Root?" he asked walking over to the table and placing one of his tattooed hands on the map Root was studying.

"Do I look like your mother?" he asked trying to move Arie's hand with no success.

"Maybe if your hair was a little longer." I caught the corners of Logan's mouth twitch into an amused smile, even though his eyes stayed glued to his computer screen. "No," Arie shook his head. "now that I think of it she was much taller. And less like a small bird."

Now Root shoved Arie hard and chuckled. "You better watch it or I'll bite your kneecaps off." Then he stood up, nudging past Arie and going over to open the refrigerator.

"Hey," Melody chimed. "You should make something fantastic for Hailey's first day here."

I smiled feeling my cheeks get hot as I finished scraping something crusty off the stove top. Root nodded in agreement. "This looks like a job for...ham!" he exclaimed, disappearing behind the open fridge door.

"Blek!" Keeta cried as she hit the bottom of the stairs. "That's disgusting. I don't want to eat a slimy, dead pig."

"Keeta, I don't get it," Root said. "You hate animals, so why are you a vegetarian?"

She crossed her arms over her chest. "I'm not so fond of you either, but morally speaking, it would still be inappropriate for me to kill and eat you."

Root turned to me just then. "If you can't tell, we all love each other in this place. How does ham sound to you?"

I smiled and tossed the washcloth into the sink. "Ham sounds great," I shrugged.

"Where are the pickles?" Melody asked as we all sat around the fire, balancing our plates in our laps. "I can't have a ham sandwich without pickles."

Root shook his head. "Pickles are cucumbers soaked in evil," he said with his mouth full. "I refuse to associate them with my cooking."

I smiled along as everyone else laughed, but when my eyes landed on Jack, I felt the smile fade. He sat across the fire from me twirling his ring around his finger, ignoring the plate of food on the floor next to him. What must he have been feeling? The sound of Sy and David coming down the stairs caused him to lift his head and our eyes met for a second before we both glanced in their direction. Keeta and Logan scooted over to make room as David sank down onto the couch, a miserable look on his face. He was rubbing at his wrist like it was in pain. Remembering back to how it had seized on him when he'd shaken my hand, it wouldn't have surprised me if he was in a great deal of pain.

"So," Sy exhaled as he walked over to join us and handed David a plate of food. "Anything interesting happen today?" Then he looked at me. "Have you been caught up with everything."

His direct question caught me off guard. "Uh," I put

my fork down. "Yeah. Yeah, I'm good now."

With a satisfied nod, he continued on. "I already talked to Keeta. Anyone else?"

"Were we going to talk about what happened to Ben?" Melody asked quietly. We all looked at her then immediately to Jack to see his reaction. His eyes were glued once again to the ring in his hand.

Finally noticing the silence, Jack lifted his head again and looked around the circle. "You guys can," he muttered. "I'd rather not."

"It might help though, Jack," Sy said assuredly.

"Help what?" he snapped. "Ben died. He's gone. There's nothing more to say about it." Then he stood up, leaving his untouched food on the ground and trudged down the stairs to his room.

I wanted to go down after him, but something told me that Jack wanted to be left alone for a while. Even if it meant sitting and staring at my plate of food while feeling everyone's eyes shift to me. Finally, I shoved the last bit of ham into my mouth then got up quickly and took my plate to the sink. Then I just stood there chewing until I heard Melody start talking quietly to Arie. My shoulders sagged in relief as the conversations started back up and I felt it was safe to duck out.

When I got downstairs and into Jack's room, I found him lying on his bed on his stomach with his head facing the wall. I couldn't tell at first if he was still awake, but then I noticed a flash of silver and saw that he was still fidgeting with the ring. I went and sat down on the edge of my bed – Ben's bed – facing him. "Are you alright?" I asked, my voice barely above a whisper.

"I'm fine," Jack said flatly.

I scuffed my shoe across the floor and bit the inside of my cheek. "Do you want to talk about it?"

"Nope."

The next morning I woke up to an empty room. There was no note from Jack this time, but I didn't know if that was because I knew my way around now or if he was still brooding over the night before. Figuring it was probably a little bit of both, I got up and headed out into the hallway. The silence told me everyone was either not awake yet or already upstairs. On my way past the bathroom, I glanced at myself in the mirror and stopped. The girl staring back didn't quite look like how I felt. Dried, shiny streaks ran down from her eyes and over her cheeks. Her mouth was turned down in a defeated frown, like she'd never smile again. I stood like that for a while longer studying this broken girl. My reflection. Sure I was exhausted from what had happened over the past couple of days, but this girl looked like her whole world had come crashing down around her. Maybe it had.

"You were crying in your sleep last night."

I turned my head to find Jack on the first step, leaning against the wall. "I was?" I asked looking back at my reflection and feeling a bit embarrassed.

"Yeah," he said. "You kept waking me up. Thanks for that."

"Why didn't you wake me?"

Now Jack walked up behind me and stood, staring at his own reflection over my shoulder. "You just would have started right back up when you fell asleep again."

"If there is any similarity between you and a decent human-being, it is pure coincidence," I muttered and ran my fingers through my hair so I looked a little less terrifying. I caught the corner of Jack's mouth twitch into a quick half smile. Of course he found this all amusing. "I'm going upstairs," I finally said and trudged past him, purposefully catching his shoulder with mine. Without looking back to see the smug grin on his face, I started up the stairs wiping the dried tears from my cheeks then holding my head high.

The main floor was unoccupied, at least I thought, until I glanced at the hammock in the corner to find Melody and Arie with their lips locked together. We briefly made eye contact before I turned away embarrassed. "Morning," I said as nonchalantly as I could.

"Hi, Hailey," Melody said with a guilty smile. "How did you sleep?"

I tried not to notice her completely distraught curls or the fact that her gauzy top was slightly crooked. "Not as good as I thought, apparently," I said glancing at Arie as he ran his fingers through his frazzled blond hair.

"What do you mean?" Melody asked me, the look on her face changing to concern.

I shook my head. "Nothing," I said too quickly. "What's for breakfast?"

The morning continued on basically the same as the one before. Not too long after I had joined Melody and Arie upstairs, Root appeared, rubbing his eyes and put his glasses on before going into the kitchen to start cooking breakfast. Logan, David, Sy and Keeta arrived shortly after that, all looking like they hadn't slept very well. Especially David. I tried not to stare as best I could, but I couldn't help glancing over at him every so often as we ate breakfast. His mouth was frozen in a creepy, forced smile making him look like a puppet.

"Weird, huh?" Root whispered leaning in close to me.

I looked down at my food, feeling bad that I had been caught. "Yeah, I guess."

"It's all because of Eli's lousy chip," he muttered stabbing at a link of sausage on his plate.

"Alright, guys," Sy said and stood up to take his

plate to the sink. "Business as usual."

Everyone else finished eating and started preparing for the day. Root, with a map fixed under his arm, and Logan, with his laptop, headed over to the big kitchen table to start researching and planning while Keeta grabbed her backpack and went straight for the stairs to the bottom floor. Jack managed a glance my way before he grabbed poor David by the arm and pulled him toward the stairs as well, probably so they could start on something else that apparently needed to be fixed. After Sy had disappeared back up to his room, it was just Arie, Melody and I again. I sat on the arm of the couch and brought my knees up to my chest.

"So are you guys going back out to get more supplies?" I asked trying to make conversation. Attempting to clear up any awkwardness from earlier.

"We couldn't fit everything in our packs yesterday," Arie said. "So we're headed out for a second trip."

"Does that happen a lot? Jack was telling me you guys usually only go out like once a week."

"We try to only go once a week," Melody explained grabbing two more backpacks out of a closet in the corner. "We alternate days so it's harder for anyone to track us."

My breath caught. "You're being tracked?"

"Calm down, Hailey," Arie laughed and took a pack from Melody. "It's just a precaution."

"Yeah, we've never had any reason to believe we were being followed." It was weird seeing such a small bubbly girl with a big, tough looking pack slung over her shoulders. Especially paired with the easy-going smile on her face.

I nodded hugging my knees tighter against myself. Arie put a hand on my shoulder. "We'll see you tonight," he said giving it a gentle squeeze. Then I watched as he disappeared down the stairs with Melody closely following. Once the last of her bouncy curls were out of sight, I looked around and realized that, besides Root and Logan intently focused over at the table, I was alone.

I wasn't really sure what Sy's "business as usual" meant in my case, so I wandered down the stairs to the first floor.

The tree room was still just as magical as it had been the other times I had seen it. I made my way over some of the roots coming up through the floor and stood at the base of the tree by the small planter box. Looking down at the bright flowers, I frowned and took one of the petals between my fingers. Fake. Of course they were fake. Who would have remembered to come down here and take care of live flowers? I put my hand on the gray bark of the tree's trunk. It looked so old and tired. With everything that had been happening, who would remember to take care of this old tree? The thing that had given Sy and the rest a chance to stay here, to be protected.

Carefully, I took a hold of a branch above my head and pulled myself up onto it. It was a strong enough branch so I felt okay to reach up and grab the next one. Two more and I was as high as I could go. I sat back on this branch with my back against the window and looked back behind me out at the courtyard. The wall blocking us from the alley was just a bit taller, so I couldn't see anything past it. There was a new blanket of snow on the ground and I watched as a stray cat jumped down from on top of the fence and landed softly on its feet, burying itself up almost to its neck.

A smile cracked across my lips as I remembered the first time my parents had taken my brother and I to go skiing. It was a foggy day up on the mountain so none of us could see very far in front of us. I was having trouble just trying to keep my skis straight while Ryan tried showing off by speeding past me down the slope. He had disappeared into the fog in front of me and when I finally did catch up to him, I found a human-shaped hole in an embankment barely off course. A very cold, very embarrassed Ryan fell out of the hole onto his back and my parents and I just lost it.

Remembering all this, thinking I would never get a chance to make memories like that again caused my stomach to sink and tears to come to my eyes. I looked back again at the cat as it scampered back over the fence while I bit my lip to keep it from quivering.

"Sleeping again?"

Startled, I whipped my head around almost losing my balance, to find Jack standing in the doorway with his hands in pockets. "Geez, are you training to be a ninja or something?" I snapped settling back against the wall again. "Why do you keep sneaking up on me like that?"

"'For the lulz', I suppose," Jack said with a smirk.

"Are you crazy?" I asked and stepped down carefully onto a lower branch. "I could have fallen and broken my neck."

He walked in and stopped at the base of the tree. "I wouldn't say crazy. Maybe an eccentric who looks good in jeans." I rolled my eyes as I continued back down the tree. "Besides, I would have caught you if you'd fallen."

My feet hit the ground and I turned around brushing myself off. "From back there? What, are you a vampire?"

"I sure am," he said after a moment. Then he brought his hand up and carefully wiped a tear away from my cheek with his finger. I hadn't even notice it there. Too caught off guard to react, I stared with my mouth open, words waiting behind my lips to come out. They didn't get a chance to though. "On weekends I moonlight as a disco ball for that seventies club off the freeway."

With a scoff, I stepped back out of his reach. "I have bathrooms to clean," I muttered and walked out past him, trying to keep my head held high for the second time that morning, even though I felt like curling up into a ball on the floor.

I tried losing myself by cleaning the second floor bathroom, for the second time, smothering my thoughts with the smells of bleach and Windex. While scrubbing the shower wall, I pictured Jack's face on each little tile and scratched and scratched at it with my sponge until only my reflection glared back at me.

As I stabbed at the inside of the toilet with the toilet brush, I heard footsteps coming up the stairs and down the hall. I turned around in time to see Melody rush past the doorway. I dropped the brush and stuck my head out about to call her name, but she had already disappeared up the stairs to the main floor. Amazing smells started wafting down from the stairwell and I picked up all the cleaners and dirty rags and followed the aroma up the stairs. I found Melody talking to Keeta, animatedly flinging a wooden spoon around above her head. Keeta nodded every so often, only half concentrating on cutting the vegetables in front of her and not her fingers.

"What's going on?" I asked feeling like I'd warmed up to at least Melody since I'd arrived.

The two looked at me as if they hadn't heard me come up the stairs.

"Arie hasn't come home yet," Keeta said, her face hinting at worry.

Melody's expression was full-blown anxiety as she stirred the pot on the stove vigorously.

"We had cut the list in half and split up," she explained shaking her curly head. "I went to a new location and Arie went where we usually go for supplies. We were supposed to meet up back here two hours ago."

"He'll get here," Keeta said reassuringly, putting her hand on Melody's shoulder.

"I hope so. He's never been late before," she muttered turning back to the stove, her flowy sleeve hanging dangerously close to the burner.

By the time dinner was served, Arie still hadn't shown up. I could tell by the way Melody was pushing the food around on her plate that she was worried about him. Worried about her partner.

After dinner was over, I helped Keeta clear the table while Jack built up a new fire. David sat on the couch wrapping his arm. Jack had informed me that earlier he had spasmed, wrenching his hand sideways and fracturing his wrist. Root and Logan were talking quietly with Sy in the corner. Logan had the map pinned against the wall with one of his hands and was tracing a highlighted line with his other. Sy nodded every so often pointing somewhere else on the map, then Root would make notes in a notebook.

Arie still hadn't shown up by the time we'd all settled down onto the couches. Jack stood against the wall, his hands in his pockets and his shoulders slumped forward. Sy pulled up a stool and sat beside the fire in front of us.

"So, Jack came to me earlier today and told me it was okay if we wanted to do a small memorial type service for this brother," he started. "We all know what happened to Ben a few days ago. It's a tragic thing when someone so young goes so suddenly. Just know that he died a hero." I looked over at Jack. He had his eyes glued to the floor and his jaw clenched. His hands were still stuffed in his pockets, but I imagined they were clenched tightly as well.

Sy went on to say what an asset Ben had been to the group. How helpful he was and always welcoming to the newcomers. Hearing all these things made me wish I had known him. But then what would I have thought of Jack? Knowing his personality and how he had been treating me, so erratically, would I have wished he was gone instead of Ben? Immediately, the thought made me feel riddled with guilt. How could I wish someone dead over another? Over a person I had never even met. Jack wasn't a bad person. I just couldn't help but wonder.

"Is there anything you want to add?" Sy asked him quietly.

Jack just shook his head and only lifted it for a second to meet my eyes. I looked away, the guilt stabbing at my stomach. I'm a terrible person, I thought to myself. I couldn't focus during the rest of the meeting. All I could do was watch Jack and try to will some of his pain away. I wished I had something to say. Something to assure him, maybe.

By the end of the meeting, there wasn't a dry eye in the room. We had a moment of silence that stretched on for several minutes. I suppose it wasn't total silence. The sound of sniffing and clearing throats was a constant, as well as the crackling of the fire.

Sy excused himself after a little while and disappeared upstairs. David followed after him, the spasms having left him exhausted. The rest of us stuck around a while and I listened while they shared the few memories of Ben that they had. Melody stayed silent, still worried about Arie's absence. Jack was quiet too, staying back against the wall probably wondering if he could disappear without anyone noticing.

Slowly, people began to retire down to the second floor to get some sleep. Jack seemed relieved when he was able to go downstairs without saying a word to anyone. I was the second to the last to leave. Melody stayed behind watching the fire burn out, sick with worry for her missing companion.

A couple of hours later, the sound of her coming down the stairs woke me from my troubled sleep and I listened as she closed the door behind her. Jack's steady breathing in the bed next to mine brought the pangs of guilt back into my chest.

I had been laying in bed wide awake for an hour or so when I heard a crashing noise downstairs. I sat bolt upright just picturing Paulson or Adams kicking in the door and barging up the stairs, bullets flying.

"Jack," I whispered as loudly as I could.

He stirred, but didn't wake up. I got up from my bed and shook him hard.

"Jack!"

This time his eyes flew open and he pushed me off of him. "What the heck, Hailey!"

"Shut up!" I squeaked. "Listen."

More ruckus came from down below us. Whoever was here, was on the stairs. It sounded like they were stumbling around drunk. Jack got up quickly and headed to the door.

"I'll check it out," he said his hand on the knob. "You stay here." Then he disappeared into the hall, closing the door behind him quietly.

I got up off the floor and went over to the door. I opened it a crack to see Jack starting down the stairs, his back pressed against the wall. When he got to the landing below, his eyes grew wide. He went down to whoever was making noise and I heard more commotion.

"Hailey!" he called appearing again from around the corner. "Come help me."

I watched as he started up the stairs with a slumped person in tow. I recognized the tattoos snaking up his arms. The person lifted their head revealing Arie's dirtied face. I rushed to help hold his weight.

Just then the door to Root and Logan's room opened

and Root came out rubbing the sleep from his eyes.

"Help us out, Root," Jack grunted pulling a half conscious Arie down the hallways and toward his room. Root woke up immediately, put on his glasses and rushed over to us. "Hailey, go get Sy," Jack ordered.

I moved so Root could take my place under Arie's arm. His dark curly hair was a disheveled mess and would have been grounds for a joke or two if not for the dire situation at hand. I ran up the stairs taking two at a time and rushed across the meeting room. When I hit the top floor, I headed straight for Sy's room.

"Sy!" I yelled hoping he would be awake before I got there. "Sy! We need your help!"

When I turned the corner, he was coming out the door pulling on his shirt as fast as he could. "What's the matter, Hailey?" he asked me sounding concerned.

"Arie's hurt," I said breathless.

"He's here?"

Sy took off down the hall before I could answer. "He just came in. Jack has him and we think he's hurt bad," I explained trailing after him.

We headed down the stairs and into the meeting room. Melody was stoking a new fire she must have just lit. Root was already there and Arie was on the couch, his hands against his eyes as he tried to keep from crying out in pain. There was a dark red stained piece of cloth wrapped around his leg and secured with a belt. Blood was seeping out from beneath the cloth.

"What happened?" Sy asked getting down on his knees next to the couch to examine Arie's wound.

"We don't know anything," Root replied calmly. "But the front door was wide open."

Sy locked eyes with him and held his gaze as if they were having a telepathic conversation.

"Jack is outside now securing the perimeter," Root

said aloud. "Arie hasn't said anything though about what happened."

Sy carefully undid the belt around Arie's makeshift bandage. Even as he gritted his teeth to keep quiet, a pained grunt escaped when Sy unwrapped the cloth revealing a wide, dark bullet hole interrupting an inked spiral on his calf . Blood still flowed freely from the wound. I had to look away to keep my churning stomach from unleashing its contents.

"It looks deep," Sy said to himself touching the skin around the hole. "I don't see a bullet in there."

Arie groaned something unintelligible. We all looked at him. His face was dripping with sweat and his eyes were fluttering as he tried to keep from passing out from the pain.

"I..." he started slurring. "I took it out." His words were muddied as he tried to keep a hold on reality.

"He took the bullet out himself?" Melody gasped in terror.

"This needs to be cleaned before it becomes infected," Sy said staying calm. Then he turned to Melody. "Mel, I need you to go get the medical supplies from my room. Bring aspirin, alcohol and bandages. Now!"

She could only nod as she backed away from us then turned and ran up the stairs, disappearing onto the top level. We turned our attention back to Arie and Sy as he began tearing away the bottom part of the boy's shorts. This caused Arie to let out another pained cry. Sy pulled the fabric back revealing another bloodied bandage wrapped tightly just above his knee. When he undid this one, it revealed a long, deep gash on the inner part of his leg cutting through the image of an eagle's head. The blood spurted out when Sy took his hand away. The man cursed under his breath and shook his head.

"What is it?" I asked wishing Jack was there with me.

"His artery was nicked," Sy explained. "Put pressure on this, Hailey."

I put my hand over Sy's and pressed hard as soon as he removed it. He grabbed the belt from the other bandage job and wrapped it tightly around Arie's thigh above the gash. Root stayed over by the fire, throwing sticks in every so often from a small pile next to him.

"How did this one happen, Arie?" Sy asked taking a hold of the kid's head. Arie was still on the brink of consciousness. Sy had to repeat himself.

"A tree branch," Arie finally groaned. "to...hide in."

"He must have climbed a tree after he got shot," Root said.

"How are you going to fix his leg?" I asked staring at both bleeding wounds.

Melody came down just then. "Don't come any closer," Sy said to her. She stopped where she was still holding the bandages and bottles in her arms. "Root, go get those from her."

He did as he was told. Sy then sent her back upstairs to grab the rest of the medical supplies. I wondered for a minute why he hadn't let her near Arie. Then I thought about seeing the two of them cuddled up in the hammock that morning and knew. Sy didn't want Melody to see him like this. Especially since he didn't know if he could save him. Root brought the supplies back to Sy. He laid them out on the couch in front of him. Bandages, a pair of latex gloves, a scalpel, aspirin, a bottle of water and rubbing alcohol.

"Hailey, I'm going to need you to keep Arie calm," he said to me as he pulled the gloves on.

I nodded and had Root go to the kitchen area to fetch me a cold washcloth. Then I kneeled down next to his head. Even though I had only known Arie for a couple days, a motherly instinct took over and I began to gently stroke his forehead with the cold cloth, pushing his light wet hair off his skin. I put a couple aspirin in his mouth and gave him a sip of water from a bottle.

Sy took his time cleaning the bullet hole with the rubbing alcohol. Arie groaned again at first then began to quiet down as the aspirin took effect.

Melody came down about a minute later with a pack of more medical supplies. Sy pulled the edge of Arie's shorts back down over the gash so she wouldn't see it.

"Thank you," Sy said not looking away from his work. "You can leave that here. Go find Jack and make sure he doesn't need help."

Melody nodded then locked eyes with me and held my gaze until I gave her a reassuring smile. Then she disappeared downstairs with a flutter of material. My smile broke as soon as she was gone and I focused again on cleaning the dirt and sweat from Arie's face.

Sy quickly had the first wound cleaned, sewed shut and expertly bandaged before getting up and going to the kitchen. He came back with a spoon in hand and set it on the edge of the fire.

"What are you going to do with that?" I asked.

"I'm going to use it to stop the bleeding," Sy replied digging through the medical kit until he found a pair of tweezers.

I watched him carefully fish out splinters and bits of tree bark, wiping blood away every so often as it trickled out of the gash. Arie's face was pasty and slick with sweat by this point.

Finally, he was done. "Get the spoon for me," he said, "and use the washcloth. It'll be very hot."

I did as I was told and retrieved the red-hot spoon for him. He took it from me, holding the end in the washcloth as I had. The metal sizzled against the damp cloth.

"Try to keep him from flailing around too much," Sy said to Root and me gravely.

We both nodded securing Arie's wrists down to at his sides. I watched as Sy touched the hot spoon to the wound causing Arie to let out the most horrendous scream I had ever heard in my life. My attempt at keeping his arm down was futile. He was much bigger than me, therefore much stronger and it didn't take a lot of effort from him to rip his arms from my grasp.

"Almost done," Sy yelled over Arie's animalistic screeching. Root gritted his teeth against Arie's strength.

Finally, Sy pulled the spoon away leaving the cut blackened and ugly, but sealed nonetheless. I helped him clean the blood off Arie's leg then he and Root carried him down to his room.

With all that excitement finally over, I fell back onto the couch exhausted and watched the fire slowly start to die. A few minutes later, Jack came up the stairs.

"Is he going to be okay?" he asked and sat down next to me.

"I think so," I replied not taking my eyes from the fire.

Out of the corner of my eye, I could see Jack studying me. "Are you?" He asked. I tried to keep my feelings under control. This was all becoming too much for me. Sy had asked me to be strong while there was a screaming boy in excruciating pain in front of me. After having gone through what I had so recently. After losing everything I had ever known. Ever loved. My family. My home. The life I thought I knew.

It was no use. Once I started thinking about everything, my emotions overwhelmed me and I fell into Jack, tears freely flowing from my eyes. He hesitantly wrapped an arm around me.

I tried to hold in the whimpers and the sobs, but it was no use. Within seconds the collar of Jack's shirt was soaked from my tears and snot. He didn't seem to care though. He just took it, tentatively hugging my shoulder, telling me that things were going to be okay and that I was safe. I was finally able to calm down enough that the noises stopped. I stared at the fire as tears continued to fall from my eyes. We stayed like that in silence until the fire was just glowing embers. Jack didn't say a word, just continued holding me there with his one arm.

This was the first time since I'd met him that I felt like maybe he wasn't cold hearted and callous like I had thought he was. Maybe deep inside there was a lost boy as sad and scared as I was. Wishing he could make everything better for someone else, if not for himself. I couldn't imagine what he must have been feeling now. Having witnessed his brother's death and then having to go in search for me. No time to grieve. No time to say goodbye.

I sat up just then wiping my face with the sleeves of my shirt.

"I'm sorry," I whispered, my voice hoarse from the sobbing.

"It's alright," Jack replied just as quietly.

"No," I said. "about Ben."

He went quiet and rigid then, taking his arm from around my shoulders. I turned to look at him and found he was frozen, crouched over with his elbows on his knees just staring at the floor. I immediately regretted saying that.

After several minutes of silence, Jack stood up.

"I'm going to bed," he whispered then started down the stairs.

I didn't try to follow after him. I knew I had made a mistake in mentioning his brother. I fell over sprawled out on the couch and watched the glowing coals. More tears started spilling over and ran down the side of my face into my hair and onto the couch. How did I even have any left? I grabbed a stray chip of wood and threw it onto the coals, watching it ignite then slowly burn out. The night's events left me exhausted and feeling drained. My eyes burned and itched from all the crying and I just didn't have it in me to stay awake any longer. Sleep took over as the last glowing coal faded to black.

CHAPTER SIX

"Wakey, wakey, sleepyhead."

My eyelids cracked open to Root's big brown eyes in my face. I reeled back, startled by how close his face was to mine and sat up. He chuckled as I looked around in a daze. I was still on the couch in the meeting room. Keeta was sitting on the other end looking at notes written in a spiral notebook, Logan bent over the back of of the couch speaking quietly. Melody and Arie were on the hammock again. Arie was wincing, biting his lip trying not to cry out as Melody changed his bandages and applied medicine to the cauterized gash on his thigh. He looked a lot better, though, which loosened the knot in my stomach a little. It seized back up when Jack entered the room carrying a few pieces of wood. His eyes met mine only for a second before he focused his attention on starting the fire back up. Someone had draped a blanket over me while I was asleep and I clutched it around my body now realizing how cold the air was.

I hadn't noticed before that Root was holding out a

plate of eggs and bacon for me. I took it now from him, eying the food hungrily. As I began to dig in, Sy came down the stairs, holding David up by his good arm. I moved over letting David slump down next to me. He winced rubbing at his neck.

"What's wrong?"

He looked at me tilting his head one way slightly, then the other. "I woke up and couldn't move my neck very well."

"Is that part of the tetanus?" I whispered already knowing the answer.

"Yeah."

"Alright everyone." Sy rubbed his hands together. "Today is going to go a little different."

Jack sat on the floor in front of me, leaning back against the couch. I wished I could put my hand on his shoulder or something. But just looking at him, I knew he would pull away.

"Hailey." I turned my attention back to Sy. "You will be helping Melody today. Arie wasn't able to get the supplies he needed to yesterday so you two need to go finish the list."

I glanced over at Melody and she smiled at me. This made me nervous. I hadn't been on the streets for two days now and the thought of finishing what Arie hadn't been able to do scared me a bit. Melody seemed to know what she was doing though. At least I would be in good hands.

Sy went on to tell everyone else that today would be business as usual then put Jack with David and went back upstairs to work in his room. Melody came over and said we would be leaving in an hour.

After people had started going about their business, I went down into the second floor bathroom and locked the door behind me. I stripped down and took a shower scrubbing at my skin till it was red and raw. Then I washed my shirt in the sink and put on Jack's coat, zipping it up to my neck. I sat down on the toilet for a minute and dried my hair with a towel. I could feel a panic attack coming on as I thought about going out to finish Arie's job. I'm the least sneaky person alive. If Arie had been doing this for a while and still got caught, what made anyone think I'd be any good? My hair was still damp as I grabbed my shirt from the sink, wrung it out and headed upstairs.

Only Melody and Arie were there now. I felt a little relieved to find Jack no longer in the room. Probably off helping David with something. I sat on the floor next to the fire and held my shirt up in front of it, hoping to get it somewhat dry before we had to go.

I'm not sure how long I had been sitting there staring at the flames when Melody came and sat down next to me. She laid her head down on her knees and looked at me sideways.

"I have a shirt you can borrow while you wait for that to dry," she said with a sideways smile.

I wrinkled the material of my still damp shirt with my fingers. "Okay."

The two of us got up and I followed her down to her room. I guess all the bedrooms were set up basically the same here. It kind of surprised me how plain it was, but then again, it wasn't like this was her bedroom. What could her room at home have looked like? Melody held out one of her flowy shirts to me to put on, which I did, quickly. It felt really light, like I wasn't really wearing anything. Quickly I put Jack's coat back on and zipped it up with my shaky hands.

"It's going to be really easy, Hailey," Melody assured me. "Arie was saying they found out about the place he was going. Either one of their spies tipped them off or a suit just happened to be in the right place at the right time."

"Suit?"

"Agent."

I nodded, the sinking feeling in my stomach easing just a bit.

"Are you ready to go?"

"I think so," I said putting my hands into Jack's coat pockets.

The two of us headed down the stairs and down the hallway to the tree room. We got out into the courtyard and Melody started for the scaffolding.

"Why are we going this way?" I asked confused.

"Guess Jack hasn't told you yet." She hiked her skirt up and put a foot up onto the first bar. "The first rule of the Tree House is 'Never use the front door'."

I remembered back when Jack and I had first gotten here. He's such a rebel, I thought to myself, but didn't say it out loud. Melody was on the other side of the wall by the time I was able to get halfway up without slipping. Once on the other side of the wall, I found myself in an alley. There were dark, deserted looking buildings on either side of us. Looking back, the wall didn't seem out of place. It perfectly disguised the Tree House, keeping the alley a safe place to go in and out.

The street connected to the alley was deserted as well, but Melody didn't waste any time. She broke into a brisk jog as soon as we were out of the shadows.

"We have to move fast," she said under her breath.

I kept up with her pretty well as we hurried down the street, staying close to the buildings lining the sidewalk. She turned down another alley not slowing down. I followed after her stopping once we'd reached a ladder. My mouth dropped open when Melody began climbing up to the top of the two story building.

"What are we doing?" I asked looking up at her.

"Avoiding people," she replied from halfway up.

Without another word, I started up the ladder after her. She helped me up on top of the roof and I looked out at the tops of other buildings.

"So, this is how you and Arie get around?" I asked.

"This is how we all get around in this area," Melody replied catching her breath. "Unless it's night, we use rooftops. Come on," she said. "The bus stop is only a couple blocks from here."

I watched in horror as Melody ran toward the other side of the roof then jumped and cleared the ten foot gap landing on another roof. After taking a deep, shaky breath, I broke into a run, going as fast as I could. When I reached the edge, I pushed off hard and sailed through the air. I cleared the gap by a long shot and landed hard on my feet then fell forward, catching myself by rolling over my shoulder. I mentally thanked my old soccer coach for teaching us how to fall properly all those years ago. Melody helped me up and I brushed myself off.

"You alright?" she asked me.

"Yeah," I replied out of breath.

"Bend your knees and don't stop running once you hit the ground," she explained. "It'll help you stay on your feet."

I nodded and we continued on to the next roof. After a couple of jumps, I was beginning to get the hang of it. I had just landed somewhat gracefully for the first time, when Melody stopped.

"We're almost there," she said going to the edge of the building.

There was a ladder going down into another alley. She started down it and I followed after her. Once we reached the ground, I leaned back against the wall rubbing at my sore legs. My throat hurt from overexertion and my head was still swimming with adrenaline. "I just need a minute," I said to Melody.

She nodded with an understanding smile then leaned against the wall next to me and took a small notepad out of the pocket of her skirt. I hadn't realized before what good shape she was in. This had been her job since she'd gotten to the Tree House. No wonder she was barely breathing hard.

"What's on the list?" I asked straightening up and stretching my back.

"We still need to get medical supplies," she said. "Especially since we used what we had left on Arie last night."

"Where do we need to go?"

"There's a medical supply store a few miles into the city," Melody explained putting the notepad back in her pocket, "hopefully this one isn't being watched."

Without another word, the two of us rounded the corner. There were a few people on the street, but none of them looked very suspicious. I followed Melody down a couple storefronts then the two of us headed down another alley and came out the other side on a busier street.

"This way," she said and turned left, walking toward a bus stop.

There were a couple people there waiting, sitting on the bench or leaning against the pole with the schedule on it. I tried to look inconspicuous, which would have been more believable if I wasn't trying.

The bus pulled up and we shuffled on with the crowd, taking a seat near the front. I stared out the window watching as the buildings grew taller and the streets became more populated. A few more minutes and we were in the heart of Seattle. Tall skyscrapers plunged the streets below into shadows. Everything was gray, made of concrete and metal. The only colors were those of the bright yellow taxi cabs and the designer clothes in storefront windows.

"Hey," Melody said quietly, "look there."

I looked at where she was pointing to out the window as we passed another tall skyscraper. The space between this one and the next revealed another tall building a few blocks back. This one was white with hundreds of windows.

"That's Eli's company," she whispered.

I felt a shudder pass through my body. That's the place I had been taken to when I was still a newborn. The place they would surely take me to again if I was ever caught. Only this time, I wouldn't come back out.

"How much longer?" I asked shifting uncomfortably in my seat.

"Just relax, Hailey." Melody laughed. "We still have like forty minutes."

I sat back against the seat staring out the window. I couldn't help thinking about Jack and what had happened the night before.

"Do you know what happened to Jack's brother?" I asked curiously.

Melody shrugged and shook her head sadly. I nodded in reply. The skyscrapers began to shrink back down again as we continued further across Seattle.

Stepping off the bus, I found myself standing on the street corner of a suburb similar to my own. This confused me.

"Where exactly are we getting these supplies from?" I asked Melody.

"Medical supply store," she murmured looking down at small drawn map in her notepad.

"What's that?"

"Directions," she said. "Only Arie has been to this

place."

We started walking, Melody checking her map every so often to make sure we were going the right way. Houses turned into small shops after a couple turns. It was mid-afternoon by the time we walked into a little medical supply store.

A bell dinged as the door closed behind us. The store was small. There were a few rows with different types of bottled pills and the back wall was lined with packages of bandages, gauze and medical instruments. An older man sat behind the counter wearing a white coat.

"Good morning," Melody chimed with a bright smile.

"Good morning, girls," he replied.

She turned to me. "Get the Vicodin," she breathed pressing a forged doctors note into my hand. "Tell him that you are picking up a prescription for Allison Baker."

I nodded as she started for the back wall, humming cheerily to herself. The panic was welling up in my stomach again as I approached the counter. Stay calm, I told myself, I'm sure he gets this every day.

I plastered a smile onto my face. "I need to pick up a prescription, please," I said. Oh gosh, he'll see right through my facade.

The man smiled and nodded, "Name?"

"Allison Baker."

"One moment," the man said then turned and disappeared into a back room.

I could just see it now. He's calling the company to let them know we're here and they'll have the place surrounded in seconds. My heart began to thump loudly in my chest as I thought of all the ways I could be killed once I was caught. Maybe they would do it fast. A gunshot to the head or one quick twist of the neck. Or maybe they would make me suffer for running or for getting a couple of their guys killed. Maybe they would take me back to their medical center and do tests on me. Take my blood, or inject poison into my veins.

"Here you are, my dear," the man said, snapping me back to reality.

He placed the bag containing the pills onto the counter. I stared down at the bag. Another couple of bags joined it on the counter and I looked up to find Melody standing next to me. She pulled out a couple of twenties from her pocket and put them on the counter.

"You can keep the change." She smiled. "Have a nice day."

I smiled too then followed Melody out the door and back onto the street. My shoulders relaxed and I exhaled heavily once we made it outside. I hadn't realized I'd been holding my breath for a while. As Melody turned, headed for another bus stop, I stopped short. A girl had been leaning back against a stop sign across the street smoking a cigarette. Now she stood straight up, her mouth open, and a look of sheer astonishment in her eyes.

I stared at her unmoving. She looked young, ragged, and sick like she lived on these streets. Her long white blond hair was braided and tangled, a knit beanie was pulled down over her eyebrows and her clothes were dirty and rumpled. But her eyes were big and alert. It seemed like she had been searching for something. Or waiting for someone. My eyes narrowed. Why was she looking at me like this? As if I was the last person she thought she would ever see.

Before anything else could happen, the girl shoved her hands into the pockets of her leather jacket and walked quickly down the street, head down to hide her face. I looked after her, watching as she turned a corner and disappeared down another street.

I turned back around shaking my head. The people

in this city are nuts.

Melody was halfway up the street by the time I reached her. The walk and bus ride back across the city was uneventful. I kept what I had seen to myself figuring what with everything that had happened with Arie, Melody didn't need something else to worry about.

The bus let us off back at the same stop we had gotten on at. I didn't really know what time it was, but guessing by the setting sun and how tired I was already feeling, I guessed it was close to six. We had already been gone for almost four hours.

"I'm starving," I said stretching my back once my feet had hit the pavement.

Melody chuckled. "Hope you aren't too hungry," she said. "We still have a little ways to go."

We started walking the opposite direction of where we had come from originally. I'm guessing we were taking a different route home, just to be safe. A few blocks down, we stopped at a convenience store to get some water. I downed mine pretty fast having not realized how thirsty I really was.

Now with a sloshing belly, I was feeling sluggish, almost sick. Melody started pulling ahead of me and by the time I had turned to follow her down another alley, she was already half way up the ladder.

I jogged to catch up then made my way quickly up and onto the roof. Once there, I continued to try and clear the alleys without biting the dust. I made it across two before a white blur from a few roofs over caught my attention, causing me to fall, landing hard on my knees. Melody stopped and hurried over to me.

"Are you okay?" she asked worriedly.

"Yeah," I replied out of breath, fighting to keep the water down. My eyes searched frantically in the area I swore I had seen something. Someone.

"What's wrong?"

I continued searching. Scanning the rooftops for movement. There, just a few buildings away, I saw another flash of white hair.

"We're being followed," I squeaked trying to keep my voice under control.

"We need to get down," Melody said quickly, pulling me to my feet and racing for the nearest ladder.

I followed hastily, slipping on the first rung. Just before my view of the rooftops disappeared, I caught the sight of the crazed girl running and jumping like we had been toward our rooftop. The two of us hit the ground at a run and raced out of the alley. Melody was a few feet in front of me and seemed to be cutting through alleys and breezeways in no particular pattern. I tried to keep up with her as best as I could, but like I said before, she had been doing this for a while now and was in much better shape than I was. It also didn't help that my stomach was still full of water.

After several blocks of weaving in and out of streets, Melody was half a block ahead of me, and I was getting tired.

It only took her another block before she realized that I was no longer following her. By this time I was sitting in an alley on a small concrete porch, trying to catch whatever ragged breath I could.

"We have to keep going," she said glancing around the corner.

"Just give me a second," I gasped

Melody sat down next to me. "I think we lost her for now."

I watched her breathe in deep a couple of times and push her blonde curls back from her forehead.

"You were in track, weren't you?" I asked sarcastically.

"Took first in the 800 meter and 3200 meter my senior year, why?"

"Never mind," I muttered resting my head on my knees.

Melody stood back up and held her hand out. "Come on, before they catch up." I reluctantly took her hand and let her pull me to my feet. "Almost there," she assured me and we started jogging, picking up the pace quickly.

After a couple of turns, I began to recognize where we were. My pace and breathing were starting to even out and the distance between Melody and I was getting smaller. We rounded a corner and ended up on the street connecting to our alley.

"Thank God," I breathed slowing down a bit.

Melody kept pace with me, our speed decreasing until we reached a fast walk.

"See?" she said between breaths. "That wasn't so hard."

I let out a noise somewhere between a chuckle and a groan, causing her to laugh. As we were about to turn down the alley, I glimpsed something down at the other end. I shoved Melody to the other side of the opening.

"She's there," I whispered, my stomach feeling nervous.

Melody's eyes widened, then she took my hand and broke into a sprint, pulling me behind her.

"Where are we going?" I asked trying to not trip.

She didn't reply. We turned the corner sharply, causing my arm to wrench from it's socket then snap back into place. I yelped and Melody let go, not slowing down. I followed close behind, keeping my eyes glued on the opening to the street a block down, waiting for the girl to appear. By the time we had reached the front door, the street was still empty. Melody flipped the latch and threw herself against the door. The two of us crashed inside and shut it behind us. I, once again, found myself gasping for air, only now Melody joined me. Both of us sat back against the door, silent except for our heavy breathing.

CHAPTER SEVEN

"I thought," I gasped, "we weren't supposed to use the front door."

Melody let her head fall to the side so she was looking at me, "Couldn't really use the back way with her watching us, could we?" she asked panting hard.

Neither of us moved or said anything else as we tried to catch our breath. My shoulder throbbed, but didn't seem as badly hurt as I thought it would be.

After a couple of minutes, we both got up and started up the stairs. Melody continued up to the third, then fourth floor to give Sy our findings. I, however, stopped at Jack's bedroom door and went in. The room was empty so I locked the door, stripped off Jack's coat and Melody's shirt, and laid down on my bed in just my bra, exhausted. As I buried my face in the pillow, I realized something. I was laying in a dead man's bed.

Before my thoughts could become any more depressing, I closed my eyes and tried not to think of the scared, big eyed girl. I was half suspended in dream land when loud, angry yelling boomed from the floor above me.

Suddenly wide awake, I threw Melody's shirt back on, grabbed Jack's coat and hurried out the door and up the stairs, taking two at a time. When I reached the top, I found Melody, Sy and a very red-faced Jack.

"What do you mean, you used the front door?" he screamed, eyes wide. "In the middle of the day?"

"Well, we couldn't very well go through the alley!" Melody yelled back. "What else were we supposed to do?"

"Keep running! Lose her!"

"Jack, calm down," Sy said quietly, "Mel, did anyone see you come in?"

"No," she replied matching his tone.

"Yeah, that you could see," Jack muttered clenching and unclenching his fists.

Melody shot him a dagger of a look. "You think I'm an idiot."

"Well, you aren't exactly proving that theory wrong," he spat, sarcasm dripping from his words.

Melody's jaw clenched tightly as if she were trying to lock her mouth shut.

"As long as everyone is safe," Sy said, finally breaking the tension.

Jack shook his head in disgust. "For now," he grumbled then stormed off up the stairs to the top floor.

The three of us stood there for a few moments silent. It was almost as if I could still feel the walls vibrating from Jack's angry foot stomps. It could have been my imagination, but I swear I saw the branches along the walls retreat, trying to get away from the anger that filled the room.

Melody turned to Sy, her eyes shining. "I didn't know what else to do," she whispered with a hopeless shrug.

"I know," he replied putting a reassuring hand on her shoulder. "Jack is having a rough time. You need to understand."

"Well, he doesn't need to take it out on me." She pulled away and disappeared down the stairs to the second story. Arie limped after her.

The sound of her door slamming made me jump. Sy and I looked at each other waiting for the other to say something. "I think I'll go check on Jack," I said quietly then started up the stairs toward the roof.

At first when I got up to the roof, it looked empty. A horrifying thought went through my mind. What if he had jumped? I raced over to the ledge. A streetlamp cast a dim light on the dark street below. Nothing.

"Don't worry." I whipped around to find a Jack shaped outline leaning against a beam. He stepped away from it. "I wouldn't do something stupid," he said standing next to me.

I studied his profile in the dim light. His eyes stared hard out into the night at the distant skyscrapers and traffic on the interstate. "How would I know?" I asked folding my arms over my chest.

"Sorry," he muttered.

"You won't let me know anything about you. I had to find out about Ben from Melody," I said. "You can't keep everything a secret, Jack. It'll destroy you."

He shivered. "I know."

The freezing weather made me grateful that I had thought to grab Jack's coat. Though now I wished I had borrowed one from someone else so he could have his back. I knew that if I offered it to him, he would refuse. I didn't know, though, if it was because he didn't want me to deal with the frigid cold or if he felt that he deserved to.

We were both quiet for a while. Maybe he was trying to decide whether or not to trust me with his secrets. Maybe he was still fuming from the argument with Melody.

"She was just trying to make the best decision," I said quietly.

Jack turned to look at me. "What?"

"Melody," I said. "She was just trying to think on her feet. I probably would have done the same thing."

He let out a pathetic chuckle and looked back out at the skyline. "That's why you clean toilets."

I bit my lip to keep from lashing out. I could see right through his front. "You try so hard to make people hate you," I whispered, afraid if I raised my voice, I wouldn't be able to stop yelling.

"Is it working?" he asked.

"You don't understand," I said. "You may be trying to make me hate you, but I'm trying to make me hate you too." Jack fell silent. "I'm going to get something to eat," I said, finally. "Want anything?"

He still didn't say anything. I must have hit a nerve. His walls were back up and here I thought I'd finally cracked the surface.

I hadn't even noticed I was clenching my fists so tightly until I got down to the meeting room and felt the skin on my palms ache under my nails. I had never been so angry at someone in my life. It wasn't so much that I was angry at him for being so frigid, but rather for being so mean to himself.

Keeta, Root and Logan were all sitting on the couches talking and eating. David sat at the table picking at his food, rubbing his jaw in pain.

"Hi David," I sighed grabbing a plate of chicken and mashed potatoes and taking a seat next to him.

He waved with his free hand, keeping the other one

on his jaw.

"Has Jack always been a complete jerk?"

David nodded, the corners of his mouth twitching like he was trying to smile. I smiled back sadly remembering that one of the side effects of tetanus is lockjaw. I realized for David to open his mouth would be extremely painful. My chicken suddenly needed my undivided attention.

The two of us picked at our food in silence. When I ate what I could, I took mine and David's plates to the sink and washed them, carefully putting them up in the cupboard where they belonged.

I considered bringing Jack something to eat, but decided against it. He could get his own lousy food.

Not knowing what else to do, I went downstairs to Jack's room and laid in bed staring up at the ceiling. It was cold down here. I pulled the blankets up to my chin and closed my eyes, not really intending to fall asleep. Only when my mind began to wander did I recognize how tired I really was. Having spent most of the day running or jumping across rooftops, my muscles were starting to ache. Even with the maddening conversation with Jack still fresh in my mind, sleep took over, though it was a shallow and fitful sleep.

I woke a couple of hours later. I only knew it was still early because the sound of the fire above my head hadn't died down any, meaning there were still people up there keeping it going. There was no way I was falling back asleep. I was wide awake. With a moan from my aching muscles, I swung my legs over the side of the bed and sat up. Maybe Jack had cooled down enough to be civil. I put on my shoes then got up, dragging the blanket with me. I still had Jack's coat on, but maybe he would finally take it if he knew that I would be warm enough.

The scene hadn't changed much from the last time I

was in the meeting room. Keeta, Logan and Root were still on the couches, Keeta debating with Root about something. I couldn't really hear what they were saying. Melody and Arie had joined them. Arie had his bad leg up, draped over Melody's lap. The two of them were chatting with Logan. Well, mostly Arie. Melody still looked upset.

David was still over at the table, but Sy was now sitting across from him wrapping the wrist that wasn't already bandaged. David's eyes were red rimmed and his hair a disheveled mess. It looked like he had been tearing it out.

I walked through the room without saying anything to anyone. I really just wanted to make sure that Jack still hadn't "done something stupid," as he had said so sarcastically earlier.

When I got up to the roof, Jack was still standing where I had left him. I'm sure he had moved during the time that I was asleep, but the dangerous ledge seemed to be his favorite place to wallow.

"Still here?" I asked, my words cracking from sleep.

He jumped at the sound of my voice, whipping around to make eye contact. I saw something flash in his hands. The ring.

"Of course I'm still here." His teeth chattered. "Whoever followed you two could be out there just waiting for me to turn my back. It would take two seconds..." He twirled the ring on his finger.

I unzipped his coat and took it off. When I offered it to him, he shook his head.

"Jack, stop being stupid," I said sternly, still holding it out.

He stared at me, narrow-eyed, for a few seconds before finally taking it from me and zipping it up to his chin. "Thanks," he muttered, the bottom half of his face hidden by the collar of his coat.

"I would say no problem," I said sarcastically, "but you seem to like making simple things difficult."

This got a chuckle out of him.

"I'm sorry, Hailey," Jack said quietly.

It sounded genuine enough. I made sure to keep my eyes locked on the city lights in the distance.

"I know," I replied then sat down, dangling my feet over the edge. Jack joined me still holding the ring. I watched him for a minute as he just stared at it, turning it over in his hands. "You have to tell me," I said.

Jack looked at me, a hint of sadness in his eyes. "It was Ben's," he said softly then held it out to me.

I made sure to be very careful as I took the ring, my fingertips brushing against his for just an instant. The blue stone in the center sparkled brilliantly in the moonlight. Looking closely, I saw that the markings surrounding the stone were, in fact, those you would find on a class ring. One side said, in simple text, "Ben" while the other had the year he graduated high school.

"This is his class ring?" I asked.

"Yeah," Jack replied. "The stone is a family heirloom apparently. Our parents had it put in when they had the ring made."

"And you didn't get one?"

"Only one family heirloom," he said. "It goes to the oldest son."

"But aren't you and Ben the same age?" I asked confused.

"He's older by a few months."

"So," I started. "Why do you have it?"

"Well," he plucked it from my hand, "I am now the oldest."

I nodded looking down at the street below us. I wondered if that girl was out there watching us. Just out of the light's reach. A chill ran over my skin and I pulled the blanket tighter around my body.

"I think you should go back inside, Hailey," Jack said having noticed me shivering.

"I'm okay," I replied.

"Now who's the stubborn one?"

I looked at Jack. He raised an eyebrow and flashed a crooked smile. "What happened to Ben?" I asked changing the subject.

The smile wiped clean off his face and he looked back down at the ring, suddenly enamored with it. "Hailey..."

"I'm sorry, Jack," I said. "I know it's hard."

"No," he whispered. "I'm just...scared."

This caught me off guard. Left me speechless for a good ten seconds. "Of what?" I finally asked.

"I've always been alone," he explained thoughtfully. "Even when Ben was alive. He was a leader. I was always one to stay back. Blend in with the scenery."

My stomach fluttered nervously. This was a side of Jack I hadn't seen before. "And now?" I asked.

"And now..." Jack looked at me. "How do I fill shoes that I don't want to fill?"

"No one is asking you to take charge, Jack," I said wishing I had the nerve to reach out and touch him. To put a reassuring hand on his hand, resting on the ledge only inches from mine.

"David is dying, Hailey," he said sadly, "and everyone knows that Sy is next. It would only make sense for me to take on the responsibility of the group. But I'm not sure I can live up to my brother. "

I could hear in his voice how scared he really was. How unprepared he felt.

"You don't give yourself enough credit," I said shaking my head. "The others here look up to you."

Jack let out a chuckle. "Seriously," he muttered. "Seriously."

"How can you know? You've been here for three days." Jack asked me shaking his head.

I smiled keeping my eyes locked with his.

Before I had the chance to answer that question, Sy's voice erupted up through the makeshift chimney.

"Jack!" he yelled. "Get down here!"

The two of us jumped up and raced down the stairs to the third floor. The scene caused a scream to escape from my throat. Root, Logan, Sy and even Arie with his bad leg were struggling with David, who was on the floor convulsing. His back was so arched, it looked like his body was trying to bend in half.

"Jack! Now!" Sy shouted over the sound of David's screams of agony.

Without a word, Jack hurried over and helped hold his friend down. All I could do was stand and watch in horror along with Melody and Keeta. Intermingling with all the shouting, was the sound of bones breaking. Keeta ran over to the boys and pushed her knee down on David's chest, trying to force him down flat. Nothing was working. He continued to cry out, blood vessels bursting all around his eyes. I had to look away to keep from screaming again, and to keep from getting sick all over the floor.

Melody wrapped her arms around me and pulled me against her, turning away, shielding both of our faces from the horrific scene unfolding in front of us.

A loud bang tore through the commotion and I whipped around to see what had happened. David had gone silent and the boys had backed off leaving Sy standing over the man with Jack's pistol in his hand.

We all stared in wide-eyed silence. "It had to be done," he finally whispered staring down at his friend's lifeless body. "He's not in pain any more."

He handed the pistol back to Jack then fell back against the wall, staring down at David.

The room was silent. No one said a word. The only sound I could hear was the crackling of the fire. This was how I was going to die. What had Eli done? It took a while before anyone moved. Finally, Jack stirred walking past Sy and pulling him by the arm to the corner. He started whispering hurriedly, glancing at David's body every so often. I couldn't hear anything either of them were saying.

At last, Sy turned to look at his friend's body then nodded his head. Jack put a sympathetic hand on his shoulder then called for Logan and Root to help him and the three of them disappeared down the stairs.

"What's going on?" Keeta asked, her voice cracking.

"They are going to get David out of here," Sy replied then kneeled down next to his dead friend and closed David's eyes with his hand.

"I can't be here," Melody whispered and hurried down the stairs to her room. Keeta and Arie went after her leaving Sy and I alone with David.

I was still frozen in place from shock. The horror of the situation was making my heart pound and causing my ears to ring. This thing that had done that to David...was in me. This disease that would erupt in twenty years. How long did Sy have? Months? Weeks? Days? He was a ticking time bomb. Without saying a word, I walked over and slumped down on the couch. The fire was still going so I leaned in close, staring into the flames, hoping they would burn away the images carved into my brain.

A while later, I heard Jack and Root come back up the stairs.

"Is Logan in the car?" I heard Sy ask from behind me.

"Yeah," Jack replied quietly. "Did you want to say anything before..."

"He won't hear me, Jack," Sy interrupted. "David's not here any more."

They didn't say anything else. As Root and Jack carried David's body to the stairwell, I looked away from the fire and locked eyes with Jack. He stared at me, his eyes were red like he had been crying. I held his gaze for a few seconds before turning my attention back to the fire. The two disappeared down the stairs with David's body.

I watched the fire die down to coals before the sound of footsteps coming up the stairs broke my trance. Jack walked slowly across the room to Sy with the rest of the group coming up the stairs behind him.

Melody, Keeta and Arie joined me on the couch, Melody laying her head on my shoulder. I put a hand on her back in an attempt to comfort her. The other boys sat around the table with Sy.

What could have been going through Sy's mind at this moment? Having just seen his friend die such a horrible death and knowing he would soon follow. I'm sure everyone was thinking the same thing I was. I looked around at my grave faced friends, all of them either deep in thought or too miserable to speak.

I couldn't get the images of David, delirious with agony, out of my head. I could still see his eyes, speckled red with broken blood vessels, his lips purple with strain as he tried to fight his own contorting body. The sound of breaking bones resonated in my ears causing my own back to throb and my teeth to chatter.

"No." Melody whispered. I turned to look at her. She was staring at the stairwell. I nearly jumped out of my seat when my eyes locked on the familiar wide eyed face of the crazed girl from the suburb.

Before anything else could be said, Jack was across the room, whipping his gun out and cocking it. He stopped only a few feet from the girl, arm extended, the barrel inches from her head. The rest of us jumped to our feet.

"Who are you?" he asked, his words cutting like daggers.

"Jack, put that away," Sy commanded.

Jack ignored his orders. "You have ten seconds," he spat, finger on the trigger.

The girl was staring with disbelief at the gun pointed at her head. "I-I I'm one of you," she quivered. "I'm one of you! I'm a patient!"

"Jack, put the gun down!" I had never heard Sy raise his voice like that before.

"Shut up, Sy!" Jack yelled back then turned his attention to the girl again. "How did you find us?"

"I followed her," she replied pointing at me with a trembling finger.

I looked away biting my lip to keep the tears back. This was too much.

"Your name?" Jack asked narrowing his eyes.

She was silent for a moment. Staring back at Jack with her big eyes, trying to find the right thing to say.

"Three seconds!" he snapped impatiently.

"It's Hai...Hailey Roemer!" the girl blurted out.

My breath caught in my throat as every eye landed on me. Had she said my name on purpose or was that by chance? If this girl was a spy...

I could just see it. In seconds this place was going to be swarming with the company's agents. How many of us would they kill on the spot? How many would they take with them, dragging my friends away from the one place we felt safe. The girl's gaze snapped me back to reality. It seemed to hit her that she had made a mistake.

"Wrong answer, sweetheart," Jack muttered as he pressed the tip of the gun to the skin right below the edge of her beanie. Right between her eyes.

"Please," she pleaded, tears streaming down her face. "I'm sorry I lied. My name is Anna. Anna Foster."

"Root?" He turned looking at the dark haired kid still frozen by the table.

"You don't understand," Anna whispered.

"Shut up," Jack snapped then turned to Root again.

He was frantically typing away on Logan's computer. After several tense seconds, Root looked back up from the screen.

"She's not on the list," he said sadly.

Jack turned back to Anna. "Didn't think so."

"Please, if you would let me explain," she cried shaking her head and trying to back away.

"Sorry."

"Jack!" Sy boomed. "Stop!"

"Don't tell me what to do, Sy!" Jack shouted. "She could get us all caught!"

"You don't know enough to just kill her!"

My eyes shifted over to Root, who sat slumped forward in his chair, head in his hands.

"Do you want to play twenty questions with a spy?" Jack asked using the tip of the gun to keep Anna pinned to the wall.

"If she's innocent, do you want to be responsible for spilling her blood?" Sy asked, his voice lowering a bit.

Jack shook his head angrily. "Did you want to be responsible for David's?" he asked through clenched teeth. "It's only a matter of time before I'm responsible for yours too!"

Silence fell on the room again. The tension was unbearable. Melody sat next to me, tears flowing freely down her face. I felt my own eyes begin to burn, but I was too afraid to move. Jack and Sy held each others' gaze, trying to stare the other down. Finally, Sy exhaled, shaking his head in defeat. He turned and began heading up the stairs to the top level. I saw Anna's eyes grow even wider as her only hope of survival vanished. Jack turned back to look at her again.

"Look," she said quickly pulling up the sleeve of her jacket. There was a fresh gash in her arm. It was dark and bleeding. "I was being used by the company," she admitted. "I was supposed to lead them here, but I couldn't go through with it."

Jack stood there, expression unchanged. "Go on," he said.

"I had a tracking device in my arm, but I cut it out and ditched it," Anna explained. "Please," she whimpered. "I have nowhere to go. The company will find their GPS in a dumpster two miles from here. I'll be just as wanted as you."

"Bull," Jack growled.

"Jack, please," I cracked. Everyone looked at me. No one else had said anything for the good part of five minutes. I held Jack's gaze trying to keep myself composed. "I can't watch another person die tonight."

I could see something in him grow cold. As if I had betrayed him. As if he knew that everyone else would back me up instead of him. He shook his head, eyes filled with hurt.

"Anyone else?" he asked sarcastically looking around the room. No one said another word. He uncocked the gun and brought it down to his side. "We're leaving tomorrow at sundown," he said then turned to glare at me. "You're watching her tonight," he said with disgust. "If anyone needs me, I'll be on the roof keeping all you children safe."

With that, Jack stomped past me, taking his coat

from the arm of the chair and disappeared upstairs, leaving us all in stunned silence.

CHAPTER EIGHT

Anna hadn't moved from her spot against the wall even after everyone else had cleared out. I sat on the couch watching her. An hour later, her eyes were still glued to the stairwell that Jack had gone up.

She looked green and sickly. Her face glimmered with sweat.

"Do you work for the company?" I asked putting a log on the fire. Anna's eyes flitted to me for a second then settled back on the stairs. Her pale mouth stayed clamped shut. "Is your arm hurt?"

This time she didn't even look at me. Alright, so she didn't want to talk. Even though, without me, her brains would be splattered across the wall. I began to wonder what Jack was doing. I imagined he was probably standing on that ledge looking out at the city feeling sorry for himself. Maybe twirling Ben's ring around his finger wishing he were there. Wondering if he had made the right decision.

This night was dragging on. I guessed it was around

three in the morning. All of the windows were boarded up so the light from the fire wouldn't catch anyone's attention. Though it was a means of keeping us safe and undetected, it was pretty inconvenient and made the situation even more depressing.

I noticed the first aid kit still on the table from when Sy had been bandaging David's arm. I walked over and snatched it up.

"Let me help you," I said and stopped in front of the girl showing her the kit.

She finally looked away from the stairs and down at the box. With a nod, Anna lifted the sleeve of her leather jacket.

"Let's sit over here," I said taking her shaking arm. She resisted at first, but then let me lead her to the couch. We sat down and I examined her wound. It was deep and looked jagged and painful. "What the heck did you use?" I whispered trying to wipe some blood away with a piece of cloth.

"A rock."

Now, I could see small bits of dirt and debris in the cut. I cleaned it out as much as I could and wrapped a bandage around her arm. Only once I was done did I look up and see the tears streaming down Anna's pale face.

"Why are you crying?"

The girl peered at me through her stringy, white hair. Her mouth trembled and her hands shook. "I'm so scared," she whispered looking down and picking at the skin around her nails.

"You're safe here." Anna's eyes shifted up to the ceiling. "Jack won't hurt you," I assured her, though her eyes didn't leave the ceiling. "Are you hungry?"

She shook her head and laid back against the couch, pulling at the bandage on her arm thoughtfully.

I left her alone after that and she finally dozed off,

bony fingers still holding the bandage. I fed the fire and tried to keep busy so I wouldn't fall asleep. It didn't seem completely unlikely for Jack to try and off her while I was out.

Through the hole in the ceiling, I watched the sky fade from black to gray. Jack still hadn't come down from the roof when the others started filing in sleepily. Root, Logan and Arie shuffled to the kitchen and started scavenging through the cupboards and refrigerator while Keeta and Melody went to sit in the hammock. Melody buried her face in her hands, still upset about the previous night's events. Anna continued to sleep through the noise until the sound of footsteps coming down the stairs from above jostled her awake. Her eyes were wide as she waited to see who was coming down. Her body relaxed with relief when Sy emerged. He looked awful, like he hadn't slept at all.

"Is Jack planning to make an appearance this morning?" Keeta asked irritatedly.

"I don't know," Sy mumbled and sat at the table, opening a notebook. He took a pen from his shirt pocket and began writing, his head perched on his free hand.

Root sat down beside me tearing into a chicken sandwich. I leaned into him. "What's Sy writing?" I asked watching the man scribble erratically on the pages in front of him.

"Couldn't say," Root replied with his mouth full. "He usually writes in his room."

I waited for Sy to tear himself away from the journal long enough to give us our daily duties, but an hour passed and he was still writing, pulling at his hair and muttering to himself. Anna bent toward me, her eyes set on him too.

"I've seen this before," she whispered in my ear.

My eyes fixed on hers. No one else around seemed

to have heard what she'd said. I took her wrist and pulled her up and toward the stairs leading down to the second story. Only once we reached the first floor did I let go of her.

"What did you mean by that?" I asked walking into the room with the tree.

Anna didn't reply at first, just stared in awe at the far wall. I couldn't really blame her. Everything about this room seemed magical. The sun filtered in through the grimy windows, illuminating the particles in the air and creating shafts of light. I almost expected a few woodland creatures to pop out from the wall and start singing.

"They've had me locked up at the research center for a few months now," Anna started, reaching up and pulling a leaf down from one of the lower branches. She twirled the stem between two of her fingers making it spin like a ballerina. "The people there," she continued, "aren't very nice."

"What did they do to you?" I asked.

Anna sank down at the base of the tree and rested her forehead on her knees. "I was one of their test subjects," she muttered into her stomach.

I leaned against the trunk. "I don't understand."

Anna lifted her head and tugged at her beanie. "I was their freaking lab rat!" This caused a string of ragged coughs to escape her throat.

"Like literally?"

"They kept me strapped down to a table and stuck needles in me," she said. "Filled me up with weird diseases then tried to erase them again with microchips."

My breath caught in my throat rendering me unable to speak as she explained this to me. I stood there in disbelief while she began hacking up a lung. Once she calmed down again, Anna took her hat off revealing big bald patches where her hair had fallen out. She roughly wiped her face with it then tugged it back down on her head. I closed my eyes, trying to clear the images from my mind.

"How did you get out?" I choked.

"They said they'd let me go if-" she coughed again before going on. "If I led them to you and the Tree House."

"They know about this place?"

"Yeah." Anna nodded. "They just don't know where it is."

"And you took out your tracking device so-"

"They still have no idea," she finished.

"Well, that's comforting."

"They seem to know who you are though," she added then let out a pathetic cough.

I turned my head to look at her. "What do you mean?"

Anna stood up shakily and leaned back against the tree. "I heard your name mentioned a lot while I was there. It stuck with me," she said. "I guess that's why I said it was my name last night. I didn't figure the girl with that name would be here." Now she was talking quieter. More thoughtfully, like she was talking to herself. "I should have known though." Her lip twitched. "Why else would they have mentioned you if you weren't at the Tree House...?"

"Anna?"

Her head snapped in my direction and she stared at me with her wide glassy eyes.

"Was there anyone else like us there?" I asked. "Maybe a boy with dark hair? A boy named Ryan?"

"There were a few others there," she replied nodding her head. "I never saw them or caught their names, but..." Her voice trailed off.

"But what?"

I waited while Anna looked up again at the tree, her face catching the light. "But I could hear their screams."

A shudder passed through my body. This was the first time I entertained the thought of Ryan being dead with a spark of hope. What could the company be doing to the people they had captured? How many others were there?

"I'm really tired," Anna whispered with her hands on her knees.

"You can sleep in my room," I replied and took her hand, pulling her behind me out of the room with the tree.

I helped Anna take her jacket and shoes off. She was wearing only a thin tank top, but when I offered her something warmer, she refused. After the girl was asleep, I made my way up to the roof. Once again, it looked empty, though I knew it wasn't.

"You must be a magician."

I rolled my eyes. "Why do you say that?" I turned around to find Jack sitting up on the roof over the stairwell.

"Well, you must be able to be in two places at once. Otherwise you wouldn't be up here," he said sarcastically.

"She's asleep, Jack."

He jumped down from the ledge, landing hard on his feet in front of me with a loud crack. His eyes burned into mine, but I refused to look away. We stood there in silence with a cloud of tension surrounding us for several moments. I clenched my hands into fists, forcing myself to hold his gaze and stand my ground.

After a while, Jack's eyes narrowed. "You gonna kiss me?" he snarled, his voice like daggers.

Finally, I looked away, crossing my arms to keep myself from punching him in the face. "Who left your cage open?"

"What do you expect, Hailey?" he asked me, his voice softer, but no less angry. "You made me look like an idiot."

"Because I told you not to kill Anna?" I threw my arms out in frustration. "Someone had to be your conscience. You can't just go around waving your gun all over the place and shooting anyone you don't like."

"I needed you!" I looked at him, my mouth still open, words waiting in my throat to be thrown back at him. "On my side," Jack added. "I needed you on my side."

Again the two of us were silent.

"No one ever questioned Ben," he said shaking his head and twisting his hand into his hair. "If he were still here..." His hand clenched into a fist as his face grew tight. Jack turned away from me, throwing his arms down in frustration.

"Jack."

"Ya know." He whirled back around. "It would have made so much more sense for me to be the one bleeding to death in the snow."

I looked down at my feet, feeling guilty for that thought having crossed my mind a couple nights before. My stomach churned.

"I'm sorry," I whispered then looked up to see Jack staring at me. For a second, time stood still. It took Jack two steps to close the gap between us, he caught my face between his hands and suddenly his lips were against mine. The churning in my stomach grew into a full on hurricane as he kissed me. I felt the heat rising in my face and tears stung my eyes. I couldn't tell you how long it lasted. But when he pulled away, it had started to snow.

He stared at me again, the hatred hadn't left his eyes. My lips still tingled and my face was still hot, my head still swimming.

"Hailey, I need you to go now," he said, his voice lower than normal.

I opened my mouth to argue.

"Go!"

My teeth snapped shut and I backed away into the stairwell. Jack slammed the door in my face leaving me to look through the small window. I watched as he paced quickly back and forth, his hands tugging at his hair. Suddenly, he swung violently and his fist connected hard with one of the concrete pillars. I whirled around and took the stairs two at a time until I reached the bottom step. There I sat down and leaned against the wall breathing heavily.

I played the kiss over and over in my head trying to make sense of it all. Of the look in Jack's eyes before and after. Both were looks of animalistic hatred, the first more like a wolf about to attack his prey, the second like a dog at the mercy of its abusive owner. Had I done something wrong? I couldn't even remember if I had kissed him back. It had been such a different kind of kiss than I had ever experienced.

A loud bang and a crash snapped me out of my head. It sounded too close to gunfire for my liking. I ran back up the stairs to find the window broken. I peered through expecting to find Jack laying on the ground with the gun lying next to him. Instead he was leaning back against the pillar, his head down and one hand cradling the other.

A long crack snaked down the column next to his arm from when he had hit it. The anger began welling up in me like bile, but I kept it down and just stared as Jack rubbed his swollen, split knuckles with his other hand. I turned and started back down the stairs before the urge to burst through the door, arms swinging got the best of me.

I turned the corner almost running into Sy.

"Sorry," I said still huffing. "I didn't hear you

coming."

His head lurched hard to the side and he stared at me. His eyes looked wild and bloodshot.

"Are you okay?" I asked him.

Sy's hands twitched and he shook his head again. "Yeah," he said. "Yeah." Then stumbled past me and shut himself in his room.

I'd only known him for a few days, but from what I could tell, this wasn't normal. Trying not to dwell too much on it, I continued down the hall and down into the meeting room. It was pretty hectic. Boxes were scattered everywhere as people began to pack things up for the night's departure. So it seemed Sy really had checked out and now everyone was looking to Jack to be their leader. Just like he hadn't wanted.

This seemed to be the case for the rest of the morning. Sy never made an appearance even as we ate lunch. Keeta made sure to bring him up a plate in case he didn't plan on coming down for dinner either.

I took a box with me down to Jack's room planning to wake up Anna and pack the few things he kept in there. Being careful not to startle her, I turned the knob slowly and eased the door open. Only after I turned on the lantern and brought it over to the bed, I realized Anna was not in it.

"Anna?" I swung the lantern around thinking she was hiding in a corner. The room was empty. I tried not to panic, telling myself that she was just in the bathroom or something. After investigating, I found that to not be the case either. I ran down the stairs and into the tree room. "Anna?"

I had to find her. If she had gotten out and made it back to the company...

I really had to find her.

Knowing I couldn't use the front door, I ran out into

the backyard planning to scale the scaffolding. Once I got out there, the sight stopped me in my tracks.

Snow was still falling and dripping from the tree limbs. The bench was dusted lightly with white as well as the girl laying across it. She was on her back, one arm dangling over the side, hand brushing the ground. Her hat lay beneath the bench and her white hair was cleared from her face, slicked back by the wet snow. With skin cold and pale like granite and huge glazed eyes staring at me, I knew she was dead. A trail of blood stained the corner of her mouth making a small sticky puddle on the bench right below.

I lowered my head and bit my bottom lip to keep it from quivering. As I looked down, I spotted something silver in the snow at my feet. I picked it up and it sparkled in my hand, the blue jewel shimmering in the light. I turned my eyes up and shielded my face from the bright sky. Four stories up, Jack sat on the ledge, his feet dangling over the edge, his face peering down at mine.

"She's dead!" I called up to him. "Happy now?"

He didn't say anything back, just tilted his head a little then disappeared from view. This frustrated me more than it should have and I gritted my teeth, letting out an angry growl. I slumped down onto the bench at Anna's feet and stared down at the ring in my hands. Thoughts of the boy I never knew, invaded my mind.

"How in the world did you put up with him?" I whispered.

I stayed there shivering in the cold for a long time while I tried to decide between getting rid of Anna's body and going in to face Jack. I knew he would be all kinds of smug about her having died out here; most likely having suffered a cold and painful death when he could have put her out of her misery the night before. Everything in me didn't want to let him win.

After a few more minutes of arguing with myself, I went inside to find someone to help me. Anyone, but Jack. As I made my way down the hall to the stairs to the meeting room, I ran right into the person I was trying to avoid.

"We need to go," he said to me.

I turned as he started down the hall past me. "Are you going to tell me why?"

Jack didn't say a word until he got to the bottom. "Let's go!" he called up.

I had to force myself to follow after him and by the time I reached the bottom step, he was already out the back door. Once outside, I saw Jack starting his descent on the other side of the wall, completely ignoring Anna's body on the bench.

"This whole keeping me clueless thing is getting very old," I said hurrying to catch up.

Jack met me in the alley leaning against the wall with his hands in his pockets. He started up the ladder to the roof without saying another word and I followed suit. Once at the top of the ladder, he helped me up. Before he had the chance to go anywhere else, I grabbed Jack's arm, pulling him back to me.

"What are we doing?" I asked sternly.

"Ya know, I'm starting to regret saving your life. I could've left you there; maybe then my endless headache would go away."

I pursed my lips waiting for him to answer my question.

"Sy needs us to do something for him," he finally said.

I let go of his arm. "So we aren't leaving tonight?"

Jack shook his head. "Not until this is done. No."

CHAPTER NINE

Human emotion is a dangerous thing. It can take over a person's mind. Eat them up inside. Rip their heart out making them feel ravaged and raw. Make them sick and keep them awake at night. Push a person over the edge. Even someone as level headed as Sy. It can lead people to do unthinkable things to other people. Even to their own family.

I had never been so angry at anyone in my family. Not to the point that I wished them dead. I couldn't imagine Sy being so angry with anyone, let alone his own godson, to the extent that he would leave them for Eli's agents to find. To kill quickly, if the kid is lucky.

But what had caused his change of heart? Why were Jack and I now scaling buildings, trying to reach this boy, Matthew, as fast as possible. Hoping we weren't too late.

Jack had filled me in about our mission between jumps as we hurried over rooftops. Sy had given him an address and a letter and urged him to find his godson and bring him back to safety.

When we hit street level, I expected to hail a taxi or find a bus. Instead, Jack headed into a large department store.

"What are we doing here?" I asked him.

"We need disguises," he said holding the door open for me.

"Disguises? Aren't we just going to tell Matthew the truth?"

"Sure." Jack shrugged putting his hands in his pockets. "I'll just tell some complete stranger that there are crazed men in suits trying to murder him, and even if he does succeed in avoiding his well-dressed assassins, he'll still die a violent and sudden death once he turns forty." Then Jack whirled around and stuck his hand up. "Go team!"

I pushed his hand away from my face again. "I guess you're right," I muttered trudging down the aisle.

My attitude didn't phase him as he headed briskly toward the mens section. The two of us, with the help of one of Sy's many credit cards, walked out of the store looking like a couple of very young detectives. Jack looked the part; I just looked like a kid trying and failing to be Inspector Gadget.

"I look ridiculous," I said pulling my hair back into a low ponytail, hoping that would help me look more professional.

Jack stopped walking and turned to look me up and down. The corners of his mouth twitched a bit, I think from him trying to hold back a smile. "Just try to stay behind me," he said and took the fedora off his head, pulling it down onto mine.

The two of us got on a bus and took a seat near the back as far away from anyone else as possible. Of course, our get-ups caused a few head turns. Some gave us curious looks, others amused. I hoped this Matthew kid was somewhat more gullible than the people on the bus.

Jack kept his face to the window for the first few minutes of the ride. I stared at his profile. At the shape of his cheek. The wisps of black hair that curled around his ears. At the small freckle on his temple. The way his eyelashes fluttered when he blinked. Everything about his face seemed charming and inviting. That is, until he opened his mouth.

When he turned his head to look at me, I, at first, continued to study his features. Only after another few seconds and an upward twitch of one of his eyebrows did I realize my staring probably seemed weird to him.

I shook my head and looked down.

"Sorry," I muttered knotting my fingers together. "I was just thinking."

Jack shifted in his seat. "That could get you into trouble."

The bus turned a sharp corner causing me to fall into him. My heartbeat quickened as I felt his breath on my cheek. Why did I have feelings for this lunatic? Why couldn't my body understand what this boy was doing to my emotions? To my head. I sat up quickly and looked out the window across the aisle.

"Sorry," he muttered. I snapped my head back around to look at Jack. He seemed to be waiting for me to say something. "Uh," he stuttered on, "about Anna."

I sighed. "It's okay."

Jack nodded then returned his attention to the window. This infuriated me. Everything he did seemed to make me angry. I wondered if he knew that. I wondered if he was aware of how his roller coaster of an attitude was making me crazy.

"You're not a nice person," I finally whispered.

He nodded again not looking at me. "I know."

The rest of the ride was a silent one. Once the bus

came to a stop, Jack got up and I followed him to the front. Neither of us spoke as we walked down the sidewalk of a residential street. He dug into his pocket as we turned down a driveway and pulled a black folded case out, holding it out to me.

I took it and opened it to find an authentic looking detective's badge. I closed it again with a snap and fastened it onto my belt.

Jack knocked hard on the door. "Just follow my lead." I nodded. "And let's hope they are all still alive."

My stomach churned at the thought of what could be waiting for us on the other side. I imagined opening the door to find a brutal murder scene. The house ransacked and blood smeared over the walls and floor. Perhaps the agents were waiting for us inside.

To my surprise, and relief, a small woman opened the door. The wrinkles lining her face seemed too deep for her to be the mother of a 21 year old.

"Can I help you?" she asked us cautiously, the door open only a crack.

"Mrs. Castle?"

The woman nodded and the nausea in my stomach died down a little.

"My name is Detective Andrews and this is my associate Detective Clark" Jack flashed his badge and I followed suit, almost dropping it. "We were wondering if we could have a quick word with Matthew," he said.

The woman's face grew cold. "Is this a joke?" she asked narrowing her eyes. My heart quickened. Were we too late?

"I'm sorry, ma'am, I don't understand," Jack shook his head confused.

"Matt is serving his third year of ten in prison," she said. "You would know that if you really were detectives." My throat closed up. "I'm going to need to see ID."

Jack hadn't given me any sort of ID. Other than those badges, we had nothing.

"Mrs. Castle," Jack started. "I'm so sorry, I meant to ask for your husband, Mark. Is he around?" He began reaching into his coat like he was going for his ID, but the woman stopped him.

"Oh it's alright, dear," she said waving her hand. "We've just been under a lot of stress."

"It's just been one of those days," Jack chuckled lightly and straightened his jacket.

"Mark, honey," Mrs. Castle called back into the house. "A couple detectives are here to see you." She opened the door the rest of the way so we could follow her into the house. "Come with me," she said.

Jack and I exchanged a look as we went into the house.

We sat down together on a small couch in their living room. The place was homey enough. Decorated like the rooms you'd see in home and garden magazines. Even with the relaxing atmosphere, the two of us stayed sitting upright, ready to jump up and get out of there at a moment's notice. We still weren't in the clear. Jack seemed charming enough, but the second I opened my mouth...

An older man came in the room shortly after we sat down and took a seat in a chair across from us. Mrs. Castle bustled around behind him tidying this, straightening that.

"What can I do for you, detectives?" Mr. Castle asked rubbing his hands together nervously.

Jack clasped his hands together as well. "We are building a profile on your son, Matthew, so we can better understand his situation and motives. Could you tell us a bit about him?"

Jack had given me a small notepad earlier and I pulled it out now. I dug around in my coat for a pencil unsuccessfully.

"Uh," I stuttered. "Do you have a pencil?"

Mrs. Castle grabbed one quickly from a desk and I took it hesitantly.

"Thank you," I whispered.

As Mr. Castle began telling us about his son, I jotted down what I could. Only a few lines in, Jack interrupted.

"I'm very sorry," he said pulling out a cellphone. "I need to take this." A cellphone? Couldn't that be traced? He flipped it open and brought it to his ear. "Andrews...Are you sure? We'll be down ASAP." He turned to me. "We need to go," he said putting the phone back in his coat. "I'm sorry, Mr. and Mrs. Castle. We're needed for a suspect ID. Thank you for your time." The couple nodded a little confused.

Jack motioned with his head for me to stand and I followed him out. When we reached the door, he turned back to look at the still confused couple. "You will be contacted shortly about continuing the investigation."

"Thanks again," I called back as Jack hurried me down the driveway.

When the door was closed, he took my arm and we jogged down the street.

"Wait," I yelled pulling my arm away. "What about the Castles? They need to know that they're in danger. We need to get them to safety," I said.

"They'll be fine."

"Jack!" This stopped him dead in his tracks. "Would you please stop doing this to me," I asked, my voice squeaky with anger.

He took me by the shoulders. "They're all safe. At least for now," he said to me. "With Matt in jail the company isn't going to bother him. Not for the next few years. There's no need to go after his parents now." His eyes stayed on mine. "Okay?"

I nodded then breathed deeply until I could keep myself under control. "So what now?" I asked as we started walking again.

"We need to get to the jail."

"And what about that cellphone?" I asked. "Have you had that this whole time?"

Jack pulled the phone out of his pocket and tossed it to me. I opened it to find a cartoon cat staring back at me. The whole thing was made of cheap plastic.

"We just needed to get out of there," he said with a chuckle. "Always have a way out."

By the time we reached the jail, visiting hours were over for the day. Jack refused to go back to the Tree House without having given Matthew the letter from Sy so that night we found ourselves in a cheap diner only a few blocks from the jail. We sat there in silence for a bit, sipping at our water and picking at our food.

I wanted so badly to bring up what had happened earlier that day. I wanted to ask him why he had kissed me if he so obviously hated being around me. Why I felt like I had done something to make him treat me the way he was.

"What do you think Matt did?" I asked breaking the silence. Jack shrugged running his fingers down the side of his glass. "Do you think it has to do with why Sy wanted him dead?"

He shrugged again. I shook my head and looked down at my food. This boy was wearing me out. Being around him, trying to figure him out was making me tired.

I gave up any effort to talk to him and we ate our food in silence. That night, we stayed in a motel near the jail. The only time he said anything to me was when he had to. I went to sleep feeling like I knew Jack even less than I had when I first met him.

I was in the middle of a falling dream when I was woken up by something landing on my mattress. My eyes snapped open to find a pair staring back at me and I sat upright.

"Jack?"

He was laying on his stomach next to me, his hands on either side of his head. "I've been thinking," he said.

I pulled the blanket up to my chin and laid back against the pillow. "About what?"

Jack didn't say anything at first. Instead he brought his hand up to my face and moved a strand of hair back, brushing his fingers across my cheek. I sighed and shook my head in an attempt to push his hand away.

"You really need to stop doing that," I whispered looking up at the ceiling.

Jack dropped his hand back down on the bed. "I know," he replied. "I'm being a jerk."

"Any particular reason why?"

It took a few silent moments for him to answer. "I don't mean to be like this."

"Yes you do," I chuckled halfheartedly. "Otherwise you wouldn't be."

"Okay," Jack said. "I don't want to have to be like this." I turned onto my side and propped my head up on my hand. Jack stared straight ahead, his nose almost touching the headboard. "I'm just angry."

"At me?"

"No." His voice came out flat.

The two of us laid there for a while not saying anything. My eyes focused on the clock on the table behind Jack's head. 2:47 glared back at me, the colon, separating the numbers, flashing with every second that went by. My heart began to pound in my temple as Jack's body heat soaked into my skin. I hadn't realized how small this bed was. Surely not built for more than one average sized person. I watched as the flashing dots synced up with my heart in a way that made me feel a little sick. My vision was getting blurry, my surroundings pulsing in and out of focus with every beat. A dull pain started blooming behind my eyes and I closed them to try and get it to fade away. As I laid there, hearing Jack's steady breathing and trying to steady my own, I began thinking about Sy.

He had been so normal when I'd met him. So composed and authoritative. It was crazy how abruptly he'd changed after David had died. How disturbed he suddenly was. How sick and afraid. His eyes had seemed so wild, so animalistic.

Sleep began taking over my mind as I imagined Sy morphing into a scared little rabbit, running down the halls of the Tree House, Paulson and Adams chasing after him with a syringe filled with more microchips. He turned a corner to find himself in another endless hallway and kept running, running running down into the dark.

I had never stepped foot in a jail before that day. Even as a guiltless person I felt trapped the minute we walked in the front doors and stepped through the metal detectors. Jack seemed to know what to do so I followed him to the front desk. I watched as he said something to the woman behind the desk then started leafing through a small stack of papers she handed to him. I eyed a chair against the wall and went and sat down in it.

After a few more minutes, Jack walked over to me.

"You stay out here," he said. "I'll go in and talk to Matthew and give him Sy's letter."

I nodded folding my arms across my chest and

leaned back against the wall. Jack sensed how uncomfortable I was. He placed both his hands on the arm rests on either side of me and leaned in close.

"I'll be quick," he said to me. "Then we'll be out of here."

I nodded again then watched as Jack walked through a doorway and spread his arms and legs out so an officer could pat him down. Before he disappeared through another door, Jack turned and gave me a quick smirk. My stomach churned nervously as I recalled waking up next to him that morning.

There was a window looking into the visitors room and I got up and watched from where I stood as Jack sat down at a small table and folded his hands together. A few minutes later, a buzzer went off and the sound of a heavy door unlocking reverberated off the walls. A boy in a gray jumpsuit took a seat at the table across from Jack. This must have been Matthew. He looked our age. Would be if he was also a patient, I suppose. His light brown hair was cropped close to his head and his face was clean-shaven.

Matthew looked confused as Jack started talking to him. I couldn't tell exactly what he was saying, but I figured it was about Sy and the company. Matthew rested his elbows on the table and held his head in his hands. This must have been a lot to take in.

I felt kind of bad watching through this window like I was at a zoo. Jack turned his head and made eye-contact with me. I stepped away from the window and returned to my chair, picking up a magazine and flipping through it without actually reading anything. I must have gone through that magazine four times before finally getting up and going over to the window again. While I stood there, I looked down the hall and eyed a payphone next to the vending machine. I should call Ryan, I thought to myself.

It was safe enough, right? Being at a jail and all.

I got change out of my pocket and dialed Ryan's number. My stomach churned a bit when it went straight to voice mail.

"Hey Ryan," I said quietly. "Um...this is Hailey. I just wanted to let you know that I'm safe." A tear ran down my cheek. "I made it to the Tree House. I've been kind of hoping you would show up, but..." I leaned back against the wall. "Anyway, we're leaving tomorrow. Leaving Seattle." An image of Root tracing his finger along the map came to mind. "We're headed east. I don't have my cell phone or anything, but...but I'll call you again when we get to where we're going. Okay, I love you. Bye" I hung the phone up and wiped the tears from my face.

Just then a little boy turned the corner and headed my way. I watched as he put a dollar bill into the vending machine. It reminded me that I hadn't eaten anything yet that morning.

The little boy retrieved his treat then toddled back down the hallway and into the waiting room. I stood staring at the food items behind the glass for a long time before finally settling on a bag of chips. My stomach was still feeling gross and I needed something to calm it down.

I sank to the floor next to the vending machine and opened my chips. They smelled like salt and oil, making my stomach feel even worse. All I wanted was to be back at the Tree House. No, that was a lie. All I wanted was for this to be a dream. Just a ridiculous nightmare that I would wake up from at any second.

I would just open my eyes and be in my bed, in my room, at my parents' house. I'd throw the covers off and get up and go downstairs to find my parents and brother, visiting from Nashville, sitting at the table, a fresh pot of coffee just waiting to be poured. Then the four of us would sit there and Ryan would tell us all about how school in Nashville was going. How cute the girls were and how hilarious his teachers were. Then he would ask me how college was going.

"Fine," I would say. "Boring, but fine."

And we would laugh. And snow would fall outside the window and it would be a wonderful, perfect morning. A morning with no evil microchips. No guys in suits kicking down the door. No Tree House. No Jack...

The door to the visitors room flew open, hitting the wall with a loud smack. I snapped my head up to find Jack standing in the hall, his head moving rapidly as he searched the waiting room with his eyes. Soon, they fell on me and he hurried my way.

"We have to go, now," he said with urgency and pulled me up.

"What's going on?" I asked. "What's wrong?"

Jack shoved the letter into my hand. "Read this," he said and led me out the front doors.

As we hurried to the bus stop, I began reading Sy's letter to Matthew.

Matthew,

I have received all of your letters. It took me a while, but I read every single one. Everyone of them cried out for forgiveness, but my hardened heart would not hear it. Matthew, from the deepest part of me, I forgive you. We all have regrets in our lives. Believe me, I have my fair share. You were just at the wrong place at the wrong time. It's been hard to live without my wife for the past several years, but I have managed. I trust that you will never drink and drive again.

As you've heard, I've been dealing with another battle. The company is getting more tactical and they have shown no mercy whatsoever. I assumed you were out of jail, but judging from your last letter, you may have chosen to stay for your own safety. If you are out, please trust my friend, Jack. He and the rest of the patients will take good care of you. If you are still locked up, be careful as I don't know how desperate the company is to get to you.

If you're reading this letter, I am already gone. I have watched several people die at the hands of this terrible disease and it's horrifying. It has become too much to bear and I wanted to make peace with you before I went.

All is forgiven. Good luck, Matthew.

Your Proud Godfather,
-Sy

CHAPTER TEN

"What do we do?" I asked Jack, my breathing quickening. "What do we do? What do we do?"

"Stop!" he yelled. "Just shut up!"

I snapped my mouth shut, rested my head against the wall of a building and concentrated on calming down. Once my heartbeat had substantially slowed, I looked at Jack again. His cheeks were flushed and his hair was a mess from him twisting his fingers through it.

"I'm sorry," I whispered.

Jack didn't say anything in reply, though his pacing began to slow down and he looked at me. I could only imagine what was going on in his brain. First he loses his brother, then David and now Sy, who had been like a father to him. And the rest back at the Tree House were still waiting for orders. Oh no. Had one of them found Sy's body yet? Had anyone been there when he killed himself? I couldn't think about that. Not with Jack here. Not like this.

I leaned back against the wall and shoved my hands

into the pockets of my jacket. The wind was bitter, making my face hurt. Jack walked out into the middle of the street.

"Where is the bus?" he growled turning to look both ways down the street. He stopped short his eyes fixed on a phone booth down the block. Jack jogged down to it and I made my way over, watching as he fumbled anxiously for some change. By the time I reached him, he was talking frantically to someone.

"Is he there?" he asked into the phone. "What? What do you mean, he's gone...?" I closed my eyes imagining the worst. "Sy just up and left...?"

My eyes popped back open.

Jack slumped his shoulders. "Alright," he said sadly. "We'll be back tonight... No, I can't... I need time...Just start packing. We'll leave tomorrow morning..." Then he hung up.

I put my hand on his arm expecting him to brush me off. Instead he put his hand on mine. "I'm sorry, Jack," I said quietly.

He didn't respond, just gripped my hand tighter. His face turned up and his eyes locked with mine. The sound of hydraulic breaks snapped us out of the moment.

"Let's go," Jack said.

He didn't let go of my hand, even as we stumbled down the aisle to an empty seat. Even as the bus took sharp corners, pushing us into each other. Even as it came to a stop a half a mile from the Tree House. Finally, our hands separated, only so he could help me up a ladder and onto the roof of a tall building.

We took our time getting back to the Tree House. Sy was gone and Jack didn't want to face the fact that he was now in charge. The lives of the rest of us were in his hands.

By the time we did get back, the sky had begun to

darken. Inside, people were dragging to finish getting things together. The air was heavy with sadness causing everyone's shoulders to sag and heads to hang a little lower than normal. While Jack helped Root and Logan check our route for the next day and tie up any loose ends, I headed upstairs to Sy's room. When I got there, I found Melody and Arie sitting on the floor by his desk with papers scattered in front of them. Melody looked up at me. Her face shimmered with tears, but she managed to smile weakly.

"We're just trying to figure out what to take with us," Arie said to me, putting an assuring arm around her.

I nodded and went to sit down by them.

"I think I need to help downstairs," Arie said then got up and limped out of the room leaving Melody and I alone.

"How are you holding up?" I asked her.

She shrugged. "Okay, I guess. I can't imagine what Jack must be feeling."

I didn't say anything.

"I can't thank you enough for being here for him, Hailey," she said. This caught me off guard. "I mean, I know Jack is being kind of a jerk, but you can understand that."

"Understand what?"

Melody looked up from the mess on the floor. "Ben died saving Jack's life," she said. "He blames himself for it."

It all made sense now. Of course Jack felt guilty for his brother's death. If he hadn't been there, it never would have happened. Perhaps if they hadn't been out looking for me it never would have happened...

"I have to go find Jack," I said and got up and out of the room before Melody could say anything else.

I was stopped at the bottom of the stairs by Keeta.

"Hailey, could you help me make dinner?" she asked me. "I wanted to do something special since this is our last night here."

I agreed reluctantly as I caught Jack's gaze from across the room.

Dinner was a weird mix of emotions. Everyone was sad and confused about Sy's leaving, but excited and anxious about the next day's departure. I couldn't help glancing at Jack every so often and he caught me a couple times, the corners of his mouth twitching. What had changed in us? That morning we had essentially hated each other. But now, now butterflies fluttered in my stomach as he looked at me. A different type of look than I'd seen before. Different from his sarcastic, demeaning stare.

As we ate, Root filled us in on what the morning was going to look like. We were to leave as soon as the sky was light enough. Everything needed to be packed in the van before then and we weren't stopping until we were well out of Seattle. The conversation faded into the background as I began thinking of living life on the road. I was basically going to be a fugitive. We all were.

"Are you alright?" Melody nudged me.

"Yeah," I replied snapping back to reality. "I'm fine. Just a lot to take in." I smiled nervously.

"I know," she said. "But we're going to hide out in the mountains. It'll be like an adventure. New scenery, ya know?"

"The mountains?" I grew more nervous at the thought of hiding out in freezing, dark caves for the rest of my life.

"It'll be okay, Hailey," she assured me.

I nodded not feeling any better. I felt like I needed to hear that from Jack. Glancing over at him again I caught him staring back, concern in his dark eyes.

I waited until Jack was snoring softly in his bed beside mine before I let the tears start flowing. It felt like I had been bottling everything up inside for the past five days and now the dam had cracked and everything was pouring out. I didn't want to leave in the morning. I didn't want to leave the one place I finally felt safe to go live in the mountains. This was the longest I had ever gone without talking to my family and now I didn't even know if I was ever going to see any of them again. I didn't even know if any of them were still alive. A sob escaped my throat and I clutched the pillow tighter over my face letting out a frustrated cry. Just then, two hands gripped my pillow and pulled it and me up. I lowered it from my face to find Jack sitting on my bed in front of me, his hair disheveled from sleep. He opened his mouth to say something bu before he could get a word out, I fell into him, burying my face into his chest. His arms wrapped around me and pulled me tighter against him as he leaned back onto the bed.

I continued crying, the tears spilling from my eyes with no diminish. My arms found their way to Jack's neck and my fingers tangled into his hair. His cheek brushed my forehead and he brought a hand down to wipe my tears away. As they subsided, I pulled back from Jack's chest and looked up at his face. Even in the dark I could make out his features. His eyes, sharp and staring straight into mine. Dark and intense like two black holes. The shape of his lips, so close to my lips. Dangerously close.

They brushed against mine sending electricity down my spine. My heart pounded in my ears. Or was that his heart? Jack's breathing became shaky as he brought one of his hands up to touch my face.

"Everything will be alright, Hailey," he whispered. "I'll keep you safe."

With that, he pressed his lips against mine and suddenly I was falling. My stomach tightened and my head spun as his mouth moved on mine. My thoughts began swirling together creating splotches of light that flooded my vision and caused my ears to ring. Goosebumps covered my skin making me shiver even though, with Jack's body pressed up against mine, I was feeling feverish.

His hand felt rough like sandpaper, but moved gently up and into my hair, pulling my face even closer to his. By this time, the tears on my face had dried and any doubts I had before about hiding in the mountains vanished from my mind. I knew I would be safe with him. I'd go anywhere with him. Whether it be the mountains, the jungle. I would live at the bottom of the ocean with this boy. Nothing scared me now.

Logan slammed the back door of the van and rattled the handle, making sure everything was secure. He made his way to the front where Root was checking the engine and climbed in the driver's side seat. Arie's legs stuck out from underneath while he checked for leaks and Jack and I were leaning back against the side watching this all happen. His hand brushed mine causing my heart to skip and my mouth to twitch up into a smile.

The sun was just coming up over Capitol Hill which meant we needed to get going soon. Melody and Keeta came out just then carrying a couple shopping bags of food.

"Okay," Melody said. "Let's get out of here."

With that, we all piled into the van. Arie, Melody and Keeta took the middle bench, Root was co-pilot and Jack and I climbed in the back. I couldn't believe I was leaving Seattle. It hadn't been long enough for everything to really sink in. One minute I was a normal girl, living a normal life. And now I was running for my life. The only friends and family I had now were in this van. Root turned around in his seat.

"Let's get this show on the road," he smiled.

Then the van started and we took off down the street. I think Logan was the only one paying attention to the road. The rest of us were turned around in our seats looking back as the only safe place we'd known began to shrink in the distance. I felt my eyes well up with tears, but then one reassuring squeeze of my hand from Jack made it easy to blink them away. Even though I had only been there for about a week, the place felt like home to me. I could only imagine how the others must have been feeling.

Now, being on the road, I felt vulnerable and out in the open. I began feeling anxious to get out of Seattle and leave it all behind. As we neared the end of the block, it all really started sinking in. This was going to be my life. At least for a while.

The sound of squealing tires caused us all to jump in our seats. We looked forward in time to catch a glimpse of a car flying past us in the opposite direction. I turned back around to watch it speed down the street and come to a screeching halt in front of the Tree House. My stomach dropped and I nudged Jack in the ribs. He was already turned around watching, along with everyone else. A dark figure stepped out of the car and stood in front of the Tree House looking up at it. We were at the end of the block now and Logan had turned on his blinker. He stepped back down on the gas and as we started to turn, the man jerked his head in our direction. I instinctively ducked down so he wouldn't see me. What could the chances be that the company had finally learned the location of the Tree House and sent an agent over as we were leaving? And what could one guy do to stop us?

It had to be a coincidence. It had to be. We continued down the road, the Tree House and the man disappearing from view.

I turned back around taking a deep breath to calm myself down. Jack put an arm around me.

"Relax, it'll all be over soon," he said. "Just another couple hours and Seattle will be behind us."

"I know," I said. "I'll relax then."

I had just managed to get my heart back down to normal when Logan swerved hard pushing us all into the side of the van.

"Forget how to drive, Logan?" Arie asked only half joking.

"No, this guy just cut me off," he replied irritated.

My eyes shot up and I was looking at the same car that had parked in front of the Tree House.

"We need to get out of here," I said, my voice quivering. The driver of the car stuck his hand out the window and motioned for us to pull over to the curb. I leaned into Jack. "It's the same car."

"Logan!" Jack yelled. "Get us out of here, now!"

Logan floored it and we surged forward past the car. Sure enough, it sped up too and followed us.

"Careful," Root said. "We don't want to get pulled over."

"Well, what do you want me to do?"

Jack slammed his hands down on the back of the seat in front of him. "Just lose him!"

My head began to spin as we wove dangerously in an out of traffic and down side roads. We shot out of an alley onto a busy street.

"Cop ahead!"

Logan let off the gas and laid on the break. As we passed the police car, Jack and I both looked back waiting for our pursuer to race out of the alley behind us. We made it to the end of the block without any sight of him.

"I think we lost him," Jack said turning back around. "How much longer till we're out of the city?"

"Another 25 minutes or so if this traffic ever picks up," Root replied looking down at the map resting on his bouncing legs.

Logan turned onto a less congested street. I took a deep breath and kept my eyes glued to the rear windshield.

"You alright?" Melody asked from behind me.

"Yeah," I replied. "I'm just making sure we-"

Before I could finish my sentence, I was jerked out of my seat and slammed sideways into Jack. I had no control as I was thrown back down, hitting the side of my head hard against the sliding door. The sound of shattering glass rattled my eardrums and light exploded in my vision. Then all I could see was black.

Once the van came to a stop, I opened my eyes to find a bunch of formless blobs moving around frantically. I shook my head and immediately regretted it. My skull throbbed and black patches appeared in my vision.

"Hhhhhlllyyyy!"

I blinked hard and squinted at the blob right in front of me.

"Hhhlllyy ccccnnnnnnooooohhhhhheeeeerrrrmmmmmmmm?"

The ringing in my ears began to subside and my vision slowly started to clear. Jack's concerned face came into focus.

"Hailey," he said. "Can you hear me? Are you alright?" He tapped his hand against my cheek repeatedly.

A trickle of red ran down the side of his face and his bottom lip was bloody. I brought my hand up to touch the blood on his cheek. He put his hand on mine, a look of relief washing over his face, and got up to help me out of the van. I stepped out into a deserted alley.

"Stay here," Jack said and disappeared around the side of the van.

Only us and the other car were in sight. Everyone else was already out and evaluating each others' injuries. They all looked to be okay. Just a few cuts and bruises here and there. The front passenger side of the van was completely crushed and buried in the side of concrete building. My eyes immediately went to Root, who had been sitting in the passenger seat. He was leaning against the van, a large cut snaking down the length of his leg.

"Don't shoot me! Let me explain!" I heard from the other side of the van.

I hurried around the back and stopped, my jaw falling open. Jack was standing facing me, his arm extended out in front of him, pointing his gun directly at the head of the guy in front of me. The driver of the other car. I stared at the back of his sweatshirt. The words "Belmont University, Nashville, Tennessee" stared back at me.

"Ryan?"

CHAPTER ELEVEN

He turned around to face me. The side of his face was bruised. His skin was pale and he was thin, but this was my brother.

I reached him in two bounds and threw my arms around his boney shoulders.

"Ryan, I can't believe it's you," I cried clutching him so tightly I thought I might break him.

"It's me," he replied and buried his face into my hair, clinging to me like I was life to him. "Man, am I glad to see you."

When we pulled away, I stepped back so I could take a better look at him. What I saw made me feel weak in the knees. My brother's dark hair looked dull and brittle, thin in some places. His skin was yellow and papery and his eyes were foggy.

"What happened to you?" I whispered.

Ryan blinked his filmy eyes and clasped his hands together. "More than you could imagine."

"Hailey," Jack interrupted. Ryan and I both turned to

look at him. "We really need to get moving."

"You're headed out of Seattle?" my brother asked.

Jack nodded.

Ryan's head shook back and forth quickly. "You can't," he said. "You can't leave Seattle."

I turned my attention back to him. "Why?"

"There's a GPS in the chip," he explained. By this time, everyone else had come around to our side of the van. "If you get more than a few miles out of the city, it will activate and they will be able to track you down."

This caused a stir among the group.

"Are you serious?!" Root exclaimed.

Ryan shook his head again, "I wish I wasn't." Just then sirens erupted in the distance.

"We need to get out of here and back to the Tree House," Jack said putting the gun away. "I say we all split up for the time being. Take different routes and arrive at different times." Then he turned to me. "We need to go."

I looked at him then at Ryan. "I'm going with my brother."

"Well," he bit the inside of his cheek thoughtfully. "Do you know the way back?"

I nodded and smiled confidently.

Jack's eyes didn't hide his jealousy very well, but he nodded anyway, knowing full well that there was no use in trying to change my mind. We all headed out of the alley and split up; Melody, Arie and Keeta heading for a restaurant in hopes of hiding out for a bit, Root and Logan going north, Jack trudging off deeper down the alley on his own and Ryan and I taking off down the street, south.

"Where's Mom and Dad?" Ryan finally asked after we had been walking for a few minutes. I just shook my head and gripped his hand. He cursed under his breath then clenched his hand tighter around mine.

Again, I took the time to look at my brother. To really let everything sink in. "What happened to you?" I asked hoping to get a full answer this time.

Ryan shook his head. "They're working on something," he said quietly running his hand over a thin patch of hair. "I wasn't the only one they caught either."

"I know," I replied remembering Anna's dead, blank stare. How long had she lived after being let go? "Are you feeling okay?" I asked in a panic.

"Yeah," Ryan replied. This made me feel a little better. "I mean, as well as I can, I suppose."

Just then all in a line, two police cars, an ambulance and a firetruck passed us, sirens blaring.

Ryan let out a chuckle. "They're in for a surprise," he said. "Not too many times does a hit and run involve both drivers running." A smile cracked on my face. Of course Ryan would find a little bit of humor in a situation like this.

The air was unnaturally warm for a winter day and the sun was beating down, melting the slush that muddied the gutters and causing the bottoms of my pant legs to drag and trip me. I had so many questions I wanted to ask my brother. What had they done to him? How had he known about the GPS? And what else did he know?

"Ya know," I started, staring up at the buildings surrounding us. "I've only done it a few times, but we travel by rooftop around here."

Ryan looked up after me, squinting in the bright light. "Huh. I'm gone for just a few months and my sister's turned into a flying squirrel."

I laughed. "Yeah, and that charming trigger happy boy was Jack."

"What is he, your guys' bodyguard or something?"

I bit my lip. "He's kind of become our leader of

sorts," I explained. "After David died, and then Sy up and disappeared..."

We stopped walking and Ryan looked at me with his clouded eyes. "I've heard those names before."

"They were two of the patients from the first trial," I said.

"Yeah," Ryan nodded. "And then the company lost track of them."

"Yeah." The two of us said nothing for a few seconds. Then I opened my mouth. "Ryan, how did you know about the Tree House?"

My brother let out a heavy sigh then licked his cracked lips. "Believe it or not," he started. "I've been in Seattle for the last week with the company."

"You were in Seattle before all this? Why didn't you tell me?" I asked, my throat tightening.

"Crap." Ryan grabbed my arm and spun me around so we were facing the opposite direction. "Walk this way." I looked over my shoulder to find two familiar agents standing on the curb a block down watching traffic. He pulled me back around. "Don't stare," he whispered. "This is near where I dropped my tracking chip."

I gave him a puzzled look. He pulled his sleeve up revealing a dark and bleeding wound similar to Anna's. I tugged his sleeve back down for him and the two of us hurried away from Paulson and Adams. When we reached the end of the block, I looked, again back over my shoulder.

"They're gone," I said with relief.

"No," Ryan whispered. "No no no no."

"What is it?"

Ryan flipped the hood up on his sweatshirt, covering his head then pulled mine up over my hair too. "They're headed this way in a black car," he explained putting his arm around my shoulders. "Keep walking." Then he clutched his hood shut. "Do this."

I copied Ryan making it look like I was trying to shield my face from an imaginary cold wind and slumped my shoulders forward. Even in my current situation, with my brother's arm around my shoulders, I felt safer. There was an alley just ahead past a small bistro.

We made it past the window just as it shattered into a million pieces. Ryan and I shielded our faces with our arms and looked back. Paulson had gotten out of the car and was crouching behind the door reloading a pistol.

"Hailey, run!" Ryan shouted and picked up one of the empty metal chairs from on the sidewalk. He hurled it at the car as I took off down the alley.

Ryan was close behind and we slid around the corner in time for a bullet to bite into the brick building where we had been seconds before. We shot down the alley and came out on another busy street. I turned my head to find Paulson coming after us trying to steady his arm and take aim. There was another alley a block down and we headed that way, dodging the few pedestrians on the sidewalk. When we reached the alley, I followed Ryan to a ladder.

"Climb," he ordered.

I scurried up the ladder as fast as I could and managed to slip up inside a metal covering just as Paulson came into view. Ryan had gone farther down the alley and was now trying to climb a chain link fence. I watched in horror through a hole in the covering as his sweatshirt snagged and Paulson grabbed his shoulder yanking him back so he fell onto the ground. I bit my lip to keep from calling out to him. Then Paulson stepped back stopping under me and I thought my cover was blown for sure.

Ryan got to his feet and brushed himself off. "Keep

going, Hailey!" he called down the alley.

"Okay, kid," Paulson said. His gun was pointed at Ryan's head. "Try to run and I'll make it hurt."

My brother was hunched over, his hands on his knees, as he tried to catch his breath. "Yeah? Well, it doesn't matter now," he said. "The others know you can't track them unless they leave Seattle. Have fun trying to find a bunch of needles in this haystack of a city."

"Where's the girl?" Paulson asked, his voice sounding irritated.

"She went down the alley."

Paulson's eyes narrowed. "You're lying.

Ryan just shrugged.

"Adams," he said. "Did she go down the alley?"

His partner came out from around the corner on the other side of the fence. "I haven't seen her," he said with a hint of arrogance in his voice.

"Where are you hiding, child!" Paulson called, his voice echoing.

"Her name is Hailey," Ryan said.

My heart was pounding in my ears by this point. As soon as he looked up, my cover would be blown. He took a few steps toward Ryan and I could feel my heartbeat slow just a little. I was safe for a few more seconds, at least. My relief was short lived as I watched Paulson push Ryan down to his knees and press the gun into the back of his head.

"Hailey," he called. "I hope you don't mind if we bury your brother here in a garbage can."

I wanted to open my mouth so bad. Through the crack, I could see Ryan shift his eyes up to my hiding place. He was staring at me, telling me to keep my mouth shut. I couldn't let my only remaining family member die, though. Just as I was about to climb back down and show myself, I watched Adams go down behind the fence. As he dropped, Jack appeared behind him. Paulson was too busy taunting me with Ryan's life to notice Jack walk over to the fence and grin.

"Should I kill him here, Adams?" he asked with a smile. "Or should we rough him up a bit and take him back to Eli?"

When he heard no reply, Paulson whirled around in time for Jack to lift his gun and pull the trigger twice. The agent fell to his knees, crying out in pain and grasping at the bullet hole in each of his thighs. Ryan crawled away from him and scrambled to his feet.

"Come on out, Hailey." He called for me to come down and I did as he said.

Once I hit the ground, I saw Adams on the other side of the fence, out cold, and Paulson writhing on the pavement, Ryan circling him. Jack was leaning against the fence watching us through the wire, his free hand was twisting around the silencer on the end of the gun. Paulson had dropped his pistol when he fell and now tried to reach for it. As his fingers touched the handle, Ryan's foot came down hard on his hand.

"You don't need that," he muttered and picked it up.

Paulson was gritting his teeth against the pain and glaring up at Ryan. "Go ahead and kill me," he growled. "There are plenty more of me out there." he said. "You'll be dead sooner or later." Ryan put the gun inside the pocket of his sweatshirt. "I'm sure you remember what happened to you back at Eli's," he continued with a pained grin on his face. "Remember everything we put in you. It's all eating you away and you'll soon be gone."

"Shoot him!" I cried. My own words shocked me. My brother calmly walked over to a pile of trash and picked up the broken leg of a chair. "What are you doing?"

"Ryan," Jack said from the other side of the fence,

"Let's go. We need to meet up with Root."

He continued back toward Paulson, gripping the leg like a baseball bat.

"Let's go, Ryan," I said urgently looking at the fallen man. Paulson stared in horror and began to back away as best as he could. Ryan came at him and swung the leg hard catching the agent's wrist, causing him to fall on his side. "Ryan!"

He hit him again, this time in his knee. The sharp crack echoed off the walls along with Paulson's screams of pain. The blows rained down on him, one after another, each as damaging as the last. The sound of breaking bones and cries for mercy rang out. Jack was up and over the fence by this time and he was trying to hold Ryan back to no avail. I stood frozen in horror as I watched my brother beat this man to death.

By the time he finally stopped, blood was flowing from every orifice on Paulson's slacken face. His eyes were swollen shut and a huge lump was forming on his cheek. Jack checked his pulse.

"He's dead," he said quietly.

Ryan stood there breathing hard, still gripping the bloody chair leg in his white-knuckled fists. I began to back away, horrified at what I had just seen. Suddenly, a hand clamped onto my throat and a gun pressed against the side of my head. My breath caught and my back arched at the touch of the cold metal. Adams's ragged breath rattled in my ear.

"Don't follow us," he rasped at my brother and Jack.

They stood there with their mouths open not knowing what to do. My eyes began to fill up with tears as we backed toward the street.

"What do you want?" Ryan asked.

"Her."

Jack stepped forward. "What do you expect to do?

Just walk out onto a busy street with a hostage?"

"I'll figure it out!" Adams yelled, his voice wavering.

I could hear the uncertainty in his words. His partner was dead and now he had to make all the decisions himself. His hand tightened on my throat making it hard for me to breathe. I looked pleadingly at my brother and Jack. Don't let him take me, I thought. As I looked at Jack, the corners of his mouth twitched upward. It was just for a second, but I caught it.

"We could always knock him out again," he said to Ryan with a sheepish grin.

Adams chuckled in my ear at Jack's remark. "Could you now?"

"Yeah."

With a loud grunt, Adams loosened his grip on my neck and he and his gun dropped onto the ground. I whipped around to find Root standing there with a chunk of concrete in his hand.

"Good thing I just happened to walk by," he said and tossed the rock aside.

"Yeah," I gasped rubbing at my neck. "Yeah, good thing."

Ryan hurried up to me and took my face in his hands. "Are you alright?" he asked searching my eyes. I nodded swallowing hard then hugged him tightly.

I pulled away. "Your sweatshirt," I said.

He looked down at his blood spattered clothes, then hastily took out the gun, shoving it into the back of his jeans and pulled the sweatshirt up over his head and threw it in a dumpster. Now, now wearing just a black t-shirt I could see how skinny he really was.

Jack walked up beside us and nudged Adams with his foot. He turned to Root. "Can you get another car?"

He nodded. "I'll come find you." Root turned around

and hurried out of the alley in search for a car.

"Let's get out of here," Jack said bending down to pick Adams up. "Maybe we can get some information out of him." Ryan bent down to help and the two of them put his arms around their necks and hefted him up. "There's a bar across the street and few buildings down from here. We can wait in there for Root to come back with the car."

As the four of us headed back out of the alley, I turned to my brother. "What if he wakes up?"

Ryan pulled Paulson's gun out from his jeans. "We'll keep him quiet with this," he replied, his clouded eyes wild.

CHAPTER TWELVE

As we headed out of the alley, Ryan stumbled almost dropping Adams. I took his place under the man's arm while he sat back against the building.

"Are you alright?" I asked feeling worry coat my words.

My brother nodded. "I just need a second."

Jack shifted his grip on Adams's arm. "We'll wait for you in there," he said nodding at the bar.

Ryan waved it off. "No," he straightened back up. "No, I'm okay."

He tried taking my place again, but I refused to let him hold Adams's weight, even though I was stumbling. We managed to get out of the alley and back onto the street. I couldn't get the image of Paulson's death out of my head. The look in my brother's eyes as he beat the man to death. Those clouded, poisoned eyes.

"Hey," Ryan said shattering the disturbing images. "Sorry about that back there." He took Jack's place and I turned my head to watch as Jack dragged Paulson by the arm, over to the pile of trash and covered him as best he could.

"I don't know what came over me."

I looked over Adams's slumped head at my brother. "I know."

Jack came back then and traded places again with Ryan.

We managed to cross the street and get inside the pub without anyone stopping us. A few people stared as we dragged the unconscious man through the doors and more stopped talking and turned their attention to us as we found a booth in the back and dropped him into it. Ryan and I sat across from him while Jack sat next to him and tried to act as normal as possible. A waitress approached our table cautiously.

"Is he alright?" she asked eying us.

I opened my mouth to answer.

"He's just had a bit too much to drink," Jack said. She met his eyes and her face softened. "A friend is coming to pick us up." He flashed a charming smile and I felt a pang of jealousy in my stomach.

"Oh," the waitress flushed. "Well, can I get you anything while you wait for your friend?"

Before any of us could answer, a couple police cars rushed past the windows, sirens blaring. A shudder ran down my spine. Had someone already found Paulson's body? Ryan put an assuring hand on mine.

"Coffee is fine," Jack said then put his arm around our unconscious companion.

When the waitress had gone, Ryan turned to me. "It's okay, Hailey," he said. "You've been evading the company this long, the police are just as clueless."

I turned my attention to Jack, who had his eyes fixed suspiciously on Ryan. Why was he staring at him like that? Could it have had something to do with his episode back in the alley? It's true, lashing out like that was very out of character for my brother. He'd always been more of a laid back person. Even when faced with confrontation, he kept his cool. What had changed in him? What had the company done?

My train of thought was broken when a hot cup of coffee was placed in front of me. I looked up to lock eyes with the waitress.

"Thanks," I said quietly.

When she left again, Ryan shook his head and stared into his coffee. "I'm sorry, guys," he said not making eye contact. "I don't know what came over me back there..."

"He deserved it anyway," Jack started. And now at least I know you're on our side."

My brother looked up, finally. "Were you worried?"

"Can't be too cautious." Jack shrugged and giddily took a big drink from his mug.

I raised an eyebrow. "What are you so happy about?" I asked him.

Jack looked at me like I was crazy. "Hailey, we got one!" he whispered not even trying to hide his excitement. "We can finally get some answers." His eyes drilled into mine. "I'm getting so sick of running. We're fighting back."

He was right. It was good that we were finally doing something. We had to save ourselves. No one else was going to do it for us.

Jack leaned into us. "Act natural," he said then motioned with his head toward the door.

Ryan and I both turned our heads to look in that direction. Two police officers and a paramedic had wandered in and were scanning the room. I immediately looked away. My coffee seemed much more interesting than what was going on around me. I could feel their eyes, like lasers, cutting across the room and burning into the side of my head. With an unconscious man and a sickly looking boy in our booth, we couldn't be more conspicuous.

"Excuse me." The three of us looked up to find the paramedic standing at the end of our table. "Is your friend alright?"

Ryan and I both looked to Jack.

"Yeah." He nodded. "Just had a little too much to drink."

The paramedic studied Adams. "Mind if I take a look at him?"

Jack shrugged and got out of his seat. The paramedic sat down beside the unconscious man and took a penlight out of his shirt pocket.

"Sir?" he said. "Sir, I'm just going to examine you, make sure you're alright."

Adams, still out cold, didn't respond. The man carefully opened an eyelid and shined the light in. My heart hammered in my chest and I glanced over at Jack. He was standing there with his arms folded. The muscles in his jaw became visible as he clenched and unclenched his teeth nervously. Ryan drummed his fingers on his legs under the table.

"Well," the paramedic said after a while. "Technically, I could have him taken in for public intoxication." My heart sped up as I watched him put the penlight back in his pocket. "But," my stomach churned. "I won't say anything if you get him home immediately."

"We have a friend coming to pick us up," Jack said, his arms still folded over his chest.

Just then, the door jingled and Root walked in.

"He's here," I blurted and looked at the door.

Root found us quickly and came over to the table. His expression hinted at worry when he noticed the police off in the corner and the paramedic standing by us.

"Are you guys ready to go?" he asked trying not to sound too anxious.

"Sure are," Jack replied clapping him on the back.

That was a little overkill, in my opinion. The paramedic didn't seem to notice though and we wasted no time getting to our feet and taking a hold of Adams's arms to pull him out of the booth.

"So what's going on, anyway?" Root asked.

"We can't say much right now," the paramedic answered. "But it seems there was an accident just down the street."

We all shared nervous glances.

"If I can have all your attention, please," a police officer bellowed from the front entrance. He waited for everyone to quiet down. "We are investigating a possible homicide and are checking all the diners and cafes on this street for anyone that may have seen or heard anything suspicious." This caused a stir in the crowd and it took a few moments before the officer was able to speak again. "If you could all just stay in your seats, my partner and I are going to come around to each table and ask a few questions."

The four of us froze where we were. What could we do? They would notice, for sure, if we tried to sneak out the back, especially with an unconscious man in tow. After exchanging glances, we slid slowly back into our seats. Root squeezed in next to my brother and I, squishing me against the window. Jack and I locked eyes as the police officers made their way toward us. When I looked to Ryan, he shrugged and shook his head.

"How are you folks doing?" he asked us. We all muttered in reply that we were doing okay. "What's with your friend?"

Jack was the first to say anything. "He's a tad drunk," he explained. "Our friend here was about to take us home when you told us to stay seated."

A moan escaped Adams's mouth and I choked, coffee burning my throat as it went down. Ryan whipped his head sideways to look at me. I pursed my lips and tried not to make another sound. The cop already looked suspicious enough. I prayed silently that Adams wouldn't wake up. I could only imagine what would happen if he did. Jack, Ryan and Root all went pale as our hostage began to stir. With how sick my stomach suddenly felt, I'm sure I was just as pallid.

"We should get him home." Jack said trying to hide the anxiety in his voice.

The four of us looked at the officer in hopes that he would agree. Instead, he stared at us with his stern gray eyes, the wrinkles in his forehead growing more prominent. His mustache twitched as he continued to study each of our faces. Adams slowly began to come to. His eyes creaked open and he blinked a few times.

"What's going on?" he slurred, holding his head.

"Sir, your friends here say you've had a bit too much to drink," the officer said.

Adams looked around at us, something still not quite clicking in his brain. How hard had Root hit him? "Friends?"

Both Jack and Ryan instinctively began to reach for the guns tucked under their shirts. Just then an explosion erupted from across the street causing the glass windows to shatter. Everyone dove to the ground, including us and the officer at our table. My hands flew up to cover my head as pieces of debris rained down on us. Even as glass continued to pelt us, Ryan tugged me to my feet and pushed me forward. He was herding me to the back exit. Ahead of me was Jack, Root and Adams. who was still stumbling around dazed.

Once we had made it out into the alley, Jack pulled

his gun out and shoved it into Adams's back. We hurried out toward the street where a car was waiting for us. Root jumped into the driver's seat, Ryan got in next to him and the rest of us piled into the back. Only when we were well out of sight of the diner, I felt it was safe to talk.

"What was that?" I exclaimed my ears ringing from the explosion.

"Always have a way out," Root said out of breath. "You taught me that," he said looking at Jack in the rear view mirror.

Jack smirked, even with his gun jabbing into Adams's side.

I put my head down on my knees in an attempt to steady my swirling head. I had never imagined explosions to be that loud.

"You did that?" Ryan asked.

Root smiled. "I put a small C-4 charge on the corner of the building across the street from the pub." He held up a cell phone. "I triggered it with this," he said then handed it to my brother, who tossed it out his window.

"Will someone tell me what is going on?" Adams yelled from beside me.

Jack jabbed him hard in the side with his gun. "We'll ask the questions," he said.

The ride was quiet after that. The only sounds were sirens in the distance, surely headed to the pub, and the rumble of the engine. It made me wonder where Root had gotten this car. Was it actually one of ours or was there someone out there now calling the police to report a theft? Who were these people I was riding in this car with? I had never been in trouble with the police in my lifetime. Then within one day I had become an accomplice to grand theft auto, murder and kidnapping. Not to mention Root had just about taken out a whole city block. What had I gotten myself into?

My thoughts were interrupted when we pulled into an empty parking lot. I didn't recognize anything around us. The back of a tall, crumbling, brick building lined one side of the lot, while an alley and a line of more buildings bordered the other side.

"Is this the Tree House?" Adams asked looking out the window.

Jack reached across him, unlocking and opening the door, then pushed him out with his gun. I watched from my seat as Adams stumbled onto the pavement with Jack behind him. Was he going to kill him? Ryan rolled the window down so we could hear what was going on.

"Take off your clothes," Jack said holding the gun to the agent's head.

Adams's hands were out, palms open. "Are you kidding?"

"Do I look like I'm kidding?"

Without another word, Adams began removing his clothes. First his jacket, then shirt and pants, and laid them on the ground and backed away standing only in his boxers. I could feel heat rising up into my cheeks. He had a belly that hung down over his waistband. His shoulders were small and weak and his arms and legs looked like sticks. He had kicked his shoes off and now had just black calf length socks on. An empty holster rested on his ankle. I felt a pang of guilt in my chest as I realized I felt bad for this man. He was just following orders. But then again, he had been part of the reason my parents were dead. He could have even been the one to put a bullet in each of their brains. The guilt was replaced by anger. It took all I had not to go out there, take the gun from Jack and end him myself.

Jack picked up the man's pants and searched the pockets, dropping the contents back on the ground next to the rest of his clothes. A wallet, a few coins and a small pocket knife. Then he dropped the pants again and circled Adam's, looking him up and down, checking for any kind of wire or tracking device. Jack stopped at his arm and grabbed his wrist, holding it up toward the light.

"What's that?" He asked pushing his wrist up into the man's face.

Adams looked at it nervously. "It's an ID chip."

Jack threw his arm back down and bent down to pick up the small pocket knife. "You're lying," he said.

"I can turn it off," Adams said backing away. "They won't be able to find me."

Jack chuckled as he flipped the blade open. "That's a load of crap," he said and motioned for Ryan to get out of the car.

My brother got out and went to stand by Adams, taking hold of his arm.

"Let me do it," our hostage pleaded trying to pull his wrist free.

Jack tossed the knife to him. "Be my guest," he said. Adams looked at the blade he was holding nervously. He looked back up at Jack. "I knew a girl once who got hers out with a rock. Don't be a wuss."

After a few more seconds of staring at the knife, Adams threw it hard at Jack, missing him completely, and took off running in the opposite direction. Jack and Ryan went after him.

"Hold on," Root said to me then threw the stick shift into gear and floored the gas. We raced forward, past Adams then swerved, coming to a stop in front of him, blocking his exit. Ryan tackled him to the ground and while he held down Adams's arm with one knee, Jack dug into his flesh and cut the chip out. Adams let out a pained cry, making me feel sick to my stomach. I sunk down in my seat and closed my eyes. Would this ever be over?

Finally, Jack pulled Adams back into the car, still in

his underwear, then threw in his clothes after him and got in on the other side. I scooted as close to the window and as far away from them as possible. Blood was streaming from the open wound, staining his boxers dark red. Sweat poured down the man's face as he gritted his teeth in pain. Jack ripped the sleeve off of Adams's shirt and tied it around the man's head covering his eyes.

"Let's go home," Jack said to Root and we pulled back out of the parking lot.

CHAPTER THIRTEEN

The rest of the ride home was uncomfortably quiet. Root dropped us off in the alley behind the Tree House then went to get rid of the car. Jack kept his gun jabbed into Adams's back as we all made our way up and over the wall then we met up with Arie in the first floor entry way. He had a short chain in his hands. I don't know how he knew to meet us down here with that, but I didn't dwell on the fact as I watched him limp after my brother and Jack through a door and down some stairs into a dark basement. He stopped, as the other disappeared into the blackness, and turned to look at me.

"We aren't animals, Hailey," he said.

I nodded, then watched Arie turn back around. I kept my eyes on a tattooed skull peeking up at me over his shirt collar as he continue down into the dark, the chain in his hands swinging from side to side like a pendulum.

Jack didn't come back up for a good portion of the day. I stayed up on the third floor, keeping some distance between me and that basement. I helped Melody and

Keeta unpack our food and put it back in the cupboards. Then we got lunch prepared and Keeta volunteered to go down and let Jack and Arie know. I was grateful for that. This whole time, Ryan stayed over on the couch staring into the fire, picking at the skin around his fingers. Whenever I looked over at him, I was immediately reminded of Anna and the half-crazed, fear riddled look in her eyes. He seemed to be lost in memories of his time with the company. I wanted to ask him what really happened. I wanted more than the vague answers he was giving me. I wanted to know if he knew what their plans were.

When I sat down next to him, he didn't move. His eyes stared deep into the fire like his mind was a million miles away. "Ryan?" I whispered and touched his hand lightly. He flinched jerking his hand back, and made a fist like he was going to hit me. The two of us stared at each other for a moment. Then my brother quickly dropped his hand and looked back to the fire. I shifted in my seat glancing back to find Keeta and Melody watching us as they continued to put the kitchen back together. "Ryan," I said again, though I didn't touch him this time. "You said earlier that you've been in Seattle for a while now. What did you come back for?"

At first Ryan stayed silent, the flames reflecting in his clouded eyes. Then his mouth opened with a click of his tongue. "I wanted to surprise you and mom and dad," he said quietly then turned his head to look at me. "You know, for Christmas."

I nodded feeling my throat close up. I cleared it quickly and blinked. "So what happened? How did you find out about the Tree House?"

"I'll get to that," my brother started looking down at his hands. "Actually, I've known about us and what we are for a couple weeks now."

My breath caught in my throat. "What?" I croaked. "How...?"

"Mom and Dad told me," he said. "They were going to tell you soon too. Actually they were going to tell us both at the same time, I guess." I couldn't believe what I was hearing. "But they skyped me in Nashville and told me about the trial."

"Why did they decide to tell you before me?" I finally asked, my voice still shaking, though from sadness or anger, I wasn't so sure.

"I guess the company called them and said they needed me to come in for some more testing," he continued shaking his head. "Biggest load of crap I've ever heard in my life."

"What do you mean?"

"Again, I'll get to that," Ryan said and scratched his head causing bits of hair to sprinkle down onto his pants. He brushed the hair off his lap carefully. "Anyway, I had Sam pick me up from the airport."

I scoffed. "You still talk to that idiot?" I muttered disgustedly.

Ryan let out a chuckle. "Yeah, I guess. So, he picked me up and we ended up getting drunk and arrested."

"Seriously, Ryan?" I shook my head angrily. "What made you think drinking with Sam was a good idea?"

"I don't know," he shrugged sadly, "I just missed everyone, I guess. Things just got out of hand."

"So you went to jail?"

"Only till the next morning. I was too afraid to call you guys so I just stayed there all day and night. While I was there, I met this kid, Matthew."

I sat up straight at the mention of his name. "You met Matthew?"

Ryan nodded. "Do you know him?"

"He's Sy's godson. Jack and I went to visit him at the

jail yesterday to talk to him and give him a letter. I guess he was in there for hitting and killing Sy's wife." My eyes settled back on the fire again.

"Yeah, he told me that," Ryan said. "He mentioned that his sentence would have been over by now, but he wanted to stay in there longer."

I lifted my head again to look at my brother. "Why would he want to stay in jail past his sentence?"

"I guess it's safer in there than it is out here," he replied with another shrug.

"So he knows about everything then? The Tree House and what Eli is doing to those of us that he catches?"

"Yep, he knows it all. Apparently, Sy was keeping him well informed."

And here all a long I had thought Sy was keeping Matthew in the dark about everything. I glanced at my brother's face to find him staring again into the flames. He tapped his thumbs anxiously against his knees, unable to keep still for even a second. "So, how did you get caught?" I asked.

Ryan's stopped drumming on his knees just then and sat completely still. I thought for a moment that he hadn't heard me or that he was lost in a memory again, but then he opened his mouth. "They were waiting for me."

A shudder went through my body at the thought of Ryan walking out of the jail only to be grabbed and shoved into a car. Then I remembered the message he had left on my phone. "But wait, when you called me..."

"I'd managed to get away from them. I jumped out of their car when we were at a stop light and they didn't catch me again until that night," then Ryan laid back against the couch and closed his eyes. "I never should have left Nashville," he whispered and exhaled heavily.

I laid back with him and rested my head on his bony

shoulder. "You're safe now, though," I said and patted his hand reassuringly.

"It doesn't matter now."

I sat up again. "Don't even say that," I snapped. "You're here and we're going to figure out some way to get you better."

Ryan didn't even open his eyes again to look at me. Instead he just pursed his lips together in a mock frown. Even through the exhaustion and the sickness, he still found the strength to taunt me. With a roll of my eyes, I laid back again and once again rested my head on his shoulder, crossing my arms over my chest.

When Jack and Arie came upstairs, their mouths were set in straight lines and their eyes were shining with something I could only describe as a mix between annoyance and excitement. The two of them sat down on the other side of the couch and talked quietly with their heads together. Probably planning the next step in breaking Adams. Root and Logan were pouring, once again, over the map, trying to find a way around the company's GPS. Keeta and Melody and prepared lunch and were now passing out sandwiches to each of us.

"Ryan?"I whispered holding a plate out to him.

He shook his head and moaned sleepily. "I'm really tired," he croaked not opening his eyes.

"But you haven't eaten yet today," I said putting it down on his lap, "At least, not since I've seen you."

"Not now, Hailey," Ryan whispered then pushed the plate off his legs and fell sideways onto the couch, exhausted.

I caught it before it could tip over and carried the plate over to the kitchen where Keeta and Melody were leaning against the counter, eating and talking about something I was too distracted to listen in on. Something was up with my brother. And seeing similarities between him and Anna, I feared the worst. Ryan couldn't die. Not after I'd just gotten him back. Sitting back down next to him on the couch, I leaned down so my head was resting on his shoulder. Then I closed my eyes and fell into a troubled sleep to the sound of his raspy breathing.

I had only just drifted off when I was rustled awake again. My eyelids creaked open and Jack's face appeared in front of me.

"Can I talk to you downstairs?" he whispered. I nodded sleepily and let him help me up.

By the time we reached the bottom floor, I was wide awake.

"How good of an actress are you?" he asked me, wiping sweat from his forehead.

"Why?"

He smiled his old smile. "Adams isn't talking and we need you to get him to."

I could feel a skeptical look cross my face. "How do I do that?"

"Just be your sweet innocent self."

My mouth dropped open before I could stop it. "Are you serious?" I asked, my voice getting higher.

"Don't worry," he assured me. "I'll tell you what to say. Just make it sound convincing."

It took a few more minutes of persuading, but finally I agreed, a lump forming in my stomach. I took my time making my way down the stairs, running through the lines in my head. I wasn't sure how Jack was expecting me to pull this off. What if Adams laughed in my face? What if I just complicated things even more? Then we'd never get any answers. We'd never be able to stop them from hurting more innocent people.

I made it to the bottom of the stairs too soon. The room I was in was completely dark except for a small square of light filtering in through a hole in a covered window. I could barely make out the shape of our captive slumped in a chair. I stepped forward and he lifted his head.

"What do you want?" he muttered shifting so he was leaning on an elbow.

My brain went blank.

As my eyes adjusted, I could see he was still in his boxers. I felt an embarrassed smile creep onto my face and Jack's voice in my head told me to just go with it. "You don't look too good," I said, my voice quivering. I hoped he hadn't caught that.

The light caught his eyes as he turned his face up to look at me. "Surprised?"

"Look," I started. I took a few steps toward him, my hands knotting together. "You could make this a whole lot easier on yourself if you would just tell us what we need to know."

"I already told your boyfriends earlier, I don't know anything," Adams said. "I'm given orders and I follow them, no questions asked."

"No questions asked," I repeated. My stomach began to churn and Jack's words went right out the window. "So, when they tell you to kill unsuspecting kids and their families you just do it, no questions asked?"

"Hey, you see it as killing innocent people, I see it as tying up loose ends," Adams said

"Loose ends?"

"Did I stutter?"

This guy was a piece of work. The churning in my stomach grew and my fists balled up, but I had to keep myself under control. "Don't lose your cool," Jack's voice came back to tell me.

"I suppose I've heard a little bit here and there," he continued. "I know the story. I know about the potential lawsuits."

"And you know this is all the company's fault," I said. "You know what you're doing is completely immoral and wrong."

Adams chuckled. "Hey, get your boyfriends to bring me my clothes, then we'll talk about immoral, sweetheart."

That was it. I found myself gripping both arms of the chair and pulling him toward me until our noses were almost touching. "Listen here, you worthless piece of crap," I spat. "If you think, for one second, that I'm going to let you hurt anyone else, you've got another thing coming." Adams seemed shaken by my change of character, but it felt good. "You have no idea what we are capable of," I continued, my teeth bared. "and if I were a pathetic worm like you, your brains would be splattered against that wall back there." I smashed my fists against the chair legs causing him to jump. "Don't even think, for a second, that I'm some sweetheart you can mess with." Then I pushed his chest hard, sending him flying backwards. The back of the chair landed hard on the floor and Adams made a horrible noise as the breath was knocked out of him. I hoped he got a concussion.

When I turned to head back for the stairs, Jack and Arie stood at the bottom, mouths gaping. "If you don't kill him," I muttered to Jack, "I will." Then I stomped up the steps, adrenaline still coursing like electricity through my body.

A while later, Jack came up. His mouth was stretched into a wide, triumphant smile that I would have found amusing if I were in any sort of mood to.

"Hailey Roemer, you've outdone yourself," he said clapping his hands together.

"Did you get anything out of him?" I asked sitting down on the steps.

Jack sat down next to me. "No, but he did say to

keep that psycho away from him, however he did use another word after psycho," he said with another smile and a shake of his head. "You looked like you were about to punch his lights out."

"I'm surprised I didn't," I muttered looking down at my hands. I felt Jack scoot a bit closer to me. "Did you hear what he said about us?" I asked feeling my throat tighten. "About my family? About you?"

Jack took hold of my chin and turned it so I was looking at him. The smile had left his mouth and now fire burned in his eyes. "We're going to make things right, Hailey," he assured me then pressed his lips against mine.

Back upstairs, Ryan was still sleeping peacefully on the couch. I sat down and once again began to study him. He looked worse than that morning, if it was even possible. His cheekbones were more prominent and his mouth looked too big. It was like something was sucking the fat and muscle right out of him. I ran my hand over his hair only to find that large patches were coming out and getting stuck between my fingers. My stomach dropped and my eyes filled with tears. My brother was dying. This was really happening. And that monster downstairs was at fault. My tears turned hot as I began to shake. I jumped up off the couch and, before anyone could stop me, I raced down to the first floor and stomped down the stairs into the basement.

The moron still sat in the chair, looking bored and inconvenienced. I'm sure he was just waiting for us to let him go so he could get back to tying up loose ends. His expression changed when he saw me coming at him, huffing and puffing.

"Hailey," Jack called from on the stairs behind me.

"What did you psychos do to my brother?" I growled and backed Adams's chair up till it smacked against the wall. "You're going to give me answers right now!"

Adams started blathering like an idiot. He wasn't even saying words. My nails were digging into my palms and before I knew it, my fist connected with his jaw, slamming the other side of his face into the wall behind him.

"What did you do to my brother!"

Before anything else could happen, hands pinned my arms to my sides and I was being pulled – no – carried backwards. I kicked my foot out and managed to catch Adams's hand against the arm of the chair. He cried out in pain as his fingers broke. My hair was all over in my face so I couldn't see exactly what was going on. I could hear Adams, though, shrieking to "get that psycho away from me" and Jack was calling for, I'm guessing, Arie to grab a hold of my thrashing legs. I was screaming this whole time, trying to pull away from Jack so I could get another punch in. This jerk deserved it. He deserved to have every last bone in his body broken. Every last appendage snapped and his eyes gouged out with a dull butter knife. I had never been so pissed in my life. This was no longer about saving lives, this was about avenging those that were lost.

I fought as much as I could all the way up the stairs. Finally, Jack took his arms from around my waist, but only after Arie had closed the door on us and locked it from the inside. I pulled away hard, still fuming mad and glared at Jack through the wet strands of hair plastered to my face. My heart was racing and my breathing was heavy.

"What is seriously the matter with you?" I asked, my voice gravely from yelling.

Jack was also breathing heavily. "We're never going to get answers that way, Hailey." He rubbed his wrists and for a split second I was worried I'd hurt him.

Only for a second though.

I shook my head. "So suddenly you're the voice of reason?" I asked. "What happened to you? You'll hold a gun to my brother's head, but not the one responsible for killing your own-"

"He can't help us if he's dead," Jack cut me off.

I shut my mouth hard, my teeth clacking together. The two of us stared the other down for as long as we could. Finally, I couldn't take it any more and my legs gave out. I sank to the floor, tears pouring from my eyes. Jack was immediately by my side with his arms around me. I collapsed into him, my tears soaking his shirt. This seemed to be turning into a regular occurrence.

"I'm sorry," I choked burying my face into his warm neck. He didn't reply so I took his silence as forgiveness. "I'm so scared of losing Ryan."

"I know."

"He's all I have left."

"I know."

Jack wouldn't let me back down onto the first floor and I would have put up a fight if he wasn't staying by my side. Even while I sat cradling Ryan's head in my lap until the sun began to set, he didn't leave me. As I watched him build up the fire, footsteps sounded on the stairs and his head turned anxiously to see who it was. Melody was just coming up, her hair wet from having just taken a shower. Jack's shoulders slumped and I felt guilt twist in my stomach. Of course he wanted to be down there. Staying up here with us girls and Ryan must have made him feel pretty useless when the rest of the boys were downstairs working at getting us answers and trying to come up with a plan.

"Jack, you don't have to stay," I whispered trying not to wake my brother.

He turned his head back around to look at me. "No, I

want to."

I couldn't help but smile. "No you don't," I said shaking my head. "I'm sure they could use your help."

He got up quickly, kissed my forehead and hurried down the stairs. I couldn't help but smile. A lot had changed.

It had only been quiet again for a couple minutes when Root raced up the stairs out of breath. He looked directly at me. "I need you to come with me," he said. His eyes told me this was urgent. I got up quickly being careful though to let Ryan's head down gently, and followed Root down the stairs. He stopped me on the second level, leaning in close. "Something happened," he whispered. "Sy didn't kill himself."

My stomach fell. "He didn't?"

"No." Root shook his head. "He stormed the company. Took out a good chunk of important people before he was killed."

"How do you know this?"

"Adams slipped up. Don't you see, though, Hailey?" he asked, his eyes shining. "We're fighting back. Something is finally happening."

I couldn't believe it. "This is amazing," I whispered. "I wonder what else he's keeping from us."

"What does it matter?" Root chuckled with a lighthearted shrug. "We aren't going down without a fight, now. Jack and everyone else is already planning our next move."

"Where are they?" He motioned with his head to Jack's bedroom door. "I'll let the girls know," I said with a smile. Root smiled back then disappeared through the door to join in on the meeting.

So, Sy hadn't given up. He knew he was going to die anyway and decided to take as many as he could with him. And now we were going to get our turn. I was finally going to be able to fight for my family. But what was going to happen now with our prisoner in the basement? I made my way down the stairs to the first floor and again down the stairs into the basement. When my eyes adjusted, I could see Adams slumped down in his chair in defeat.

I cleared my throat loudly causing him to snap his head up. His eyes widened when he saw who it was.

"Thanks for the info," I said smugly.

Adams let out a scoff and shook his head. "You all think you're so clever with your little plans and meetings. None of you have any idea what you're getting yourselves into and who you're dealing with."

I crossed my arms over my chest. "Who are we dealing with?"

"An insane man, that's who."

"Eli?"

Adams gave me a look like he couldn't believe I had said the man's name so nonchalantly. Who was this man that he could put such a look in someone's eyes?

"Yes, Eli," he said to me. "You don't know the kinds of things he's doing. Just be glad you and the rest of your lab rat friends are out here and not in there."

"What are you talking about?" I asked irritated. "What else is he doing?" The man shut his mouth, shaking his head like he suddenly decided he wasn't going to say any more. "Don't you think it's a bit late for that?"

Adams bit his lip before finally opening his mouth again. "He's working on a few other things not meant for the public."

"How do you know this?" I asked.

"Word gets around in that place. And it helps being partnered with his right-hand man."

"Paulson?"

"Yeah."

Ryan was going to be happy to hear that he'd killed someone so important. If he ever woke up... "So what is he doing?" I repeated.

Adams shook his head and sank deeper in his chair. "I've heard rumors of a chip in the making used to erase certain memories in a person's head and replace them with new ones. It's meant for military use, but I'm pretty sure if they knew we were doing involuntary human testing, they would put a stop to it."

"How far along is it?"

"Eli is still working out some kinks. It seems all of the chips he has developed just shield things instead of wiping the problem out completely. This one is still too unreliable," he explained. "His human subject has spells of remembering things that should have been erased."

Then without warning, Adams began to chuckle. I could feel anger rising in my throat. "Yeah, that's hilarious," I muttered in disgust.

"No," he said trying to control his laughter. "It's not that."

"Then what is it?"

It took him a moment to compose himself. "I just realized, you know the kid."

My eyes narrowed. "Who is it?"

Adams shook his head, a few more laughs escaping his throat. "No, no, I'm not going to tell you. I've said too much already."

Suddenly, my hands were wrapped around his neck and my nose was inches from his. "Who is it?" I yelled in his face.

His face was already red from laughing, but now veins started popping out in his forehead. "It's your smart alec boyfriend's smart alec brother," he choked.

I immediately released my grip. Had I heard him

right? "What?" My tongue was suddenly too big for my mouth and I couldn't control my lips. They moved involuntarily trying to form the words. His name escaped my throat as more of a gasp than an actual word. "Ben?"

CHAPTER FOURTEEN

"It's not true," I stammered. "He was shot. Jack watched him bleed out in the snow. He watched him die."

Adams was still shaking his head. "He's not dead; I was there."

"No. You're lying. You're lying!" With that, I spun and ran up and out of the basement. Once I hit the top of the stairs, I didn't stop, but rather kept running to the tree room and out the back door. The air was frigid and I was aware of the slush seeping into my shoes, but I didn't care. My breathing was uneven, not so much from running, and I could feel my heart pounding against my ribs. I reached the scaffolding and pulled myself up and over.

When I finally stopped running, I found myself on top of a building a few blocks from the Tree House. My breath came out sharp in clouds that quickly evaporated into the black. It was impossible. Adams had to be lying to me. He had to be. There was no way Ben was still alive. No, Jack saw him die. He saw him. And now I saw him kick himself every day because he wished it was him. I balled up the ends of my sleeves into my mouth and screamed until all the blood had rushed to my face and my lips tingled.

When I opened my eyes again, I was on my knees. Tears streamed down my face, drying and pulling at my skin. Could I even tell Jack? If it was me, I would want to know. But could I blame anyone for keeping it from me? After all, finding out he was alive so he could be dissected and experimented on would be even worse. Right?

I got to my feet again, my shoulders sagging from the new weight of the news I was now carrying. It took me a while to get back to the Tree House. I couldn't drag myself across the rooftops so I climbed down the ladder and walked the few blocks back.

Hot water rained down on me from the shower head, thawing my skin and soaking into my bones. When I had walked down the hall toward the bathroom, the sound of voices were coming from inside Jack's room. My stomach had tied in knots. Of course he still didn't know. Now, I laid my forehead against the wall in front of me, staring down at the drain and wishing it would suck me in and pull me down into the dark.

The scalding water numbed my thoughts after a while, which I was grateful for. I was able to get myself out and dried off without collapsing to the floor. Even going back out into the hall and hearing Jack's voice didn't cause my shoulders to sag. I didn't know how long this was going to last so I hurried up to the third floor to find that nothing had really changed since I'd left. I took my place, once again, on the couch next to my brother. His eyes were open again, but he was still laying down on his back.

"Hey," I whispered. Ryan cracked a smile that only

barely resembled the ones he used to make. "How are you feeling?"

"How do I look?" he croaked in reply.

I put one of my hands on his feverish cheek. His skin was so dry and tight. "Is it possible that you look even worse than you did a couple hours ago?" I finally muttered. His smile stretched a little wider for a second then retracted like a rubber band. I hadn't even noticed the tears welling in my eyes until one ran down my cheek. "I don't know what to do," I whispered.

Ryan put his hand on top of mine. "You'll be okay, Hailey," he said to me. "Jack's a leader. And he doesn't seem like a total nutcase."

A mix between a laugh and a sob escaped my throat and I became aware of the silence in the room. I guess I hadn't noticed Keeta and Melody leave.

"Listen, Hailey," Ryan said, his tone not hiding the gravity of his situation. "I know you think this is all just too much."

"Ryan.."

"No, listen to me," he interrupted. "Just please, don't stop fighting. You can't let them win. Got it?" His eyes reflected the fire in front of us making them look angry and determined.

More tears trickled down my face. Of course I will keep fighting, I wanted to say, but all I could do at this point was nod. Ryan nodded back, his clouded eyes shimmering, and lifted his arms to me. I fell into them and buried my face into his side. His chest felt hollow and his ribs were brittle against my cheek.

"I love you, Ryan," I whispered into his shirt.

His arms tightened around me. "I know."

We lay like that, arms around each other for longer than I knew. I think I drifted in and out throughout the night. Time seemed spotty. I'd open my eyes and the fire would be almost out then blink and Keeta would be kneeling in front of us, feeding the flames. Sleep only really pulled me under a few times, though I was woken each time by Ryan gasping for air, having stopped breathing while he was asleep. Each time I woke, my cheek ached from laying on his bony shoulder. But that didn't bother me as much as the sound of his heart slowing in my ears did.

When I woke again to find light filtering in through the makeshift chimney, I immediately became aware of the silence. I squeezed my eyes shut again, willing myself to really wake up. Tears seeped from between my eyelids and fell onto my brother's unmoving chest. His name escaped my mouth before I could stop it and my hand went to cup around the back of his neck. Sitting up, I kept my eyes closed, so afraid of what I might find. His hair still smelled like him. Then the dam broke and I lost it. Sobs racked my body and I shook, trying to hide my face in between in chest and his arm while sounds of hurried footsteps came up the stairs.

My eyes stayed shut, even as hands pulled my brother's cold body away and replaced it with a warm, living and breathing one. Jack's voice whispered in my ear, though I couldn't tell what he was saying as my ears were filled with the sounds of my own cries. More hands touched me and I could feel whose were whose. The small, delicate hands of Melody smoothed my hair while Root's heavier, thicker hands rubbed my back, his rough skin occasionally catching on my shirt.

Jack's grip around me tightened. He felt so different than my brother had. His chest was warm and smooth, his arms substantial and his hair felt thick between my fingers. I guess I hadn't realized just how frail Ryan had been. "It's going to be okay, Hailey."

I kept my eyes shut trying to keep my brother alive

in my mind. The touch of hands on me began to fade away as the image of Ryan's face became brighter. I realized at this point that tears had stopped falling from my eyes and the trails on my face were beginning to dry. My head was swimming and I felt like I was floating. A sea spread out around me, gray and endless and a small bird flew over my head.

"Ryan?" I called out.

The bird circled above me then dove into the water, disappearing below with a small ripple. I immediately followed, the sea swallowing me, cold water rushing into my ears. I saw the bird, a dark blob far below me, tumbling, spinning and dancing through the currents. I wanted to tell him to come back to me and that it's lonely up here on the surface, but I couldn't open my mouth, for fear of drowning. Then fingers wrapped around my arms from behind and began to pull me back. No! I wanted to scream, I can't leave my brother down there! The hands continued to pull me back. Through the water I could see the bird's shadow fade as I was pulled into darkness.

"Hailey, open your eyes," Jack's voice said to me.

"I can't."

"Please."

Slowly, one at a time, I eased my eyes open. The light seemed so much brighter than it had before and I realized I was no longer in Jack's arms, but laying on the couch with my own arms wrapped tightly around myself.

"Where is he?" I asked meeting his gaze.

Jack seemed relieved that I had woken up. "Logan and Root took his body downstairs and outside," he said. "We can bury him here if you would like."

I could only nod in reply. He helped me up and didn't remove his hand from around my waist as we started down the stairs. The descent seemed to last forever. Each step seemed taller than the last. Walking down the hallway, I was joined by Melody, Keeta and Arie. What was I going to see once I got into the backyard? It didn't take long to find out.

Cold air rushed into the tree room when Jack opened the door for me to the outside. I stepped cautiously, keeping my eyes plastered to the ground, afraid of what I might see if I looked up.

"It's okay, Hailey," Jack said, sliding his hand up to rest between my shoulder blades.

I slowly lifted my head and settled on the scene in front of me. Root and Logan were finishing digging a deep hole beneath the tree, right next to the frozen garden. It took me a moment to find Ryan's body. It was wrapped in a clean white sheet so it blended well with the blanket of snow covering the ground. Seeing my brother's body made my stomach hurt, like a rock had been dropped on it from ten feet up. But then the pain faded to a dull, manageable ache. This isn't Ryan, I reminded myself. He's just going to be gone for a while. I'll see him again. I can't give up now. I told him I would keep fighting.

None of us said anything as Jack helped Root and Logan lower the body carefully into the hole. I think they were waiting for me to say the first words, but I didn't. The silence was enough for me.

A light snow began to fall, dusting the mound of dirt that now covered Ryan's body at the base of the tree. Jack stood next to me taking a few of my fingers in his. I couldn't take my eyes off the grave. It's like I was waiting for my brother's hand to come shooting up out of the dirt. Of course, that didn't happen though. After a little while, the rest of my friends slowly started making their way back into the house. Melody and Arie went first, Melody putting her hand on my shoulder for a moment before disappearing inside. Then Logan and Keeta went in. Root stayed leaning against the tree, his arms propped on the shovel he was holding.

"Hailey," Jack said. I tore my eyes from the grave and looked at him. "If you need anything..."

"I'll be okay," I cracked nodding slightly. "Weren't you guys in the middle of planning something before all this happened?"

"You're more important than that right now."

A tear escaped from my eye before I could blink it back. "Well, I'm ready to kick some butt."

It took a bit of convincing and constant reminders that I would be okay to get everyone else back on track. I didn't want to be the reason for putting our plan on hold. Still, it seemed Jack didn't want me to be left alone. As I sat on the couch in the main room, poking at the fire, Melody sat next to me, humming to herself with a sketch pad on her lap.

"I didn't know you draw."

A smile played on her lips. "I try," she replied, her eyes not leaving the paper.

"Can I see?"

Melody hesitated for a second then flipped the book around so I could see what she had done. The lines were faint, almost like she had been drawing a ghost. I immediately recognized the small mole on my cheek, just below my eye.

"That's me." I smiled. "You're pretty great."

She smiled back shyly. "Thanks," she said. "I don't get to do it often enough, what with trying to avoid being killed and all."

"Do you have any more?"

With a nod, Melody handed the sketch pad to me. The paper felt thick and soft under my fingers. I turned the page, careful not to smudge anything. A pang hit my stomach when I saw a two familiar sleeping faces.

"Ryan," I whispered.

"I'm sorry," Melody said, reaching for the book. "I shouldn't have-"

I shook my head stopping her. "No it's okay." I looked down at the page. She must have done this while the two of us had been sleeping the day before.

"It must have been terrible," Melody whispered. I looked up at her again and caught a tear running down her cheek. "I mean, I don't know if any of my family is still alive, but the fact that you and Jack both have had to see it actually happen..."

My eyes flicked to the staircase. "Jack."

"Hailey?"

I had completely forgotten about Ben. Handing the book back to her, I got up quickly. "I'm sorry, Mel. I'll be back." Then I hurried down the stairs and into the hallway.

When I reached the door to Jack's room, I froze, arm up, fist ready to knock. What was I doing? I lowered my hand again. I guess I had never decided if I was going to tell him or not. With everything that had happened so far, could he handle it? Could he accept the fact that not only was his brother still alive, but he had left him there to be taken by the company? No. No, I couldn't do it.

I turned and slid down to the floor with my back to the door, listening to the muffled voices coming from the other side. It seemed like Jack was doing most of the talking. He'd definitely taken to his role after Sy had left. I know he hadn't wanted it, but it was true what Ryan had said about him. He really was a leader. Just then, the door opened behind me and I scrambled to my feet. Root's eyes met mine.

"Sorry, Hailey," he said surprised and pushed his glasses up his nose. "I didn't know you were here."

"It's alright."

He put his hand on my arm. "Are you okay?" His eyes were full of sympathy.

I nodded. "Yeah, Root, I'm okay."

"Anything you need?"

I was about to say no when it hit me. I couldn't tell Jack, but someone had to know. "I need to talk to you in private," I said, my voice low so those in the room behind him couldn't hear me.

Root closed the door quietly, "Sure, what's going on?"

"Not here." When we had reached the tree room, I felt it was safe enough to talk. "Adams said something to me yesterday."

"Oh yeah," Root grinned, "I totally forgot about our house guest. Anything I need to take care of for you?"

"No," I smiled halfheartedly. "It's about Jack. Well, it's more about his brother."

The grin on his face disappeared. "What happened?"

"Apparently, Eli has been developing a different kind of chip," I explained quickly. "Like a memory loss chip for the government to use or something. I'm not really sure what for, but-"

He must have known where this was going. "Is Ben still alive?"

I nodded. "They're using him to test it out." Root was silent for a few seconds. "And I don't know what to do," I finally continued. "Do we tell Jack?"

"No," he said flatly. "We don't tell Jack. It could distract him from our plan and get himself or all of us killed."

I bit my lip. It didn't feel right keeping something so huge from him, but Root was right. This was already going to be dangerous enough without distractions. "So what do we do?" I asked.

"I'll take care of it."

"Is everything okay?" Root and I turned our attention to the other side of the room where Arie leaned against the door frame.

Root straightened up. "Yeah," he said. "I was just filling Hailey in on our plan."

I nodded in agreement. "Yeah, sounds good to me," I added.

"Well, Jack wants us all to meet upstairs. We can fill everyone in at the same time."

"Right, good point." Root glanced at me. "You always were the logical one, Arie."

With a chuckle, Arie turned around and hobbled back down the hall toward the stairs. Once the sound of his footsteps had faded, Root turned to me. "We don't tell Jack."

Five minutes later, we were all sitting on the couches surrounding the fire. Just being here, sitting in the same spot I had been holding my dead brother only hours earlier made my stomach twist into knots. It was hard fighting back the tears, but I knew I had to be strong. Moping wasn't going to help. I hadn't been able to save Ryan or Anna, but maybe I could keep others from going through what they had.

Jack sat down beside me, breaking me out of my dark train of thought. "Are you doing alright?" he asked me.

I nodded. "Yeah," I said. "Let's get this thing going."

With a smile, Jack got back up. The room went silent and everyone turned their attention to their new leader. I couldn't help but grin as I watched Jack take his rightful place. "The other guys and I have spent the last couple of days trying to come up with a plan," he said. "There's no getting around the fact that we'll be exceedingly outnumbered and some of us are probably going to get hurt."

"Or worse," Keeta added. We all looked at her.

Jack pursed his lips. "But we aren't going to let that stop us, right? We know our chances going into this," he said. "I'm not going to make any of you risk your lives, but I hope you understand what we're fighting for." Once he was sure everyone was on board, which we were, Jack started in on the plan. "Root knows more about explosions than anyone else I've ever come across," Jack said.

"Good thing he's on our side, then," Arie said getting a chuckle out of everyone.

Jack smiled too. "We're going to need to create at least four big ones, maybe more. Think you can handle that?"

"Sure can." The gears in Root's head were already turning.

Over the next couple of days we were all going to be doing various things to get ready. Keeta and Logan, Melody and Arie were assigned to get a list of supplies from Root and fan out across this side of the city to get what we needed. "What do you want me to do?" I asked sitting up straight.

Jack looked over at me. "You're coming with me."

He didn't say much as he led me to a car parked in the alley behind the Tree House. Even when I asked where they kept getting all these cars, he only smiled a sheepish smile and opened the door, gesturing for me to get inside. I narrowed my eyes skeptically, but got in the passenger seat, settling into the soft black leather. This one seemed so much nicer than the pieces of junk we had been using before.

"What are we doing?" I finally asked, my voice stern so he knew I was serious.

Jack looked at me. His mouth was still stretched in a wide grin "Why, we're continuing our investigation, Detective Clark." The engine roared to life. "Now put your seat belt on."

"Someone played a little too much Grand Theft Auto in their day," I said and sat back in my seat.

He put the car in gear and we eased out of the alley. "I was never really into video games. No, I was more of a hands on kind of kid."

"Like what?"

"Football, mostly," Jack replied with a shrug.

I turned my head to look directly at him. "Football?" I asked. "You?"

"What are you trying to tell me here, Hailey?" he chuckled as we turned onto the main road and started toward the city.

"I don't know," I shrugged. "You just don't seem like the football type."

"What? Big and lacking brain cells from ramming my head into people too hard?"

I smiled. "No," I said. "You seem more independent, I guess. More like the kind of person that might wrestle or play golf."

"Wrestle or golf?" Jack repeated. "Golf was the second best answer you could come up with? What kind of person do you think I am?"

"I-" Now I stopped. What kind of person was he? "I guess I don't know," I finally said. I didn't know anything about this boy that I had spent the past week with. That I had been yelling at and crying on and kissing. That I was depending on and trusting with my life. "I really don't know anything about you, Jack."

With a smile, Jack put his hand on mine. "There will be plenty of time for us to get to know each other after this is all over. Until then, let's just trust each other to trust each other."

I nodded. "I think I can do that. Though could I ask just one thing?"

"Sure."

"Where are we going?"

Jack chuckled now and shook his head. "You're just bent on ruining all the fun, aren't you?"

Eli's building loomed up ahead like the opening of a massive cave. And somewhere inside, he was perfecting his experiments. Waiting for just the right time to come out of hibernation. And somewhere in there, Ben was suffering.

Jack pulled the car over a couple blocks short and parked, turning the engine off. My heartbeat quickened. This was getting to be a bit too much. "What are we doing here?" I asked, my voice barely above a whisper.

Jack brought binoculars up to his face. "While everyone else is out doing Root's grocery shopping, you and I are playing spy."

"And you don't think they're going to notice a ridiculously nice car sitting in plain sight all day?"

"Look around, Hailey," Jack said without taking the binoculars away.

My eyes scanned the street around us. Government buildings lined the sidewalks and parked on the curb in front were cars that seemed to have been made no earlier than last year. "Alright," I finally said, "but I'm not getting out of the car."

Jack pushed his door open and climbed out. He leaned back in and winked at me. "Suit yourself."

The door shut again before I could say anything. Ryan's words from the night before echoed in my head. Jack's a leader; and he doesn't seem like a total nutcase. I shook my head. "Don't be so sure, bro," I muttered with a pang of sadness, then got out of the car. Jack was already halfway down the alley when I caught up with him. "If I ask another question, am I just going to get another vague non-answer out of you?"

By now he had pulled himself up onto the first rung of a ladder. "Why don't you give it a shot and find out?"

"I don't really have one," I muttered. "This is more for future reference." Jack jumped back down in front of me then put a hand on either side of my face and kissed me. When he pulled away, I put my hands on his to keep them in place. "What was that for?"

"I know how you feel right now, Hailey," he replied brushing my cheek with his thumb. "And I'm sorry."

I bit my lip to keep the tears back. "It's okay," I said. "You were doing a good job of distracting me."

"Want me to continue?"

"Please." As Jack leaned back in, I put a hand on his chest to stop him. "That's not what I meant."

Jack grinned, "I know." Then he turned and started back up the ladder. After looking back at our car, fitting perfectly in with the others, I started up after him.

The building was tall enough that we could see over the rest and watch the doors of Eli's company. Jack laid down on his stomach, pulling the binoculars out of his back pocket and propped his elbows up on the ledge. I kicked a rock and watched it disappear behind a metal tube. "What are we watching for?" I finally asked.

"Anything and everything, oh curious one."

I shook my head, smiling then went and laid down on my belly next to him. Jack reached back and into the pocket of his jeans, pulling out a small, retractable telescope. When he dropped it into my hand, I turned the dinky thing over and over. "So we can afford a crazy nice car, but not a second pair of binoculars?"

"I thought you might feel like being a pirate today,"

Jack said still watching Eli's building.

"Read my mind, matey," I replied under my breath and peered through the telescope. "Land ho." Jack chuckled next to me. From what I could see, not a whole lot was happening. A few people went in and out, but for the most part, the doors to enter the building stayed shut. "Again, what are we looking for?" I finally repeated.

Jack sat up and wrestled a piece of paper out of his pocket. After almost ripping it in half, he managed to get it out, unfold it and smooth it down onto the gravel. Looking at it closely, I saw it was a bird's-eye-view of Eli's building. "There are entrances here," he pointed, "here and here. If we can figure out some sort of schedule for when people come and go, we can plan the perfect timing to get in and set off the explosives, taking out the most amount of people while keeping us safe."

I looked back up from the map and watched a couple of women in white coats as they sat down on a bench and started unpacking their lunches. One of them lit a cigarette and laughed at something the other must have said. The thought of hurting these unknowing people made my breath catch in my throat. Jack looked up from his drawing and set his eyes on me. "Are you alright?" he asked.

"Do you feel okay doing all this?" My voice was just a whisper.

Jack's hand found mine. "Hailey," I looked at him. "We're saving the world."

CHAPTER FIFTEEN

Ryan,

Without you here, I feel even more alone. At least before I still had hope that you were alive. That I would find you again and the two of us could get out of here. Now, I wish you would have just stayed away. Stayed in Nashville where you were safe. Where Eli couldn't find you. I'm so sorry I couldn't save you, but I promise you're death won't have been for nothing. I promise I'm going to fight for you. Love you, bro. And I'll see you again someday. Maybe even soon.

Hailey.

I tore the page out of the spiral notebook in my lap and started picking at the fringe along the edge. Snow from the branches above me was melting and dripping onto the hood of my coat. One drop landed on my letter and ran down the page, smudging the words a bit. It didn't matter. It wasn't like Ryan was going to be able to read it anyway. I stood up and brushed the torn bits of paper off of me. They fluttered to the muddy ground like snowflakes. I crumpled the soggy note up in my hand, squeezing it into a tight ball and walked over to the mound of mud and ice that was my brother's grave.

"This is for you, Ry," I whispered, a warm tear running slowly down my cold cheek. I tossed the crumpled note onto the mound and pushed it into the dirt with my shoe.

Back in the Tree House, I had just started up the stairs to the second floor when Root emerged from the basement. He froze when he saw me. "Hey," he said quickly and pushed his glasses up his nose.

"Hi," I watched his hands as they tapped rapidly against his sides. "What's going on, Root?" I asked him.

He didn't say anything at first, just pulled the door shut behind him then finally let out a sigh. "I said I would take care of it."

"Root what did you do-?" Before I could stop him, he hurried up the stairs past me and I heard his bedroom door shut.

What would I find behind that door if I opened it? Now I couldn't remember if I had seen blood on Root's hands. Though I guess, now there was no chance that Jack would find out about Ben. Maybe it had to be done. Maybe it was for the best. Trying not to think about Adams's lifeless body laying below in the dark, I hurried up the stairs, past Root's room and up the stairs again to the main floor with everyone else.

This place had been in a frenzy ever since Jack and I had gotten back home from the first of several stake outs on the roof of that government building. For the past few days we had sat up there for hours with a notepad and a watch, keeping track of when people left and went in which doors. By now we had an idea of where we needed to be and when we needed to set off Root's explosives. Each day while Jack watched intently through his binoculars, I sat imagining where in that place Ben could be and what he must have been going through.

How were they treating him in there? Was he awake and walking around? Interacting with the doctors like any normal human being? Or was he caged up like an animal, given attention only when they wanted to poke and prod him or pass food to him through the metal bars. Or maybe they had him drugged up on an operating table, hooked up to machines so they could monitor his brain activity without him being awake. Maybe he'd been asleep the whole time not even knowing he wasn't laying dead in the snow, only because he hadn't woken up yet. "What do you think is going on in there?" I finally asked Jack the last day of our stake out.

Without taking the binoculars away from his eyes, he let out a disgusted scoff. "Well, you saw Ryan and Anna. I'm sure there are more just like them in there."

I watched the same two women sitting on the bench out in front at the same time as the last two days. The one lit a cigarette. Smoke slithered out of her mouth like an evil genie escaping its lamp and I hoped that Ben was, in fact, laying on a table believing he was dead.

It didn't take long for Adams's body to be discovered. Arie and Logan had been checking up on him regularly and when Logan came up, pale as a ghost, my eyes flicked over in Root's direction. He was sitting at the kitchen table carefully assembling his explosives, making an effort not to lift his head.

Jack was looking at Logan, his expression filled with concern. "What happened?"

"Adams is dead," Logan finally said, his voice wavering just barely.

"What?"

"Who could have killed him?"

"Did they find us?"

I saw the worried looks on everyone's faces and realized what they must have been thinking. That someone from the company had somehow sneaked in and done it. Silenced him before he could give anything more away. Root's face was still buried in his work. I stood up without another thought. "I did it," I blurted out.

The voices stopped and every eye, including Root's, was on me. Jack's mouth was slightly open as he had been stopped mid-sentence. "Hailey-"

"It was his fault, alright?" I interrupted. "My brother is dead because of him and the Company." My fingernails were digging into my palm. "He didn't deserve to live."

No one else said another word. Who could disagree with me? Other than what he had told me, we had gotten no useful information out of him. Who could blame me? Even if I hadn't really done it.

"Okay," Jack said softly. "What's done is done." The look in his eyes said disappointment.

I looked back over at Root again to find he had turned back to his bombs. So this was his way of taking care of it? With one more quick glance at Jack, I crossed the room and hurried up the stairs, feeling all eyes still on me.

Up on the roof, looking out at the city in the distance, I really understood why Jack had always retreated up here. I sat down on the ledge, letting my feet dangle off the edge. This was where Jack had told me his biggest fear. Oh how much had changed over just the past week.

"Hailey?"

I turned my head to find Root peering around from the door. With a scoff, I turned away again and glared at the space needle in the distance. "What do you want?"

"Hailey, I'm sorry," he said hurrying over to sit down beside me. "I should have stopped you. I should have said something."

"Well, why didn't you?" I asked meeting his eyes. "Why did you let Jack think I would be capable of killing anyone?"

Root looked down at his hands ashamed and his glasses slid down his nose. "I plan on telling Jack it was me."

"When?"

"Right away," he assured me. "Look, Hailey, I'd like to think we have become friends since you first got here."

"I'd like to think that too."

"Then I will make this right. I promise."

I looked Root in the eyes. There was no secrecy, no mystery in them. "Thanks, Root."

"I told you I would take care of it. I hope you don't think I've failed you."

I shook my head and put a reassuring hand on his. "I don't," I replied with a small smile. "But don't let Jack think I could do such a thing for too long. If he thought I actually had that kind of nerve, he might try and make me useful. Really, I'm all talk."

Root smiled back. "I heard about what you did to Adams the other day."

"Oh that..."

"You about broke his jaw. You've got some fire in you."

"I'm not a killer," I said dryly, shaking my head. "I never will be."

The smile had disappeared from Root's face and he broke eye contact. "Okay," he uttered. "Okay, sorry."

Just then the door opened behind us and we both turned to find Jack looking around. His eyes settled on us and I saw his shoulders rise and fall as he sighed.

"Hailey, I need to talk to you."

Root scurried to his feet and helped me up then tried to get in front of me. "Jack, wait-"

"I need to talk to Hailey," he interrupted.

"I know, but-"

"Hailey, how could you kill Adams?" Jack asked sounding hurt. "You know we were trying to get information out of him and we were really starting to get somewhere."

"Jack-"

"I mean, sure I would expect this out of your brother, maybe even Keeta, but I thought you were different," he continued.

I brought my hands up to press against my temples, feeling the tears forming in my eyes. "Jack, I never meant-"

"I thought you understood-"

"Jack!" Root yelled. "That's enough." Jack stared at Root, astonished at his sudden burst. I was shaking now and the tears were flowing freely down my face. "Hailey didn't kill Adams. I did."

It took a moment for Jack to respond. "Why?" he finally asked.

"I have my own reasons. Hailey was just trying to save me the embarrassment."

Out of the tops of my eyes I could see Jack turn his attention back to me. "Hailey?"

All I could do was shake my head again. Then I rushed past him and hurried back down the stairs, hiding my tears behind my hands. I didn't hear the door open again after it had shut behind me. Good, I didn't want him following me anyway. Everyone else was still on the main floor and watched as rushed past them. Melody tried to reach out to me, but I pushed her hands away and disappeared down to the second level. Finally, I made it into my room and slammed the door, locking it and throwing myself on my bed. My stomach was twisting so horribly and all I could see when I closed my eyes was the disappointment on Jack's face.

Ugh. I dug my nails into my pillow and pushed it hard into my face and screamed, feeling all the blood rush to my head. This was just too much for me. Everything that had happened over the past few days; it was all just too much for me. My door opened just then – apparently the locks didn't work – and I turned away, pulling my pillow down to cover my head. "Go away!" I yelled into my mattress.

"Hailey."

I felt his hands on me. This time I didn't want them. "Don't touch me," I said, my words still muffled.

"Please talk to me, Hailey."

This time I yanked the pillow from over my head and sat up, staring straight into Jack's blurry face. "Any part of you that touches me, you're not getting back."

Jack held his hands up in defense and leaned away from me. "Listen," he said, his palms still out. "I'm so sorry. I thought-"

"You seriously thought I killed the guy?"

Now he stood back up. "You said you did. Am I just supposed to think everything you say now is a lie?"

"I don't...I don't know," I muttered then stood up to face him. "What if I had killed Adams? Would that have been just too much for you to wrap your head around? That the girl who has been through everything and that held her brother while he died in her arms. You don't think that girl would be capable of killing one of the men responsible?" I waited for Jack to say something. Instead he just stared at me. "So now you have nothing to say to me?" I asked biting my lip habitually in an attempt to keep the tears back, even though they were already there.

Finally, he just nodded, pursing his own lips then turned around and walked out of the room. After he closed the door softly behind him, I sank back onto the bed. What had just happened? I fell back and stared up at the shadows on the ceiling. The angry tears had finally stopped flowing freely from my eyes and dried making my face feel stiff. I brought my sleeve up and wiped them away, rubbing my eyes until I saw stars.

I must have fallen asleep after that because the next time I opened my eyes again, my mouth was feeling dry and my body ached. I had been sleeping with my arms over my face for a while now and as I lowered them, a sharp pain shot through my shoulders making me wince. It was pitch dark in the room now. I no longer felt fuming mad, but rather hollow and sad. The conversation I had had with Jack was coming back to me now and I couldn't help, but feel terrible for being so angry at him. The look on his face when he had left...I couldn't really describe it. I had to find him. I had to make things right.

The hall was empty and I could hear voices upstairs, so that's where I headed. When I got up there, I only found Keeta and Melody. They both stopped talking and looked at me.

"Hi," I whispered, my voice raspy with sleep.

Melody gave me a small smile. "How are you doing?"

I shrugged. "I'm feeling kind of awful, actually. Where is everyone?"

"Looking for Jack." Keeta replied.

My stomach dropped. "What do you mean?"

"No one has seen him since he went to talk to you," Melody explained tugging at her flowing skirt uncomfortably. "It's been almost two hours since the other guys left."

"Well, what are we doing here? Why didn't anyone

wake me up?"

Melody got up, probably sensing that I was about to make a run for the front door. "Hailey, we have to stay here."

"What the heck for?"

"We have a rule. There has to be at least two people here at all times. In case something happens. In case we're found out."

"Well then, I'll go."

This time she took my arm. "You can't go out there by yourself. Not now."

"The guys will find him, Hailey," Keeta assured me from on the couch. "You can sit and wait with us here."

Melody led me by the hand over to the couch and sat me down between the two of them. As soon as my butt hit the cushion, I jumped back up. "I need air," I gasped then ran up the stairs to the roof. I burst through the door, gulping in as much air as I could. It was frigid and burned, but the pain was sharp and just what I needed. My heart was hammering hard in my chest, pounding against my ribs and racking my body. My parents once told me that when I was younger, I would get panic attacks a lot, but then stopped suddenly when I hit the age of five. All this time I hadn't remembered having them or what they felt like, but now, shaking so bad I couldn't walk straight and my vision blurring to black, the memories returned. I fell down onto my knees and rested my forehead against the concrete, trying to concentrate on steadying my breathing instead of the sound of the blood pulsing in my ears.

Being chased and getting shot at didn't do this. Holding my brother, watching him die didn't do this. No, but the fact that Jack had left. The defeated look on his face. The thought that he could never come back. That sent terror crashing through me like a bull through a maze made of glass. Lightning crashed and rain started coming down in sheets as I laid there with my head against the ground. I was immediately soaked, but it didn't matter to me. Jack was out there somewhere. Alone. Maybe not even alive any more. I got on my feet, steadying myself, then ran over to the edge.

"Jack!" I yelled out into the rain. Another crash of thunder erupted, drowning out my voice. "Jack!" I stood there for a few seconds, my eyes searching the streets below me. I kept calling his name until my voice was hoarse. I didn't care if anyone saw me up there or heard me. They could think I was some crazy, homeless girl. "Jack!"

Another boom of thunder caused me to jump and I stumbled back under the cover, leaning against one of the pillars. I wrapped my arms around it, my hands balled into fists. It was my fault he was out there. I had pushed him away. I had made him leave. Again I called out his name, though it was cut short by a sob. The rain was still coming down hard and I could feel another wave of panic rising up in me. I hugged the pillar tighter and braced myself.

Then the door slammed behind me and I turned to find him, soaked and bloodied, but still alive. "Jack," I gasped and ran to him. "Don't you EVER scare me like that again!" I screamed pushing him hard. "Don't you EVER leave me like that!" My fists were flying, battering against his chest. "If you ever do that again I'll-"

Jack grabbed my wrists, holding them between us. "You'll what?" he whispered, water dripping from the hair in front of his eyes.

I ground my teeth together, feeling the panic coming on. Then, before I could stop myself, my mouth crushed against his, causing him to stumble backward against a pillar. He grabbed me to steady himself and wrapped his arms around me, pulling me closer. His lips were warm and familiar and I could feel the panic in me dying down rapidly as we kissed. He clung to me, his fingers knotting into my hair, making my knees weak.

When he finally pulled away, my head was swimming and the anger was gone. For a second I thought I saw his eyes glistening, but then he blinked and it was gone. "I'm so sorry," he whispered holding my face between his hands.

I nodded. "Me too. But don't ever do that again."

"I won't," he replied then pulled me against him again and kissed my head softly. "I promise I'll stay."

CHAPTER SIXTEEN

"Where did you go?" I asked him as I dried my hair with a towel.

We were now cramped together in the only working bathroom in the whole place. Jack sat on the edge of the tub holding a damp cloth to the bloodied side of his face. The pained look in his eyes and the way his split lip twitched anytime he moved the towel let me know that something or someone had worked him over good.

"I just went for a walk to cool off, I guess," he replied putting the towel into my outstretched hand.

I ran the cloth under the faucet, ringing out the bloody water and going back over to him. "Did you walk into a brick wall?" I asked and pressed the cloth back to his cheek.

Jack sucked in sharply, his fingers digging at the side of the tub. "Ow," he winced. "I may have gone to a bar known to attract the vermin of the city."

"And what made you think that was a good idea?"

"I was feeling a bit like vermin, myself."

I froze for a second, my hand hovering over his face. It had been my fault for making him feel like that. "I'm sorry," I finally whispered, touching the cloth more gently to his face. This time he didn't wince, but looked up at me.

"And I kind of wanted to punch someone."

"Looks more like you wanted to get punched," I replied noting the ring shaped scrape above his eyebrow. He cracked a smile causing his lip to start bleeding again. I dabbed at it carefully and shook my head. "What would it take for you to be nice to people?"

Jack shrugged. "A lobotomy, maybe. Ow! Watch it."

"Oops," I muttered not even trying to hide my sarcasm.

We were both quiet after that as I finished cleaning his cuts as best as I could. Then I started searching through the medicine cabinet for some bandages. When I turned back around, I sucked in sharply. Jack had silently gotten up and now stood in front of me, our faces only inches apart.

"What?" I finally whispered once my racing heart had steadied some.

Jack looked down at the bandages in my hand and closed his own fingers around mine. Looking back up at me, his eyes pierced into mine. "I think-"

Footsteps from above our heads cut him off and caused us both to bolt out of the bathroom. We hit the hall just as the rest of the guys came barreling down the stairs. Root was the first to see us and ran forward, grabbing Jack's shoulders.

"What were you thinking, man?" he screamed shaking him violently.

Jack shook him off. "I was thinking a stroll in the rain and a tussle was the perfect end to a day such as this."

I couldn't help but smile at the look on Root's face. Especially hearing Jack shrug this off like they hadn't been out searching for him for hours. Root stood there dripping wet, just staring in angry disbelief through this foggy glasses. I swear I could see steam rising from his skin.

"So...you're not dead," Arie finally said breaking the silence.

Jack looked at him and smirked. "Nope."

Arie nodded then put a hand on Root's shoulder. "Well, congrats. I think this one needs to cool off a bit." Then he pulled his fuming friend back toward the stairs. Logan followed after them, hesitating for only a moment to give Jack a worried, but somewhat relieved look.

I turned back to him once the rest had disappeared. "What were you going to say to me in there?"

Jack looked at me then. "Oh," he finally said. "Nothing...nothing." Then he walked past me toward the stairs. Thinking about the way he had been staring into my eyes, like he was trying to get me to see even deeper into him, I knew it wasn't nothing.

"Seems like Jack is done brooding now," Root said when the two of us had made it back up to the main floor. Arie and Logan sat on either side of him. The looks on their faces and the way their bodies were tensed made me think that they were ready to stop Root if he were to try and get up to attack Jack again. It was almost funny, especially when Jack stood nearly a foot taller than him and was probably twice as strong. "So can we finally get on with it?" he asked.

Jack smirked. "Are you finished with your hissy fit?"

"Seriously, you two," Melody scoffed shaking her head. "Grow up."

"Don't forget who's the explosives expert here,

Jack," Root finally snarled crossing his arms over his chest.

I shot him a look. "Root!"

"Oh don't mind him, Hailey," Melody said. "He's like a hormonal teenage girl in a man suit when he gets his feelings hurt"

"Alright!" We all stopped and looked to Logan, who had been sitting there picking at a loose string in the cushion. Now there was a nice sized hole and the couch's innards were piled up in his lap. "Can we just stop fighting like a bunch of eight year olds and continue with the plan? Last I checked, we were all on the same team."

"Right," Jack finally said scratching at the back of his head.

Root just settled back into his seat and glared at the fire in front of him.

The rain had stopped by the time we had finished for the night. Any snow that had still clung to the roofs before had been washed away and now everything was dark and silent. Headlights from the freeway moved forward sluggishly from the late night backed up traffic. Why were there so many cars on the freeway so late at night?

The door behind me opened and closed and I stayed where I was, not needing to turn around to know who had joined me. "So we're really going to do this tomorrow," I said still watching the cars.

Jack stood beside me silently and watched. He didn't reply, just stood there in silence. Finally I turned to look at him. His shoulders were slumped forward and when he turned his face, light from a streetlamp caught his cheekbone and I noticed a dark spot that had finally surfaced. I brought my hand up and brushed the hair from his cheek to get a better look.

"Did I make you do this?" I asked almost afraid to hear his answer.

A smile played at the corners of Jack's lips. "You can't make me do anything, Hailey," he replied just a little sarcastically, but when I went to pull my hand away, he stopped me by putting his hand on top of mine. "No," he finally sighed. "That's a lie." Then he met my eyes, his mouth now set in a serious, straight line. I felt my stomach drop. "Hailey," he said and dropped his hand, still holding mine. "You make things...difficult."

I pulled my hand back. "Difficult?" I couldn't hide the confusion in my voice.

He chuckled and sat down on the ledge. Why was this amusing? I hesitated before joining him. "When we met in that diner," he started again, looking out at the city. "I never meant to save you."

I felt heat rising in my cheeks. "Well that's good to know," I huffed.

"Let me finish," Jack said calmly. "Before you showed up, I had fully intended on getting myself plastered then finding some quiet alley to end it."

"You were going to kill yourself?" I asked feeling my heart beat faster.

Jack took the pistol out of the back of his pants and held it in his palm like it was a wounded bird. "I had one full clip left," he said. "I was going to empty it, put one bullet in, maybe play a small game of Russian Roulette. Just to see how I would feel after pulling the trigger and hearing the gun click a few times before finally blowing my brains out."

"Jack," I whispered.

"And then you wouldn't leave me alone," he continued chuckling. "You were so adamant that I was going to save you. That you would be safe with me," he looked over at me and I saw that his lip had split again.

"Good thing Ben had instilled in me to always help a damsel in distress. I had seven bullets left in this gun." He flipped the chamber open and slipped the magazine out, examining the bullets. The gun glistened menacingly in the moonlight. "One went into that guy that had cornered you behind the diner. One into David," he sucked his breath in sharply through his teeth as if the memory caused him pain. "Two went into Paulson's leg. Another was intended for Adams after we were finished with him."

"I guess Root found a more efficient way," I said, my voice shaky with anticipation.

"Yeah," Jack chuckled again then snapped the magazine back in place with one fluid motion. "One I plan on burying in Eli Scott's brain."

"So if you had killed Adams, and after you kill Eli, you'd have one left," I said. "What's that one for?"

He held the gun with his finger on the trigger and brought it up so it was parallel to his ear and pointing up at the sky. "I don't know any more," he whispered tapping the barrel thoughtfully against his head. Both of us were silent for a while. I realized I was holding my breath, waiting for Jack to say something else when my lungs began to ache and I had to exhale heavily. This seemed to snap him out of his thoughts. "All that to say," he continued. "I went out tonight with the thought that, even if I was gone, even if I wasn't the person to kill Eli, the rest of you would follow through with our plan. Root would take over as head and he'd lead you guys. But then..." He sighed, dropping his hand in defeat. "The thought of something happening to you, something that I could protect you from if I were there. It brought me back."

"You want to protect me?" I asked meeting his eyes.

Jack looked back down at the gun in his hand. "It's

not so much a want as it is...a need. I need to take care of you, Hailey."

"Look," I said waiting for him to turn his face up to me again. "I don't need someone to take care of me," I said. "I am a grown up and I can take care of myself. But...I'd like if you wanted to take care of me..."

"I don't really think I have a choice in the matter," Jack shrugged though his words were heavy.

I wrapped my arms around myself as a bitter wind picked up. "If it was a choice...though."

Jack didn't say anything for a while, but I watched the wind move subtly through his bangs, revealing just a corner of a slice healing above his eyebrow. "I thought I was just doing my job in bringing you back here. I figured once we'd made it to the Tree House, I could go back to that town and finish what I'd started." Then he looked at me again, his eyes bright. "I never meant to fall in love with you."

"You're in love with me?" I whispered, my voice shaky with nerves.

"You sound surprised," Jack replied sounding almost as nervous as me. I'd never heard him sound like that.

I looked at him. "Well, I am." Then I looked down at my hands. "When did you decide this?"

Jack looked thoughtfully out at the city again. "I think when you stepped in front of Anna to keep me from shooting her."

I chuckled. "Could have fooled me," I muttered. "Seems like you hated me."

"Not as much as I hated myself." He shook his head. "And only because I couldn't help it." Then his eyes locked on mine again. "I hated that I couldn't hate you."

Why had I never noticed the tiny flecks of silver in those deep green eyes? "Do you still wish you hated me?" I asked watching his irises glint in the moonlight. I shivered again, though this time I knew it wasn't the wind.

"Sometimes," he said and lay the gun down between us. He picked up my hand and pulled it into his lap, making me scoot closer to him. I watched mesmerized as he traced the lines of my palm with his long fingers. "Like when I kissed you up here that first time." My heart was hammering so hard by now, I knew he could hear it. "I really wanted to hate you a bit right after that."

"I'm sorry," I choked. Why was I feeling so nervous all of a sudden? Why was I feeling like I was feeling like this for the first time instead of like I had been for days now? Maybe because he finally said what I'd been feeling. I don't know how long I'd loved him. If I loved him. Maybe I was just realizing it. I don't know. I don't know. "But now..." I continued, letting my words trail off.

Jack bit the edge of his lip and narrowed his eyes like he was trying to find something on my face. After a few seconds he opened his mouth again with a smack. "I think I'm over it. What about you?"

This caught me off guard. We had been talking about him, about his feelings for me for a while now. And the sudden turn around caused heat to rise in my cheeks. Did he want me to tell him that I loved him too? Did I love him? "Isn't it obvious?" I finally croaked, pulling my hand back and standing up, brushing off the back of my pants. They were damp from the pavement and I knew if I turned around, he'd probably laugh. Instead, I backed toward one of the pillars.

Jack stood up, picking up his gun, lowered his head and peered up at me through his hair like a shy child. I'm not really sure what was supposed to be obvious to him, but I was hoping he'd fill in the blanks and that would be enough. "I'm not really sure any more," he replied finally taking slow steps toward me. Why was I backing up?

My back hit the pillar and Jack stopped in front of me, leaning his hands on either side next to my face. Then he stared at me with those silvery green eyes. I finally decided to stare back, unblinking. "Gonna try and force it out of me?" I asked keeping my focus on his eyes even though his mouth was growing closer to mine and I was so tempted to watch it.

"Do I need to?" he asked me. Now his lips hovered only inches from mine. My heart was going absolutely crazy and was racing so fast, I couldn't tell one beat from another. A strange feeling came over me just then. My head turned and my eyes shifted to the gun sandwiched between the wall and his hand. I knew what Jack wanted to hear. I knew he wanted me to buckle, to look dreamily into his eyes and profess my love for him. He wanted to make me feel like I needed him to kiss me, when really, he needed me to need him to kiss me.

Instead I reached my hand up the wall and wrapped my fingers around the cold metal barrel of the gun. "Want a confession?" I finally asked breathlessly. I couldn't really help that though. "Here I am about to put my life on the line tomorrow, go all Mission Impossible and save the world and I don't even know how to fire a gun."

Jack's lips hesitated over mine then curled up into a smile. "I couldn't imagine you firing a gun."

"Well don't you think I should learn?" His mouth was still dangerously close to mine. "You know...to protect myself."

"I'll protect you."

I put my hands against Jack's chest and shoved him hard. He stumbled back, the smile still on his face. "Again," I snapped. "I don't need protected. You're going to teach me how to shoot a gun."

Now Jack set his mouth in a hard line. His eyes were

hard and stubborn. After a while, he huffed loudly. "Fine," he said through gritted teeth and shoved his gun back into in place by his hip. "But you're using a different one."

"Why?"

"Again," he mocked, "I have two bullets left."

"You carry that thing around with no extra bullets?" I asked then shook my head. "You would."

"Jack shrugged. "It keeps me from using it recklessly. Now, do you want to learn to shoot or not?" I nodded quickly before he decided he'd changed his mind. "Alright then," he said. "Follow me."

The two of us went back downstairs then instead of continuing on to the third floor, he turned into Sy's room. I watched as he went over to the desk and began pushing. The heavy desk moved slowly until a hatch in the floorboards was revealed.

"What's down there?" I asked peering over Jack's shoulder. He crouched down ignoring me. "You know, for someone who claims to love me, you put on a spectacular act of hatred."

Jack turned around and before I could react, he put his hands on either side of my face and crushed his lips to mine. I felt heat rising up to my ears and when he finally pulled away, I was left breathless.

"Believe me, you don't want to know what I do to people I hate."

I brought my hand down and brushed his hip with my fingertips. The gun's metal was still cold, even against his skin. "Believe me," I replied. "I have an idea."

Jack let go of my face and turned back around. "This is Sy's gun cellar," he said and started down a ladder.

I followed after him cautiously. The ladder wasn't very long so it took no time for my feet to hit the floor. When I turned around and Jack flipped on the light, I couldn't help but gasp. The room wasn't very big. Maybe eight by eight, but the walls were covered with guns of different types and sizes.

"Where did he get all these?" I asked touching the cool black metal of one of the handguns on the wall next to me.

"Sy wanted to be prepared for the worst," Jack replied. "Do you like that one?"

I stepped back and let him take the handgun off the wall. He held it out for me to take and I wrapped my fingers around the grip, feeling it's weight. It felt good in my hand. Comfortable. Like it had been made for me.

"Alright," he said flipping the light switch off and plunging us into darkness. "Time to go for a little ride."

Not too much later, I found myself sitting beside Jack on one of the few late night buses. The gun under my shirt, though small in my hand, was pushing against my bone and made me feel like I had a huge bulge protruding from my hip. Jack said he couldn't even see it though. I looked over at him. He had his arm draped across my shoulders casually and was staring out at the city lights, probably deep in thought. To think this was all going to end tomorrow. Where was I going to be at this time the next night? Would I be celebrating with everyone else? Would a few of us be missing? Would Jack be missing? Would there be any of us left? The thought made my stomach churn and I snuggled up to Jack, biting the inside of my cheek to keep the tears back. Even though Jack kept his head turned away, he must have sensed something because his arm tightened around me and he rubbed my shoulder with his thumb.

He had said he wanted to protect me. How far was he planning to go? Did that mean throwing himself at any danger that came at me? Was he really planning on not making it out of there alive like he had hinted at?

"Jack?"

He turned his head and tilted it back so he could look at me. "Yeah?"

"What do you think is going to happen tomorrow?"

Jack turned his profile to me and the muscles in his jaw showed on his face as he ground his teeth in thought. "I think Eli's going to find it pretty hard to unleash terror on this world with a brain full of lead."

"What about you?"

"I know how my story ends."

I sat up and shrugged Jack's arm off my shoulders. "Could you at least pretend to care about yourself the tiniest fraction of the amount that I care about you?" I asked trying not to raise my voice. "Would you do that? Would you do that for me?"

"So you admit it," Jack smiled looking straight ahead.

"Admit what?"

"That you care about me."

This surprised me a bit. "Where have you been for the past week? Of course I care about you. What makes you think I don't?"

Jack shrugged.

"Is it so hard to believe that someone would like you?" I asked knowing my voice was getting a bit high. It tends to do that when I get frustrated.

Again, Jack shrugged.

I sat back in the seat and crossed my arms over my chest. "Well I'll tell you this much, you don't make it easy with your gloomy pessimistic attitude."

"I was born to be a pessimist. Optimism just means you lack information.," he finally said cracking his knuckles.

"News flash, my life sucks too. You know, I'm pretty sure if you asked anyone back at the Tree House they would tell you they aren't living a life of rainbows and unicorns either."

A smile cracked on Jack's mouth and he let out a chuckle. "I suppose." He looked at me again, this time seriously. "Do you love me, Hailey?"

"Can I ask you a question first?"

He didn't say anything, so I continued.

"What if..." I looked down at my hands. "What if something happens tomorrow? Something...bad. And I'm left alone. Then what?" Jack looked down at his hands for a moment. "I mean, I've already lost everyone else I love. I don't know if I can handle losing another."

Jack wrapped his arms around me again "That will never happen," he said reassuringly."I'll stay alive for you."

I lay against him, my ear pressed against his chest so I could hear his heartbeat. His words still made me worry a bit, but there was no use in worrying. I closed my eyes so it was easier to picture his heart. Full of blood. Pumping. Alive. Just how it needed to stay.

CHAPTER SEVENTEEN

"Alright, a little wider," Jack said to me pulling on my leg.

I gave a frustrated huff. "I want to shoot a gun, not do the splits," I muttered as he put my foot down.

It was almost completely dark out here and the trees blocked out the moonlight making it eerie and still. A single lamp post cast a small amount of light on us and the target on the tree about thirty feet away. The bus had dropped us off a block over and then we'd walked to the edge of the woods. I was worried we'd get caught right at first. But Jack reassured me that he came out here all the time.

"Now, you've set your feet apart," he said straightening back up. Then he slipped the gun out from the waist of my pants and put it in my palm. "Lock your elbows and hold the grip tight with both hands." I don't know why he was telling me when he was doing it all for me, holding my arms in place and wrapping his hands over mine around the gun. "And lean forward a bit. Then you're going to aim with your right eye at that target. That little bump on the end is the front site. Line that up with your target."

I closed my left eye and focused on the reflective target on the tree. "K, now what?" I asked trying to hold completely still.

Jack stood back and gave me a once over to make sure everything was right. He nodded. "Now pull the trigger slowly."

"Am I going to have time to do all this if I'm having those suits coming at me?"

"Leave the suits to me," he replied.

I dropped my arms and looked at Jack. "Seriously." I said. I didn't even need to finish. Jack knew what I was getting at. If something happened to him, how was I going to protect myself?

"Look, now you have to do it all again," he joked. "Okay," Jack said softer. "Just try to hit the target."

"Alright," I exhaled and lined myself back up with the tree. I slowly pulled the trigger back, holding my breath, waiting to hear the loud bang and feel the gun jump in my hands. Instead, the trigger released and all I heard was a click. "Jack!" I yelled smacking his arm with the gun. "How am I supposed to hit the target if there are no bullets in this thing?"

"I said I would teach you how to shoot a gun, not wake the whole neighborhood."

For a second I wanted to throw it at him, but he was right. After all, what time was it anyway? Close to ten? Surely a loud gunshot would draw attention to us. And that was the last thing we needed.

"That's a semi automatic so just keep pulling the trigger."

I lined myself back up and the gun clicked three more times. "Look at that, I'm a natural."

As I lowered it again, snow started to fall. I looked up at the sky and watched as the tiny flakes turned into huge ones and stuck to my face. Closing my eyes, I imagined I was little again, in the park with my mom and brother. Sometimes I would just stand there like I was now while other kids played on the slippery slides or threw snowballs at each other. I always just liked feeling the snow on my face. To feel the flakes hit my skin then melt, until my face was too cold and wet for me to stand it any longer.

When I opened my eyes again, Jack was looking at me. It was weird to think how much had happened in the time we had known each other. It was especially weird to think that in such a short amount of time, he had gone from being a stranger to someone I couldn't see myself without.

"How long has it been since I found you?" Jack asked me, squinting his eyes.

"I'm not sure," I replied. "It was just a couple days after I started winter break I guess. So about two weeks, I guess?" I shrugged wrapping my arms around myself.

"That's what I thought," he said with a smile then reached into his pocket. "I guess with everything that's been going on lately, I've lost track of the days." When he pulled his hand back out, Ben's ring shown from between his thumb and finger. "Merry Christmas," he said holding it out to me.

I stared for a moment at the ring. "But Jack, that's your brother's. I couldn't take it from you."

"You're not taking it from me," Jack replied with an eye roll. "I want you to have it."

Carefully I took the ring from him and held it up to the light. The jewel sparkled and the silver shined. "I wish I had something to give you," I said closing my hand around the ring.

Jack smiled. "Just try to stay alive tomorrow. That's enough for me."

"I'll try," I replied with a nod.

My heart was hammering harder than it ever had before. Harder than on my first day of college, harder than when I was running for my life with bullets flying past my head, harder than when Jack had kissed me up on the roof for the first time. This time it went through my whole body, taking its sweet time reaching every nook and cranny of my body before racking me. I felt like I was jumping two inches off the ground with every heartbeat. And I was completely drenched in sweat. Not the warm, sticky sweat like you get from a good workout. This was cold, dripping sweat. The kind that makes you even colder, makes you shiver. Makes your bones shiver.

I knew the night before that there was no way I was going to get even a wink of sleep, and now as I climbed into a van, I had yet to figure out how we were getting all these vehicles, and sat down next to Jack, my vision was going wonky and I had the sick feeling in my stomach one gets from lack of sleep and nerves. I was ready for this to be over with. It seemed like with the complete silence that had been with us since sunrise, everyone was just ready for this to be over too. Though at the same time, I felt the electric feeling of anticipation in the air. Almost excitement. Almost.

Twirling Ben's ring around my thumb nervously, I closed my eyes and tried to focus on breathing. I didn't notice the rhythmic bouncing up and down of my knee until I felt Jack's hand fall on it. My eyes snapped back open and I looked at him.

"You'll be okay, Hailey," he said to me as calmly as he could.

I had never heard his voice tremble like this before;

the emotion was beyond description. My heart lifted up into my throat so I was unable to say anything. I knew we would come to this point someday, but I hadn't thought it would be so soon. All I could do was nod.

"Buckle up, everyone," Root said adjusting the rear view mirror. "Wouldn't want anything happening to us on the way there."

"Wouldn't that be ironic," Keeta said getting nervous chuckles out of all of us.

As we pulled away from the Tree House, I looked back remembering the last time I had done this very thing. Over the past couple weeks this place had become a home to me. These people had become my family. I looked down then at the bombs carefully arranged on the floor of the van. How many of them was I going to lose?

It wouldn't have been hard to predict a long car ride of silence. I'm sure everyone was having a million things go through their heads like I was. This day meant so many different things to me. It meant possibly finding out what happened to my parents. Avenging them and my brother, Anna and David and all the others that had died from the microchip. Finishing what Sy hadn't been able to finish. Finding a possible cure for this disease that was going to kill all of us and a ton more in twenty years. Maybe even saving the world from any more of Eli's deadly experiments. And living a peaceful life with Jack.

Root turned down a street and Eli's building loomed in front of us at the end of the last block. The ride was way too short for my liking. I would have been happy to stay in this van forever with the friends I had made. But I knew I had met them for this very reason. Everything came down to this moment.

As Root turned down an alley closest to Eli's building, Jack reached back and carefully took four bombs in his hands, passing them up to Melody and Arie, the first ones to leave us. Arie placed them in a black backpack and zipped it up. There was no hesitation, no minute of silence or anything before we put our plan in motion. Root stopped where Jack and I had marked our map and Melody and Arie got up and out. As they closed the door behind them, Melody's eyes met mine. They were bright with determination and fire. She had been the first to reach out to me. She had let me borrow her flowing clothes and had taught me how to travel by rooftop. It was weird seeing her wearing black clothes. Especially pants. She gave me a small smile and a nod. I didn't know if that was to signify that I'd see her again or if it was her way of saying goodbye. Either way, I nodded back, saying it was nice to know her.

We watched the two of them jog down the street, the backpack slung over Arie's shoulder. When I turned around to face the front, I caught Keeta swiping her fingers across her cheek and I couldn't help, but feel my own eyes burning. No, I couldn't do that today. I had spent most of the night crying over the lives of the friends I had made and the risk put on them today. Now I needed to be strong. I owed it to them. I squeezed Jack's hand hard and blinked the tears away, gritting my teeth.

The second stop went the same as the first. Jack handed four more bombs up to Keeta and Logan, who put them in a black backpack. The two of them got out of the van and shut the door, giving us a nod through the window. Logan's eyes met mine for a second before he looked away again. Something about his expression made me wonder what was going on in his head. Then they headed to their places to wait for the next step.

Now it was down to Root, Jack and I. Jack turned to me. "You remember how to cock the gun?" he asked me, anxiety dripping from his words. I nodded. "How to reload it?" I nodded again. "Shoot it?"

"Yes, Jack," I said becoming aware again of the hard, cold metal pushing against my hip bone. "I could do it all with my eyes closed."

Root looked back at us through the rear view mirror. "I'm going to be dropping you guys soon so be prepared," the two of us nodded. "When I do, get to the front. You'll only have a minute before the others set their bombs off."

"We got it, Root," Jack replied putting our explosives in the backpack and zipping it up. "And you're sure these will work?" he asked holding up the small black clicker Root had given to each of us.

He nodded. "Yes, I guarantee they will work." Then he pulled to a stop before I was ready. "Out you go."

Jack nodded back and took my hand in his, pulling me out the side of the van. Once my feet hit the ground, I felt like running in the opposite direction. Good thing Jack's hand was still tightly wrapped around mine, otherwise I might have. "See you soon, my friend," he said to Root. Any trace of their attitudes toward each other from the night before was long gone.

"That's the spirit," Root replied with a smile then took his foot off the brake.

The two of us watched him disappear around the corner. Jack hefted the backpack up onto his shoulder and I heard the pipe bombs clink together, sending a jolt of fear through me. "Careful!" I hissed.

"Oh Hailey, what have we got to lose?" he asked shrugging, even though his voice was tense. "Our lives? We got those for free anyway."

I tried to stay focused on the task at hand as we made our way down the alley. Any thought of Jack or the others that entered my mind, I had to immediately push aside. There was no room to get emotional now. It would only hurt us. Maybe kill us. I couldn't be responsible for that.

When we reached the front courtyard, I paused and turned to the street behind us. It was weird seeing everything from this angle after having spent the last week looking at the building through binoculars, well, in my case, a telescope. Now the place looked gigantic in front of me. Now I felt so small. Maybe we couldn't do this. No. Stop.

I followed Jack up to the entrance and we knelt down behind a row of shrubs. "Alright," Jack said unzipping the backpack. "We wait till Root comes back around. He'll give us the thumbs up letting us know everyone else is in position. Then you know what to do, right?"

The gun was digging into my side and I almost fell backward trying to adjust it. "Sorry," I muttered. "My limbs are trying to declare independence at the moment." Then I nodded. "I know what to do," I said trying to keep my voice steady.

He took my chin between his fingers. "We're going to get through this, Hailey," he said looking me straight in the eyes. His gaze was steady and confident.

I nodded again.

Motion from the road caught my eye and I looked up to see the van pulling around the corner. "Here we go," Jack said under his breath.

With my feet under me again, I waited for Root's signal. Once he let us know the others were in place, Jack and I were going to throw the bombs in the entrance and set them off, taking out any guards we could and then booking it for the elevator. Sy and David, back when they were still in contact with Amanda, had managed to get a hold of blueprints of the inside of Eli's building. The two of us were going to get to Eli's office, and hopefully get him to hand over the cure for our tetanus and then destroy whatever new crap he was going to unleash on the rest of the world. Then Jack was going to put a bullet through the deranged man's skull and we would be back out of there, hopefully headed to meet back up with everyone else at the Tree House.

Root pulled up in front of us and we made eye contact. His hand went up to give us the okay, then I heard a loud crack and then a pop. The van lurched sideways as one of the tires burst sending sparks and rubber into the air. Jack yanked on my arm sending me sprawling on my butt. "Get down," he hissed. I fell onto my stomach and peered under the bushes. A few men had rushed out the doors and were firing at Root. I could see him trying to turn the van around, his face red and his teeth gritted. Bullets pinged against the metal body, sending sparks onto the road. When the back window shattered, I gasped clapping my hand over my mouth.

With a frustrated grunt, Jack threw the four bombs into the open doors and pushed down on the button, pulling my head against his chest, covering my other ear with his hand. The explosion rattled through me, the sound erupting in my ear drums and causing white flashes to burst behind my eyes. After the initial explosion, I looked to Jack, who was pulling me up and yelling something at me, though his words were muffled. A high ringing resounded in my ears and my vision was blurry, but I managed to get to my feet and follow him through the doors.

The air was thick with dust and I could hear bullets and shouting. I felt my gun slip out from under my shirt and Jack took it and started firing into the fog. His hand gripped my wrist tightly as we ran blindly in the direction of the elevator. Everything seemed to be happening in slow motion. As we ran, I stepped on something soft and I heard it crack under my foot. Without even looking, I knew I had just crushed a human hand. I closed my eyes and kept my head down not lifting it again until we were in the elevator and the door had closed. I fell down on the floor already feeling too exhausted to move on. Jack leaned back against the wall breathing hard.

"Well, that didn't go as planned," he said then wiped sweat from his forehead. Then he turned and slammed his fist against the wall angrily.

I got to my feet and put one of my shaking hands on his arm. "Jack," I said turning him around. "Look at me," I waited until his eyes were on mine before I continued. "Even if we lose, if we fail and the world goes up in smoke and everything we've ever known ceases to exist... I want you to know that I do love you." Jack's face didn't change and I wondered if what I said was even registering. "I've loved you for a long time, I just couldn't say it cuz I was afraid of what it meant. But I'm telling you now," I said. "Because I might not get another chance."

I stared at him waiting for something to happen. Slowly, Jack's mouth turned up into a smile, his teeth gleamed through all the dirt and dust on his face, and his eyes came alive. He took my face in his dirty, dust hands. "I know," he said, "It is good to hear you say it though."

The two of us stood there for a moment looking at each other. Finally, I pursed my lips. "Why'd you take my gun?" I asked.

Jack smiled then dropped his hands, offering the gun back to me. "I told you I'm saving those last bullets for Eli."

I laughed. "Do you have a grand speech prepared for when you pull the trigger?"

"I'm still trying to come up with that one. Believe me, though, it will be impressive."

Just then the elevator dinged and we both looked up as the last number lit up. We'd reached the top floor.

Without another thought, I cocked my gun and aimed it at the doors. I heard Jack chuckle next to me. "Who's laughing?" I muttered. "I seem to be the only one with a gun worth more than two shots, here." Jack pulled his semi-automatic shotgun out from the strap on his back. I had almost forgotten about that one. As the doors slid open, I put my finger on the trigger, ready to start firing away at the first thing that moved. Both of us were surprised to find an empty hallway in front of us. I lowered my gun and we carefully stepped out. "Where is everyone?" I asked quietly.

Jack's eyes darted around suspiciously. "I'm not sure," he replied. "I don't think we took everyone out downstairs."

"So what do we do?"

He pointed his gun to the door at the end of the hallway. "We get Eli," he said.

The two of us kept our backs to the walls on either side as we made our way down the hall. At every doorway, I whipped around, gun out and ready in case anyone was there waiting for us. We made it all the way to Eli's office without a problem. What was going on? Where was everyone? Nothing felt right about our situation. I put my gun in the waist of my jeans and brought my hand up to the knob. Locked.

"This is my master key." Jack held up the shotgun with a smirk. "Any lock opens magically when I blow a door off its hinges."

With a loud blast, the door flew open, slamming against the wall. "Was that really necessary?" I asked taking my hands from my ears.

Jack didn't reply, but rushed in, shotgun at the ready. I followed after him. Eli's office wasn't anything special. I almost expected to walk into a mad scientist's lab. Instead, I found myself standing in a square room with dark walls, dark wood bookcases on the walls and a dark wood desk in the center of it all. The high backed chair behind it was facing away from us, toward a window that looked out over the street below. I glanced Root's van, shot to smithereens. There was no way he was still alive.

"Turn around, you coward," Jack shouted bringing me back to reality. The shotgun was pointing straight at the back of the chair.

The chair swiveled around reminding me of the ending to a bad mob movie and I half expected to find Eli sitting their stroking a fluffy white cat. Instead...

The shotgun clattered to the ground and Jack stared wide-eyed and unmoving at the person sitting, staring back. My mouth dropped open.

I could hear Jack's voice quiver as a familiar name escaped his mouth. "Ben."

CHAPTER EIGHTEEN

I'm not sure why I was surprised at how different Ben and Jack looked. After all, the two had been adopted, apparently from two different places. Jack, of course, had tanned skin and dark hair while Ben was all light and snow. His hair was such a light blond, it looked almost white and his skin was pale, though I'm sure some of the paleness was due to how he was being treated here. A few bruises dotted his face and he looked thin and weak. His light blue eyes were cold as ice as he glared at his brother. The ring on my finger suddenly felt too heavy.

"What the..." Jack finally whispered taking a step toward his brother. "I thought..."

There was something in the way Ben stared that made me realize he didn't recognize Jack at all. Instead he eyed him like a lion would eye a lone gazelle.

"Jack," I said under my breath. He hadn't heard me I guess, because he continued forward. "Jack," I said a little louder. Was this what that chip that Adams had told me about was doing to him? Jack was now stopped on this side of the desk, leaning in to stare at his brother..

"Ben, it's me," he said. "It's Jack."

Ben's upper lip twitched. "I know who you are," he said through gritted teeth. Even though he looked young his voice came out deep and angry.

"I thought you were dead," Jack said trying to reach out to him.

His hand was stopped immediately when Ben grabbed him by the neck and yanked him closer. "Wouldn't that have been convenient?"

Jack's mouth dropped open. "What?" he croaked.

I watched then in horror as he picked Jack up from across the desk and slammed him down on top of it causing his head to smack against the hard wood. I couldn't stop myself from screaming his name when Ben jumped on top of him and punched him square in the face. As I went to lunge forward, I was grabbed from behind and wrenched backward, my shirt scraping my throat in the process. I felt my gun fall to the floor as I flailed trying to get myself loose, but one suit had grabbed my arms and the other was pulling me by my hair. My hands flew up trying to pry his fingers from around my ponytail as searing hot pain shot through my scalp and made my vision go spotty.

I screamed for Jack as they towed me down the hall. Through my fading vision I could see the light blur wailing on the darker blur. Finally, the hand on my hair loosened and I immediately threw both my legs back, feeling my feet connect with a pair of knees. A pained cry erupted behind me and the grip on my shirt loosened so I could slip free. Without looking back, I bolted back down the hall toward Eli's office. I didn't slow down when I got through the door. Instead I bent my knees and sprung at Ben, colliding with him and landing hard on the ground on the other side of the desk.

The impact caused the breath to be knocked out of me and I had a hard time wrestling Ben off of me as he wrapped his hands around my throat and started squeezing. This was all happening in such a blur, I couldn't distinguish any shapes as I wrestled against him, raking my nails down his face with one hand, the other pinned to the floor under his knee. My head was getting hot and felt like a balloon about to burst. My lungs were screaming for air and my tongue was swelling in my mouth. My vision became dark around the edges as I looked up at Ben's angelic, porcelain face now with four red gashes down his cheek. Had I done that? The last thing I heard was a loud bang and then everything went black.

When I opened my eyes again, Jack was shaking me, his bloody face made him barely recognizable. I sat up with a gasp, taking in as much air as I could.

"Where's Ben?" I panicked, my voice high and raspy.

As if on cue, I heard a moan from behind Jack and I peered around him to find Ben on his back with his hand clutching at his shoulder.

"You shot him?" I gasped.

Jack held my gun out to me. "We have to go, Hailey," he said quickly and pulled me up. "We need to find Eli, now."

As he turned and headed for the door, I looked down at his injured brother. "Not without him," I said causing Jack to stop dead in his tracks.

He turned around again. "He's not my brother any more," he said angrily.

"Yes he is," I replied and bent down, pulling him up by his free arm. "Ben is still in there."

Jack stared at me, astonished that I wanted to help the one that had just tried to kill me. "How do you know this?"

There was no time to explain everything. "I just know," I said putting his arm over my shoulder. Ben didn't fight me or try to hurt me. He just moaned painfully. "I may never get my brother back," I continued and pulled him with me toward Jack. "But there's a chance you could."

Jack didn't say anything more, but gave me a look like he knew I wasn't telling him something important. Later, Jack. Later. As I towed Ben down the hall, Jack stayed in front of us, pointing his shotgun wherever his eyes went. We had to step around the two that had grabbed me before. Now they were lying lifeless on the ground with gaping wounds in their chests, having surely been shot while I had been out cold.

When we reached the elevator and the doors were shut, I dropped Ben's arm and let him slump down against the wall. Jack bent down next to him and pushed his head back.

"Where's Eli?" he asked coldly, his hand against his brother's forehead. Ben stared back at him, his eyes pain filled and feral. He opened his mouth like he was going to say something, but instead reared back and spat in Jack's face. In anger, I watched Jack grab a clump of his blond hair and smashed his head back against the wall hard. "Where is he!" he yelled.

I turned away as my eyes began to fill with tears. This couldn't be Ben. He had to be in there somewhere. The boy that Jack had spoken so highly of. This wasn't him.

"Where!" Jack repeated and I heard Ben's head hit the wall again.

"Jack, stop!" I finally yelled, turning back around. Jack and Ben both looked at me then. "Just stop, I can't handle it."

Jack got up again leaving Ben glaring at me on the floor. His shoulders heaved up and down as he breathed, his eyes blazing. I could swear I saw smoke curling up from his nostrils like a dragon's. We heard a ding just then and the doors opened to another empty hallway. I took Jack's arm and pulled him out of the elevator. Then I turned to Ben, "Stay there." I said to him, "or I'll sick your brother on you."

Ben sneered sarcastically and closed his eyes. I turned my attention back to Jack who was halfway down the hall, still huffing and puffing. Slowly, I made my way toward him, looking back at Ben with every step. He stayed unmoving against the wall of the open elevator.

"Jack."

He let out a loud frustrated cry and slammed both his hands against the wall, cracking the plaster with his fists. With his head still against the wall, I watched as his mouth twisted into a strange grimace and his body shuddered. I stood where I was, afraid to come any closer.

When he finally did step away from the wall, his face was red and shimmering. "Who...is that?" he cracked stabbing a finger angrily at Ben in the elevator.

"Your brother," I replied quietly.

"That is NOT my brother!" Jack yelled. "That is not my brother." Then he swung at the wall again with his open hand "You're not telling me something!" He screamed in my face. "Why is he here?"

I bit my lip hard as my eyes began to burn. It wasn't meant to be like this. Ben wasn't supposed to be up there in Eli's office waiting to attack us. He was supposed to be somewhere, locked up, waiting for us to rescue him. This wasn't how Jack was supposed to find him. I took a deep breath. "Ben wasn't dead when you left him," I whispered.

The anger wiped completely off Jack's face just then and was replaced with absolute horror. "What?"

I could feel tears streaming down my face now, but I didn't try to wipe them away. My lips were trembling so much it was hard to form words. "Um...they brought him back here..." I continued looking down at my hands. "And...they put a chip in him that made him like this."

Jack shook his head. "That..." he pointed again to his brother. "That is another one of Eli's creations?"

I nodded hysterically in reply. "It's something he's trying to come up with for the military," I continued now just rambling on, telling everything I'd heard. "Adams said Eli was trying to develop this chip that could erase memories and create new ones in hopes of using it for our military or something, but they don't know he's doing involuntary testing so some of the people they've caught are being used to test these chips and I was going to tell you sooner, but I was afraid you would come storming in here all kamikaze like, like Sy did and then I'd lose you forever, and I know he's your brother, but I was hoping we could find a way to fix him..."

Jack held his hand up causing me to stop talking. I took a few deep breaths to get my sobs back under control. When I was finally silent again he lowered his hand. "Let's go," he whispered and started back for the elevator.

Having not said anything else, I wasn't really sure what Jack was feeling. Was he angry with me? Did he think I had betrayed him or done the right thing in keeping it from him? What was he going to do with Ben?

I still hadn't moved by the time he had reached the elevator, so I had to jog and reached it just before the doors closed. The three of us stayed silent for a few floors before Jack hit the emergency stop button and turned to Ben aiming his gun at his forehead. My eyes grew wide.

Was he really going to kill his brother? With one of his last bullets?

"Where's Eli?" he asked calmly.

The stone cold glare that Ben had kept on his face had now vanished and his skin grew even more pale, if that's possible. It seemed like he was trying to decide whether his life was more important than this information. "I-I've never even met him," he finally stammered, his eyes flitting from Jack's to mine. "I don't know where he is."

"You're lying," Jack said.

"I'm not...I swear."

He lowered his gun and tapped it thoughtfully with his finger. Without another word, he lifted it again, pointing it at Ben's unwounded shoulder and pulled the trigger, spattering Ben's shirt with blood and causing him to cry out in pain.

"Jack!"

"Where's Eli!" He yelled, the smoking barrel now pointed back at his brother's head.

"I don't know!" Ben screamed back clutching his freshly wounded arm.

Jack turned to me. "How can you tell that someone's a compulsive liar? I mean, assuming that their pants aren't on fire."

I just stared back in horror.

"I'm not lying, J!"

Jack and I turned our attention back to Ben. J? "What did you call me?" Jack whispered dropping his gun. "Did you say J?"

"Who's J?"

Jack leaned into me. "That's what he called me when we were younger. How do you remember that?"""

Ben shook his head. "I don't...I don't know."

Now Jack pinched the bridge of his nose between his

two fingers and squeezed his eyes shut. "Do you know anything, Ben?" he asked sounding frustrated.

His brother lowered his blond head in defeat. I felt my shoulders sag. That little spark of remembering Jack's nickname had given me hope. But now...

Ben lifted his head back up. "Wait." I saw Jack's face perk up. "If he's anywhere, he'd be trying to get his experiments out of here."

"Well, where does he keep them?" Jack asked impatiently.

"In the basement."

Jack nodded and hit the button to get the elevator going again with the flat of his hand. "To the basement."

"We can't get there using this elevator," Ben said matter-of-factly. Jack's and my shoulders slumped. "There's a set of stairs leading down from the first floor lobby."

This meant going back into the chaos we had left behind at the entrance. Jack and I looked at each other. Then I hit the button for the first floor. "To the lobby." I said quietly.

The ride down was silent. Ben stayed against the wall sulking, his hands covering the wounds on both his shoulders. Jack had his shotgun strapped to his back and his other gun was tucked into his waist on one side making him look dangerous, like a walking arsenal. My gun was tucked back under my shirt, ready to be taken out at any minute to end a life.

As the elevator came to a stop, Ben scrambled to one side in hopes he wouldn't be caught in the crossfire. Jack motioned for me to get to one side as well and I hugged the wall with all the buttons. As soon as the doors slid open, I tensed, expecting to be hit with ricocheting bullets. Instead everything was silent. I peeked out from my hands slowly and looked over at Jack. He had his back against the opposite wall and was holding his shotgun against his chest, loading shells into it quickly. Locking the barrel back into place, he turned his head and locked his eyes with mine. Then with a nod, he rushed out of sight and into the lobby.

I turned to Ben. "Stay here," I said to him then turned and followed Jack out into the lobby.

There were dead bodies scattered across the floor and a few suits were rushing in from different rooms. Jack had taken shelter in the hallway and was exchanging fire, shooting blindly with his shotgun. He turned to me. "We have to make it to that stairwell," he shouted motioning with his gun toward a door across the room from us. "There's too many of them," he continued. "I'll stay behind and cover you. Get down there and find Eli."

"Then what?" I screamed. "I can't kill him. What if there's more of them down there?"

Jack cursed under his breath. "You're right." Then he raised his gun and shot off another several rounds. "You get over there and wait inside the door," he finally said. "I'll follow you."

We waited until there was a lull in the crossfire then Jack looked at me and shouted "Go!" I took off at a full sprint for the door. Bullets started flying again and I covered my head in hopes of protecting it. I felt something slam into my shoulder, sending electricity, pain and then numbness down my arm. I've been shot! I've been shot! But I couldn't stop. I didn't stop until I made it inside the door and had shut it behind me. Then a cry of pain escaped my throat and I looked down at my arm. A nice sized bullet hole gaped at me through a tear in my shirt. I couldn't believe I was shot. Blood was pouring out rapidly and I clapped a hand over it, wrapping my fingers around to plug the exit wound on the other side. I gritted my teeth and rested my sweaty forehead against the wall in hopes that I could push the pain out of my mind. I took a few deep breaths. You're going to be okay, Hailey, I told myself. Ah, it hurt! It'll all be over soon and then you can go home.

Once the initial wave of nausea had passed, I realized Jack hadn't come over yet. When I made my way back up the stairs and looked out the window, I couldn't help but gasp at what I saw. At least four suits had Jack cornered and he was now firing with a handgun he must have picked off a fallen suit. His shotgun laid on the ground, surely out of shells. He needed my help or he was going to be killed.

With my good hand covering my wounded arm, I used my bad shoulder to push open the door a crack. Pain washed over me, making me feel sick and lightheaded. There was no time for that. I slipped my gun out from under my shirt and aimed the barrel out at them. There was no room to spread me feet apart like Jack had taught me and I couldn't really extend my arms out in front of me. I was able to lean into the recoil like he had said and I closed my eye, taking aim. Slowly, I squeezed the trigger.

I hadn't been ready for the gun to kickback the way it did and I almost dropped it. Luckily, I hit one of the suits in the neck and he went down. Without any more wasted time, I aimed again and squeezed the trigger. This time I was ready for the recoil and was able to fire off a few more rounds, taking out the other three suits and creating a break so Jack could run to me. He didn't hesitate for a second, instead he bolted toward me, not even trying to hide his proud smile. I opened the door so he could run in. When he was maybe ten feet from me, I caught movement out of the corner of my eye then heard a loud crack and Jack's legs were kicked out from under him.

The smile wiped clean off his face as he crashed to

the ground, blood jetting from a bullet hole in his calf. I lunged forward then, firing blindly at the other side of the room. When I got to Jack, I uncovered my wound and grabbed his arm with my slippery hand. I continued to shoot as I dragged him through the door, though I'm pretty sure I had already killed whoever had hurt him. Once the door was closed tight and we were down onto a landing, I let go of him and slumped down against the wall. He was breathing heavily, his face glistening with sweat.

Jack clutched his leg. "Ahh, that hurts!" he grunted laying his head on his knee.

"Are you alright?" I asked with a shaky voice.

He moaned again. "I just about had my leg shot off."

"So...are you alright then?"

Jack took his hand away from his calf and looked at the bullet wound. Then he sighed, wincing again in pain. "Yeah, I guess I'm alright."

I looked down at my own wound again. The bleeding had slowed a bit and now I could see more inside it. Luckily it hadn't hit my bone, but rather went through my flesh and had exited out the other side. A clean shot. I scooted over to Jack and undid the handkerchiefs around both our necks. Keeta had been right to suggest we all have one handy. In case something like this happened. Carefully, I wrapped Jack's around his shin and tied it tight, causing him to inhale sharply through his teeth. Then I let him tie mine around my arm. We were bandaged now. Only thing left to do was go down those stairs and find Eli.

I didn't want to. My head ached. My muscles ached. My arm ached. I just wanted to stay on that landing and hold Jack's bloody hand for the rest of my life. But I couldn't. I didn't know if any of our friends were still alive, but I had to hope they were. I had to believe we would see them again and that had to be what kept us going.

With a grimace, I stood up, my bones creaking from fatigue. Then I held out my hand to Jack. A crooked smile cut through the pain in his face and I couldn't describe it as anything less than admiration. When he was up on his feet, he wrapped his arms around me.

"You saved my life back there," he said into my hair.

With a smile I took one of his arms fand slid it up over my shoulder so I could support his weight. "Or I'm just prolonging your suffering," I replied jokingly. "So don't show me any gratitude yet."

The stairs were treacherous. With Jack being half a foot taller than me and twice my size, I had a hard time trying to keep him up. Any time I went to use the wall for support, a jolt of pain went down my wounded arm and I would groan. I knew Jack felt bad, but we had to get down the stairs. We needed to get to Eli so we could end this whole nightmare.

"I'm sorry, Hailey," Jack said under his breath.

I shook my head. "It's okay," I replied. "Hop." Jack hopped down onto the next landing with his good leg. "It's not like you can help it," I added guiding him carefully across the landing and to the next step. "Hop. Is your leg getting tired?"

"No," he lied. "It doesn't matter. But that's not what I mean. I'm sorry you had to do this."

"Jack, I'm here for a reason too," I said. "Hop. Don't think that I'm only doing all this for you. Hop. My brother and parents are dead because of Eli. Hop. I have my own vendetta to settle."

Jack didn't say anything to that, instead he hopped whenever I told him to hop. "Why didn't you tell me about my brother?" he finally asked me.

"I didn't want to hurt you. I didn't want us to fail."

"You should have told me."

I sighed. "Then what would have happened? Hop."

"You don't have to say hop," Jack muttered. "I think I got it by now."

"Right, sorry." I hitched his arm up and wrapped my own tighter around his waist. I guess Jack understood where I had been coming from because he didn't say another word on the matter.

When we reached the bottom of stairs, both of us sighed with relief. I didn't even want to think about what we were going to do once we were ready to leave again. Maybe we wouldn't even get that far...

"What is this place?" Jack whispered looking around.

The room we were in was pretty well lit and all kinds of machinery cluttered the floor and walls. We made our way toward the next room slowly, taking in everything as we went. As I walked down an aisle, I stared closely at the tubes on either side of me. They looked like huge, sideways refrigerators, and when I peered through a small window in one, I realized they were. I couldn't stop the cry from escaping as I stumbled back against another one. I covered my mouth to keep myself from crying out again as Jack hobbled over to me as fast as he could. All I could do was point at the refrigerator, at the little window at the end. At the human face, eyes unblinking, staring back at us.

CHAPTER NINETEEN

"What is this place?" I asked, my voice coming out in a squeak.

Jack pulled at the handle on one of the refrigerators. "This must be like a storage room or something. They're all locked."

"Well, we have to get them out!" I shrieked. "We have to save them!"

"It wouldn't do you any good."

The two of us turned to find a man standing, blocking the doorway to the next room. He was ordinary looking. Shot dark hair, average height, average build. But his dark eyes spoke of evil. This had to be Eli...

"Why?" Jack finally demanded.

Eli shrugged. "They're all dead." My stomach dropped. "Subjects of failed experiments."

With a closer look, I could see now that each face seemed to have something wrong with it. The one closest to me had dried blood streams coming from his mouth, eyes, ears and nose. The one next to him looked like she had been stung a thousand times by bees.

"You're sick," Jack spat shaking his head. "What is wrong with you?"

"Do you even have a conscience?" I asked loudly.

The two of us watched this man, this harmless looking man, walk toward us, looking at each dead face as he walked down the line. "Philosophers, theologists, and politicians can talk their throats hoarse about whether or not something is moral or right. Scientists simply say 'Yes, but can it be done?'"

"Oh," Jack continued. "So you're just a raving lunatic. Where's the maniacal laughter?"

The corners of Eli's mouth twitched, like what he had said amused him. "Maniacal laughter is both inappropriate and unbecoming." Jack rolled his eyes. "Don't you see I'm trying to help humanity? I helped you didn't I, Jack?"

Had either of us said our names since we'd been down here?

Jack let out a sarcastic laugh. "You think you saved me? You do know your lousy chip is failing, right? You do know that if you release your new and improved chip, it's just going to fail too, right?"

Now Eli stared hard at Jack, his mouth set in a straight line. I could see the muscles in his jaw moving as he ground his teeth together. Then an easy smile softened his face. "But Jack," he said with a hint of tension in his voice, "I gave you life. If not for my chip, you would have been dead before you ever had the chance to live."

Jack shook his head in disgust. "No, because of your chip, hundreds of people are going to die a violent death. What's going to happen in forty years when the new one starts to fail?"

"It won't matter," Eli replied clasping his hands together. "I will be gone."

"You'll be remembered as the one who wiped out humanity," I said angrily.

Now Eli turned to me. He hadn't even acknowledged me since he'd shown up. But now, he looked at me and I felt his brown eyes piercing into mine. Drilling into my head. "Ah," he sighed sadly. "But at least I will be remembered."

I narrowed my eyes hoping Eli couldn't see the tears forming in them. "You're a horrible person." I said bitterly.

"A lot of brilliant artists were horrible people."

"Yes, and we all pity you," Jack said. "but now you're running out of time." He pulled his gun out from under his shirt, cocked it and pointed it at Eli's head. "Where are you keeping the new chip?"

Eli glanced at the gun unemotionally as if Jack were pointing a blade of grass at him. Then he looked at me. For a few, long seconds he looked at me. Just stared. I could feel my forehead breaking out in a sweat. What was going through this lunatic's head?

"Hailey," he said at last.

I nodded hesitantly.

"Ryan was your brother, am I correct?"

I nodded again. "He's dead now because of your experiments."

"Ah yes," Eli said. "He was a fine specimen."

That was it. "My brother was a person, you psycho freak!" I flew at him, arms flailing. Before he even had time to react, my fist connected with his jaw and he stumbled back against one of the coolers. Jack grabbed my bad shoulder and pulled me back, causing me to cry out in pain.

"Sorry sorry," he hissed keeping his gun trained on Eli.

Eli straightened back up rubbing his jaw. Then he

smiled. "I suppose I do want to show you where I keep that new chip of mine. If anything to let you two see that there is nothing you can do to stop me."

"You sound so confident in yourself," Jack said disgustedly.

With an extended hand, Eli motioned to the back room. "Right this way."

I wasn't so sure about this. Obviously, Eli intended to kill us. Why else would he be so calm and cooperative about showing us his new experiment? I touched Jack's hand and when he met my eyes, I gave him a worried look. "It'll be okay," he assured me softly so Eli couldn't hear.

The two of us followed after him, leaving the room filled with bodies. Did Eli have two empty coffins just waiting for me and Jack?

When I stepped through the doorway and entered the next room, I half expected to find myself in a mad scientist's lab. I thought there would be test tubes and beakers with colorful fluids or a monster over in the corner. Maybe I watch too much television. Instead the room was almost completely bare. The walls, floor and ceiling were covered in shiny metal and in the center of the room, stood a podium, and that was it. Eli led us over to the podium. It reached almost to my shoulders and laying on top in a small glass case were two computer chips.

"These, of course, are the prototypes," Eli said to us. "The real chips are four hundred times smaller."

"Why two?" Jack asked not sounding impressed.

The man smiled at the question. "One will be injected into the right hemisphere of the brain, and one in the left," he replied all too proud of himself. "And together they will fight off every ailment known to man. I have created the fountain of youth."

This guy was delusional.

As Jack opened his mouth to say something in reply, I interrupted him. "If you created the fountain of youth, why did you say earlier that you would be gone before we saw the repercussions?"

Again the look on Eli's face turned to sadness. "It is much too late for me," he said.

"Why is that?" Jack asked now furrowing his brow.

"Back when I was first starting," Eli continued and picked up the small glass box from the podium, "I was the subject of most of my tests. This has changed my genetic makeup. If I were to implant myself with the chips, it would have adverse effects. Instead of fighting off diseases invading my body, they would team up and destroy me at a more rapid pace. At least I can help everyone else." Then he stared adoringly at his creation. " With this prototype, I will make millions of chips identical to them, and then there will be no more suffering in the world."

Then the glass box exploded in Eli's hands. He stood there in shock for an instant, watching as blood began dripping from hundreds of tiny cuts on his hands. "What have you done," he whispered. Jack stood next to me, his hand still holding the trigger back. I stared in disbelief at the shards of metal and glass on the floor at the man's feet. "What have you done!" he screamed this time, his face contorting angrily.

"I do believe I just saved the world," Jack replied putting his gun back in his waist. Then he turned and started limping out the room, his head held high.

I didn't move. I'm sure Jack had wanted me to follow him out, strut along side him. But I couldn't get my feet to move. Instead I bent down and picked up one of the larger pieces of glass, turning it over in my hand. Eli's red face was on its way to purple now and veins were standing out in his neck. He seriously looked like he was about to explode. "You will pay for this!" He screamed and charged after Jack.

As he rushed past me, I jabbed my hand into his stomach. Eli froze, his mouth still open, lips still moving, though now no words were coming out. His legs gave out and he fell onto me. I staggered under his weight before falling down to the floor with him and scrambling back away from him. Eli looked down at the big shard of glass protruding from his stomach. Blood was pooling up on all sides and staining his perfectly white shirt. Jack had rushed over to help me back up and the two of us watched Eli make a terrifying gurgling sound before his eyes went blank.

I wanted to stay there. I wanted to sit for a while and make sure this evil man really was dead, but Jack pulled me away. Kept saying "we need to go, Hailey." So, I finally let him drag me out of the room. I glanced back one more time at Eli and noticed the hauntingly sad look in the dead man's eyes.

About halfway back up the stairs, I realized Jack had been helping me up even with his bad leg. Even though I still felt a little in shock, I manged to switch places with him, putting his arm over my shoulder so he could lean on me. It took a while to get the rest of the way up, maybe because I knew there were just going to be more agents waiting for us when we got up there. Instead, the place was cleared out. The dust had finally settled and I could see clearly the drab artwork on the walls and the many dead bodies littering the floor. The tiles were tacky with blood and we had a hard time getting to the front entrance without slipping. As we neared the doors, I realized we were forgetting someone.

I put a hand on Jack's arm. "Ben."

He was still in the elevator where we had left him.

His eyes were shut and slumped over. I was afraid he was dead, until Jack nudged him with his foot and he let out a groan. The two of us each took a hand and pulled him to his feet.

When we opened the front entrance doors, I had to squint my eyes from the brightness. It had to be noon by now. Police cars and ambulances filled the streets, wheeling suits out on stretchers, most in body bags. The few that were still alive looked like they wouldn't be for much longer. Jack grabbed my hand and the three of us moved quickly down the side of the building before we could be seen. My palm stung where he touched it. When we were safely around the corner, I pulled my hand away to find a long deep gash. Jack took my hand in his carefully.

"We need to get that patched up," he said. "Let's go back to the Tree House. Hopefully everyone else will be there too."

"Except for Root," I cracked as the adrenaline began wearing off. I suddenly felt so exhausted.

"The Tree House?" Ben asked.

Jack and I looked at him. "Do you remember that place?"

For a few seconds, we watched as Ben stared hard at the ground while he dug around in his memory. Finally, he nodded slowly. "I think I do."

The hopeful look on Jack's face made me smile. Maybe he could have his brother back. Maybe things could return to normal eventually. A strange tapping noise broke the moment and we began looking around to find the source. Another metallic tap made us realize it was coming from a grate in the wall. Together, Jack and I pulled the grate from the wall. We were met with a grimy, but familiar face.

"You've got to be kidding me," Jack chuckled as he

pulled Logan out of the wall.

"How did you get in there?" I asked him feeling so happy to see at least one of our friends alive.

Logan stood up and tried to brush himself off. It didn't help though, his hands were just as dirty as the rest of him. "After we detonated our bomb," he started, "we were ambushed and I got separated from Keeta."

The happy feeling faded. "You don't know where she is?"

He shook his head sadly. "No, but I did manage to get to the main computer and wipe out all the hard drives. There won't be anything more coming out of this place. At least not for a while."

"Still doesn't explain how you ended up in the wall," Jack said, though his voice was full of satisfaction.

"I climbed in there after I ran out of ammo," Logan explained. "I've been crawling around these stupid ducts trying to find a way out for the past hour and a half." Just then he turned and noticed Jack's brother leaning back against the wall away from us. He stared for a moment. "Ben?" Ben looked up just then and gazed at him. His expression didn't change as Logan walked toward him. "I thought you were dead," Logan said putting an arm on his shoulder. "How are you, man?"

"He's having trouble with his memory," Jack said from behind him.

Logan looked back at us then at him again. "Do you remember me?" he asked.

I watched Ben. Something in his eyes wasn't right. He seemed to recognize Logan, but he wasn't the least bit happy about it. What was going on in his head. "I do remember you," he finally said, his eyes narrowed.

"Alright," Logan clapped him on the back causing him to grunt in pain. "Sorry, man," he apologized now noticing the bullet wounds in his shoulders. "What happened?"

"I shot him," Jack replied with a smile. "Twice."

"Yeah, I really think the best investment I've made is this microfiber coat, blood just beads on top and wipes right off," Ben said stuffing his hands in his pockets. Now, I could see where Jack got his sarcasm from.

Logan chuckled uncomfortably. "So is Eli..."

Now Jack was beaming ear to ear. "Hailey stabbed him."

"Yeah," I said. "I couldn't even do that though without hurting myself." Then I held out my injured hand.

Logan, being in a lot better condition than we were, gave me his handkerchief and Jack helped me wrap it around my cut.

The four of us didn't waste any more time standing on the side of the building. We made our way down the nearest alley and headed for the Tree House.

It took a while to get there what with Jack's injured leg. Especially since we stuck with alleys and deserted streets as best as we could. Four bloodied kids walking around Seattle was bound to create unwanted attention. A helicopter flew over our heads back in the direction of Eli's building. It looked like our work was going to be on the six o' clock news that night. Jack tightened his arm around me, more for comfort than need. I prayed the others would be at the Tree House waiting for us. I was just ready for this day to be over with already.

When we finally made it onto our street, my heart sank. Apparently this nightmare wasn't over. Far from it, actually. A couple black vans were parked in front of the Tree House and some agents were taking axes to the front door while a few others were pouring gasoline on the walls. They were going to destroy it.

"What do we do now?" I asked feeling the tears

coming on.

"You walk," Logan replied.

I turned around to find him standing there, two handguns pointed directly at us. My mouth fell open. "Logan?"

"I'm sorry," he said sadly. "They promised I'd get my family back."

"I thought we were your family," Jack said.

Ben stepped forward. "Now I know why I remember you. You came to talk to Eli a few days ago. No wonder I didn't link you with the Tree House."

Logan just shook his head and pushed one of the guns into my back. "I'm sorry," he said again. "I didn't want it to happen this way. I just want it all to be over." Then a tear ran down his cheek. "I just want to go home, alright?" His hands were shaking as he pushed me forward.

I looked to Jack, hoping he had a plan. Instead he just shook his head in disgust. "You're a coward. They're lying to you. Your family is dead," he spat.

Logan pushed me again. "Go on," he whispered.

With one gun in my back and the other pointed at Ben's head, what choice did Jack have? There was no way he had time to whip out his shotgun and shoot Logan before either of us were killed. He sighed then started limping toward the Tree House. The rest of us followed, the sound of Logan's sniffling filling my ears.

As we neared the agents, Logan called out to them, causing them to turn and look at us. When we reached them, he passed me, Jack and Ben off to one of the suits and lowered his guns. "I did what you asked," he sniffed trying to hide the quivering in his voice. "Now where are my parents and my sister?"

"They will take you to them," the man replied nodding to two suits waiting by the van.

Logan nodded. "Thanks," he whispered then met my eyes before turning away from us.

As he neared the van, one of the agents put a hand on Logan's shoulder reassuringly, then lifted a pistol to his head and pulled the trigger. I heard myself scream as blood exploded out the other side of his head and he fell to the ground motionless.

Arms wrapped around me and I was lifted into the air just then. I kicked and thrashed as they carried me, Jack and Ben toward the alley to the back of the Tree House. They could kill me now, I didn't care. But I was not going down without a fight. I was not going down the way Logan had.

My mind was racing and filling with memories of my parents and Ryan. It was like I was seeing two things happening at once. While the agent carried my thrashing body along the side of the building, I watched as my brother's and my little kid bodies splashed around in the community pool as Dad videotaped. Flames engulfed the Tree House as Ryan and I blew out ten candles on our birthday cake. This was right before he promptly shoved my entire face into the cake and ran away while I chased him, screaming in pain from the frosting that had gotten in my eyes. Now I screamed and kicked, rearing my head back trying to catch the man's nose, straining my arms to break free. My shoulder was throbbing and pain was shooting down my arm making me see spots.

We reached the alley and the agents stopped, dropping Jack, Ben and I. I looked around confused until I saw what they were staring at. Standing between us and the Tree House stood a very bloody, very angry Root. His hair was plastered to his head from sweat and blood and his glasses were gone. His hands were balled into fists and his teeth were bared. He looked nothing like the boy we had left in the van just that morning. This was the hulk version of Root.

"You thought you killed me," he growled. "But I am not going down without taking you with me." Then with a warrior cry, he charged at us, his eyes wild with rage.

The agents shoved us hard and reached for their guns. Just before the first one pulled the trigger, Root threw his coat off, exposing the bomb strapped to his chest. Jack, Ben and I didn't waste another second before bolting out of the alley. The sound of the guns firing cracked in my ears followed by a blast that knocked me off my feet. Time slowed down and I was flying. I felt flames lick at my ankles and then I was falling to the earth again.

I hit the pavement hard, skidding across the road a few feet before coming to a stop. For a moment I was sure I was dead. If nothing more, I was at least paralyzed. I laid there for what seemed like ever as I waited to hear more gunfire. For bullets to start flying, aimed right for me. They never came though.

I waited for a while longer as feeling and then pain started trickling back into my body. When I was able to move my arms, I slowly slid them toward me and tried to pick myself up. It hurt to breathe. It hurt to blink, but I managed to get to my knees and look around. The Tree House and surrounding area were engulfed in flames. It took me a second to realize that I wasn't directly in any harm. I had run far enough away to only be knocked off my feet. When Root's bomb had exploded, it had ignited the gasoline around the place, reaching all the way to the front and taking everyone out.

Looking to my left, I saw Jack laying on his stomach, his face turned toward me. His eyes blinked twice and then he rolled over with a groan. I made my way over to him and held his head in my lap. "Jack," I whispered. "Are you okay? Can you move?"

At first he could only groan in reply. But then he moved one of his legs and nodded. "Yeah," he croaked. "Where's Ben?"

I looked around in a panic then felt relief when I saw Ben about ten feet away, sitting holding his head. "He looks alright," I said.

Jack brought his hand up to touch my face and I held it there with my injured one, feeling true relief for the first time all day. Finally, the worst part was over and I still had him.

"We're alive," I whispered feeling tears welling up in my eyes. "We did it."

Jack's eyes shined as he smiled up at me. "If I remember correctly, you did it."

CHAPTER TWENTY

The three of us didn't waste any more time getting out of there. It wouldn't be long before the place was swarming with police and news reporters. Surely they would end up linking both the fire and the explosions at the company together. Hopefully they wouldn't link us with them though. For now we weren't taking any chances and decided it would be best to lay low for a while.

Being in such a deserted part of town, it wasn't hard to find an abandoned building to take shelter in. We were hoping that even with the Tree House now destroyed, the others, if there were any left, would come looking for us. We checked back every hour in hopes of finding someone there. It took us until sundown before finally giving up and accepting the probability that we had been the only ones to make it out alive.

After the police had cleared out for the night, Jack, Ben and I went back to see if there was anything left to salvage. I walked among the burned remains, kicking over charred parts of the place I had called home. The tree that had been growing through the walls was just a blackened stump now. The fire department had chopped most of it down so it wouldn't collapse while they were there checking everything out. Sy's arsenal was gone, of course. As well as any other hint of what had really been hidden here.

I made my way up the broken staircase onto the main floor and closed my eyes, standing in the wreckage, picturing that the couch wasn't just a charred, black pile of wood and springs and that it was occupied by the people that had become my friends. I smiled thinking about Melody's flowy clothes and curly hair bouncing as she laughed at any one of Arie's corny jokes while Keeta rolled her eyes trying to hide a smile. And while Root sat at the kitchen table, immersed in his own world of plans and data, gnawing on an apple and pushing his glasses up his nose every few seconds. Saying something to Logan occasionally, who had his eyes glued to his computer. His face always aglow from the light of the screen. Logan, who had held such a terrible secret from us.

"Hey."

I opened my eyes to find Jack standing in the doorway, surrounded by the blackness and the ruin. A tear slid down my cheek and I quickly wiped it away. He limped toward me slowly then opened his arms so I could fall into them. As more tears spilled from my eyes, I breathed in deep, smelling him. Through the smoke and the sweat, I could smell his familiar scent. It reminded me of the earlier days. It reminded me again of the memories this place held. Of the people I'd never get to see again.

"I don't even have anything to remember anyone with," I sobbed into his chest, my voice breaking with every word.

Jack's arms held me tighter. "Memories are better

than nothing," he whispered in reply. I could hear the pain and sadness in his voice, even as he tried to keep it even and strong for me.

"So much...has happened," I whispered.

"Should we talk about it?" he asked me.

"I don't know if I can," I choked again. "I---I just -love- you right now...that's all..."

Jack took my face in his hands and lifted it so I was looking at him. "Let's get out of here," he whispered using his finger to wipe my tears away.

I nodded then let him lead me out of the room, down the stairs and away from our home. Ben was waiting in a car for us and Jack helped me into the passenger seat before climbing in the back. We drove in silence for a while.

"I recognize that," Ben said finally eying my finger.

I looked down at my hand to find his ring still resting on my middle finger. "Oh." I pulled it off and held it out to him. "It's yours. You can have it back."

Ben smiled, looking just for a second like Jack, only all light. "You keep it," he said pushing my hand away. "It looks better on your hand anyway."

I slipped it back on my finger. "Thanks," I whispered.

We pulled up to a small department store and got out. People looked at us with gaping mouths as we walked down the aisles, grabbing pants, shirts, jackets and a first aid kit. After we finished checking out, we took turns going into the bathroom to change and clean ourselves up. When we all looked satisfactory enough, minus a few scrapes and bruises, we headed to the nearest diner.

I didn't realize how hungry I was until the waiter came and I ordered just about everything on the menu.

While we waited for our food, I laid my head on Jack's shoulder and closed my eyes. I must have dozed off because when I opened them again, my plate sat in front of me. I didn't remember the waiter even bringing it over.

We ate in silence and now as I looked at my food, I suddenly didn't feel hungry any more. Not with the images of Logan being shot haunting my memories. It seemed like Jack had the same idea. Ben didn't have any problem shoveling his food in though. At least one of us was coping well. It hit me right after that this could have possibly been the first time he'd had real food in weeks.

While we waited for him to finish, my eyes flitted up to the television in the corner above us. A popular talk show was on, like it was every Friday night, and it shouldn't really have phased me. Except for seeing the person she was interviewing.

Quickly, I flagged a waiter over and asked if he could turn the volume up. Jack looked up too to see what I was getting excited over.

"Many of you know of the terrorist attack that occurred this morning at E. Scott Pharmaceuticals, causing almost one hundred deaths and destroying years and years of research," the interviewer said. "Today we have Eli Scott himself, who was luckily out of the country this morning. And now he's flown home to be here with us today."

"What?" I gasped then turned to Jack to see the same look of disbelief on his face.

"I thought you guys killed him," Ben whispered, his mouth full of food.

"We did."

"Mr. Scott, why don't you tell us about how this will effect the release of your new drug?" the interviewer asked him.

The man turned and smiled at the camera. Wasn't

this the man I had killed just that morning? I turned to Jack and his brother. "This isn't right," I whispered. "I saw the blood. I watched him die."

"He was dead as a dormouse," Jack added.

Ben looked at him with narrowed eyes. "What did you say?"

"Dead as a dormouse," his brother replied. "It's an expression."

"I think you mean doornail."

"What?"

I watched as the two of them continued to look at each other. "The expression," Ben continued to explain. "It's dead as a doornail."

Jack sat back. "Well that makes no sense. How can a doornail be dead? An inanimate object can't be dead or alive. At least you can kill a dormouse."

Finally I hissed through my teeth to get the two to be quiet. Looking back up at the television, I watched as the camera closed in on his face. Something was different. I narrowed my eyes. His hair was short and dark, the same. His face was ordinary. Ordinary nose, ordinary mouth, ordinary eyebrows. But when I stopped on his eyes, I couldn't help but gasp. Remembering back to that morning. I had stared into those eyes and I remembered them clearly being brown. This man though had blue.

"That wasn't Eli," I finally whispered.

Ben leaned in close. "He was an imposter?"

"That man I killed had brown eyes," I said.

Jack looked me in the eye. "You're sure?"

I nodded. "I'm sure of it. Completely positive." The three of us sat back again when we noticed other customers looking at us funny. "This can't be happening." I whispered pressing my fingers to my temples.

We looked back up at the screen again, a sinking feeling in all of our stomachs. Eli, the real Eli, was explaining his new set of chips to the interviewer. She smiled and nodded every few seconds, but I knew everything he was saying was completely over her head. "So these chips will still be released on time in just a few short months," she finally interrupted after he had been rambling for a while. "What are you calling them?"

Eli smiled and folded his hands on his knee. "Well, I've decided to name the two chips after a couple dear friends of mine, who I believe are watching this program as I speak."

I felt a shudder go through my body. "Oh no," I whispered.

"And what are the names?" The interviewer asked obviously not aware of his dramatic pause.

Now Eli turned his face toward the camera, like he was looking directly at Jack and I. His eyes pierced into mine and though my heart was pounding in my ears, I saw his lips move, forming our names.

EPILOGUE

There is a certain point when you realize there is no returning to the way you were before. A crossroads where the life you knew and the life ahead of you turn sharply in opposite directions. Sometimes I wish that my life were a story that I had full control over. Sometimes it seems just as simple as deleting a few chapters; adding this in here, taking that out there. Redo. Retry. What would happen if I only had been this way, or had done that thing?

The sun was just rising as we hit the coast. Since the computers had been wiped clean, there was no way to activate the GPS in our chips. We could go where we pleased now. Though the only place I really wanted to be was back at the Tree House with everyone that I had loved. The only place I wanted to be was the only place I couldn't go.

It had taken me a few days to really understand my situation. I was homeless, without a family, other than the two brothers, one dark, one light, that stood on either side of me. They were all I had left.

Now the three of us were standing on the beach as the sun rose up over the water, illuminating the sky and making the clouds vibrant with color. The wind was icy and bit at the scrapes on my face that were still healing. For the first time I welcomed this pain. It meant I was alive. It meant I still had time left. Not much time though. Only twenty more years. About seventy three hundred more days before my world would end. Only about ninety days before the rest of the world would start its own descent into chaos.

My legs felt too weak to carry my weight. Jack's hand found mine as we continued to watch in silence. He was the only one who kept me from falling. A part of me wanted to push him away, shout at him and say things I would regret, in the end. This was the first and last day we could really rest. That we could just stand and watch the sun rise together. After this day, things were going to change. Things were going to happen. My brother's words echoed through my head and made their way down into the rest of my body, electrifying my limbs and making my fingers and toes tingle. "Don't stop fighting," he had said. It didn't matter how hopeless I felt. It didn't matter how tired or in pain or insignificant I felt. All that mattered was that I still had those words in my head fueling the fire deep down inside me. I could feel it growing by the minute and over the following few months it was going to turn into a blaze that couldn't be stopped. With Jack and Ben by my side, we were going to be unstoppable. Together, we were going to save the world or die trying.

ABOUT THE AUTHOR

Shay Lynam works as a humble cashier in her hometown in Washington. She lives with her husband, Mike, and puggle, Lucy and spends her free time writing and crafting. You can visit her online on www.shaylynam.com or on Twitter (@shay_lynam)

THE TREE HOUSE PLAYLIST

- Help, I'm Alive - Metric
- Strange & Beautiful - Aqualung
- Silence - Blindside
- Now - Paramore
- Look After You - The Fray
- Monster - Paramore
- Renegade - Paramore
- Open Your Eyes - Snow Patrol
- Safe & Sound - Taylor Swift ft. The Civil Wars
- My Love - Sia
- Luvstory - Sigur Rós

Made in the USA
Charleston, SC
22 March 2013